EVANGALINE PIERCE

A Crown of Gilded Thread

A fairy tale retelling

Contents

Home

Gwen smiled when the warm air rushed over her face. The heat in the house was nice, and supper needed to be made. "It's the last we'll have, and I want it to be special," she said to the feline lounging on the narrow windowsill.

A golden curl slipped from the bun at the nape of Gwen's neck as she wiped the sweat from her forehead. The fire crackled in the hearth when she stirred the logs with the poker. A whoosh of flame licked the wood as she flipped it.

The blaze heated both rooms of the cottage well. Even one with so little fuel. Stone walls Papa set himself, with the help of the neighbors, insulated against the winter winds and summer sun.

Currently, the two rooms felt too big, with Gwen being the only one to fill them. Her father, the miller, was out looking for work or grain to get the mill going again.

An eerie silence had slithered over the cottage months ago. The comforting cadence of stone grinding upon stone stopped.

Soon after the silence descended, so did the offer from the king. A courier's hand landed against the wooden door. It creaked as Papa opened it. The note passed quickly from the jeweled fingers of the courier to Papa's twisted fingers. The red wax snapped between them. His lips pursed while his eyes moved back and forth over the paper. Then Papa pulled his shoulders back, lifted his chin, and handed the paper back to the courier with a single word. "No."

Gwen sighed at the unhappy thoughts as she stirred the fire again.

Now, the second year of drought meant there would be no harvest. No harvest meant no grain. No grain meant no milling. The offer may have seemed a kindness, but there were rumors the king was shrewd and cruel.

An ember popped from the fire onto her skirt, pulling her from her memories. Her hands patted against her knees to prevent further damage to her only dress. A hole the size of a small pebble formed with blackened edges.

Gwen shook her head and smoothed her skirt. She lifted the kettle from the hearth and carried it to the water keg just outside the door. She twisted the spout as she drew her arms together over her chest. The air was crisp and cool. Clear liquid dribbled into the kettle. Quickly at first. But drop. Drop. Drop. Drop. became Drop…. Drop… Drop……… Drop. It was just enough for the soup she was planning.

Back inside, the last of the vegetables from the root cellar went in. She gave it a stir and turned her attention to the table.

Wooden bowls thudded against the wooden surface as she sat them gently in their spots. Beside each, she placed a spoon. Three places. One for her father, one for her mother, and one for herself. Of course, the place for her mother always remained empty. She didn't like to think about it, but Papa insisted it be there. He would throw a tantrum and ruin the meal if she forgot.

Tonight, especially, she wanted everything to be perfect. It was their last meal. There were no more vegetables, no more water. The thought of eating the house cat was detestable. But tomorrow, it would come to that. They would starve to death or beg the king for their lives.

She didn't know what actually became of those who begged. Once a family left the village, she never saw or heard from them again. Some said they fed the fires of the war, or served in the castle. Was that better than starving? Gwen wasn't certain.

As she thought about her fate, the door creaked open, pulling her out of despair. Wiping her cheeks, she pressed a smile on her lips and turned to face her father.

"Papa!" she said as she waited for him to appear. "Come in, I have supper almost ready."

When he didn't emerge immediately, she stepped into the doorway.

A man appeared on the threshold.

Gasping, Gwen jumped away from the door, holding her hand to her chest to calm herself.

He remained in the doorway, hunched and leaning on a cane. His thin grey hair barely covered his head. Mottled skin sagged over the bones in his face. "Hello dear," his feeble voice cracked.

Gwen took a step toward him. "Hello," she replied weakly. There was nothing in the house she could use to defend herself. Until now, there had never been any need for weapons. But the old, stooped man didn't look capable of hurting her, and he had kind eyes.

"I couldn't help but smell your delicious meal as I was passing by. Might I come in and share your stew with you?"

Gwen looked over her shoulder at the pot of soup bubbling over the fire. "My father will be home soon, and there is barely enough for the two of us."

"But you have three places set."

"Yes, one is for my…" she paused, thinking of how to explain her father's irrational insistence that they make a place for her mother. She decided it didn't matter. She would give her last meal to this man and hasten her end. "Nevermind. Please come in."

He stepped through the door. A sharp click as his cane hit the floor echoed through the small room. Gwen busied herself, pulling out a chair for him to sit. He slowly lowered himself onto the wooden and wicker seat and settled in. The creak matched the crackle of the fire.

Gwen snatched up the bowl she had just placed and filled it with vegetables and broth. When she sat it in front of him, the old man greedily slurped the liquid without another word until the dish was drained.

"Too bad there isn't a crust of bread to clean the bowl," he said as he ran a crooked finger around the rim. Gwen didn't reply from her place by the fire.

She fiddled with the locket that hung on a delicate gold chain around her neck. She couldn't bring herself to part with her mother's locket or the ring on her finger. Her father wouldn't have heard of it either. They would rather die than lose the precious heirlooms.

Gwen had developed a habit of sliding the locket along the golden filament while she was thinking. She did this as she watched him with curiosity and a healthy dose of wariness.

"Bread has been hard to come by these last few months," she replied.

"As a miller's daughter, you would know."

"Yes. I would." She stoked the fire to keep the remaining serving of soup warm for her father.

His chocolate-brown eyes twinkled up at her. "That is a lovely trinket you are wearing."

She froze in place. His words slid over her and awakened a warning from deep within her being. It wasn't the words that bothered her. It was something about the way he said it that caused concern. The covetous tone. She immediately hid it away under her apron, mentally chastising herself for having it out at all.

"Might I inquire of its origins?" he asked.

"It…it.." Gwen stumbled over her speech as she tried to come up with some lie that would keep her safe. Not being able to think of any, she decided the truth was the best and would hopefully belie the little man. "It was my mother's and only holds value for me."

He squinted and leaned toward her. After a few moments of scrutiny, he moved back again, a crooked smile pulling at the corners of his mouth. "I was only making interesting conversation," he replied. "No need to worry." His cruel smile revealed twisted and rotten teeth.

Gwen stood abruptly. "I think it is time for you to move along. My father will be home soon. You may call upon him tomorrow."

To her surprise, he didn't argue. He rose slowly from his chair, grabbing his cane from the edge of the table where he had rested it.

"You are right. Your father will be here any moment. We wouldn't want him to find you here alone with a man and no chaperon."

"As you say," she agreed, opening the door and pulling it against her as a shield. She wanted no other argument with him, only that he leave. It would be too soon if she ever saw him again.

He paused as he reached for the doorknob. "Although I wonder what kind of father would leave his lovely daughter at home alone with so many dangers lurking about."

Gwen crossed her arms over her chest. "A father who loves her enough to search for food and work where there is none."

"Perhaps he is looking in the wrong places." The man reached into his coat, retrieved a golden card, pinched between his finger and thumb, and stretched it out to her. "Please give your father my card. Maybe we can make an arrangement."

Thinking it was the fastest way to get rid of him, she politely took the card and said nothing else. The man nodded and walked out the door, whistling a light tune as if the world was not coming to an end. When he was out of sight, she let the door shut. She flipped the card in her hand. In fancy scribbles, it read Woolworth.

She stomped over to the fireplace and stood before it. Everything in her body wanted to toss it into the flames. But her mind stopped her. What if it were a legitimate job offer? What if the creepy little man was their salvation? The door creaked open behind her, moving her to action. Before she knew what she was doing, she slipped the card into her apron and stirred the last serving of their last meal.

Papa

He teetered against the door frame, barely able to stand.

"Papa!" Her steps quickened around the table and toward the door. She threw his arm around her shoulder. The weight of his lean body pressed down on her. "What's happened?"

His head lolled to one side.

"Papa. Are you hurt?"

"Ne…ver… felt…. bedder…" he slurred.

They took several shaky steps to the table. "Papa. Please tell me what's happened." But even as the plea left her lips, she knew the answer.

Gwen lowered her father into his favorite chair opposite hers at the table. The one next to the fire and facing the door. He had claimed it as his when she was very little. So that he could always see what was coming through the door of the home. And always protect her, though there had never been a reason. But with the drought, people were getting desperate. They would do just about anything to anyone.

His muscular arm thudded onto the table, making the bowls and spoons jump. He propped his head on his hand. His cheek slid up, revealing browning teeth. Her father had never been lax about hygiene, but lately he hadn't made it a priority. As his eyes slid shut, his head slipped down his forearm.

She shook him. "Papa. Are you ok?"

He lifted his head. His eyebrows climbed in unison, doing their best to pull his eyelids open. As soon as they succeeded, his eyes narrowed into slits as creases formed between them. "Why do you keep asking me that?"

Gwen took a step back. "I've never seen you like this."

"Like what?" he drawled.

"Are you sick?" She sniffed and immediately scrunched her nose. She waved her hand in front of her face. "You smell awful."

"No. The smell might be from vomit." His chin hit his chest as he struggled to keep it upright.

"You are sick?" she asked again.

He fanned a hand in front of himself, shooing her away. "No. no… the vomit isn't mine."

Gwen leaned against the wall next to the hearth. Something wasn't adding up. She pieced through her father's behavior, but couldn't come up with a plausible explanation. She lifted his bowl from in front of him. "Are you hungry? I made us a lovely meal."

"Pssh. A few carrots in some water is not a lovely meal."

Gwen's head fell forward, and she pressed the heel of her hand into her eye to keep tears from spilling out. "I know." Gwen shrugged, sloshing the vegetables into the dish, careful not to spill any. Every drop was precious. "But it might well be our last. I just wanted it to be nice."

He laughed. "You wanted to pretend it was nice."

She froze where she knelt beside the fire. Her father had never spoken to her like that. Cruel. He was never cruel. Deciding to ignore it and make the best of the situation, she finished preparing his meal and placed it in front of him.

"I was hoping you would pretend with me then."

His head bobbled, and he leaned it against the back of the chair. "No more pretending."

"Fine. Let's be honest then."

Her father rested against his hand again and picked up the spoon, filling it with the clear broth. Immediately, he released the utensil back into the bowl. His head crashed against it. Soup poured down his face and spread into a puddle on the wooden table. Gwen's mouth dropped open in shock as the liquid began dripping through the slats.

The black and white cat appeared instantly to lap up the precious liquid on the floor.

For a few moments, Gwen couldn't move. White-hot tears slid down her face to her chin. After recovering from the initial shock, she found a towel and wiped her father's face. She let the cat clean the rest. Someone might as well enjoy the meal she had spent hours anxiously preparing, wanting it to be just right.

Where did you go to come home this way? She silently asked her father. There were taverns in the town, but they didn't have money to buy drinks. She hoped he had not started a bill with the tavern owner. There was no possibility of their being able to make that right. Judging by the looks of her father, he had had many beverages.

Perhaps I'll go to the tavern myself and ask about it. Looking out the window at the ever-darkening sky, she grabbed a shawl and flung the door open. The wind howled through the trees, and Gwen struggled to keep her hair out of her face. Her skirts blew against her legs, making it difficult to walk.

Fortunately, they lived only a couple of miles outside of town. If her father had ventured into a tavern, she hoped it would be the one closest to home. If it wasn't, she would have to begin her search anew tomorrow.

By the time she reached town, the sky had gone completely dark. Lanterns lit up the buildings that lined the dusty streets. The same buildings now blocked most of the wind from harassing her.

She grabbed a fistful of her garment and stepped onto the rickety boardwalk. Her father told stories of when the town was thriving and new. It gleamed in the golden sun. But that was before. Gwen had never seen that version of her village. She was born not long after magic started its death spiral.

Papa would tell of powerful magicians with crazy abilities. Some could breathe fire, read minds, turn ordinary objects into extraordinary things. Now the king searched his land for anyone with even a whisper of the extraordinary. And if he found them, they were never heard from again.

Her boot clicked on the smoothed wood porch in front of Tilly's Tavern. She didn't hesitate at the door, though she should have. Taverns weren't safe for young women.

Gwen didn't have to open the door. Two men stumbled out, silhouetted against the bright fires from inside. The smell of smoke from hearths and pipes wafted after them. One man had his arm slung around the other and his head lolled to the side. Gwen couldn't understand anything he said. The other man was several inches taller than he was. His muscles flexed under the weight of the burden he carried. As he approached the edge of the porch, he dumped the smaller one in the street. His hands clapped softly when he swiped them past each other, as if he was getting the dust off of them. He paused for a moment as he looked at Gwen and then pulled the door open again and stomped back inside.

Gwen was able to dodge the door and slip in without a word.

Nothing could have prepared her for the scene she found. Across from the entrance, a bar lined the far wall and, beyond that, a well-lit kitchen. At either end of the room, a floor to ceiling hearth roared with fire, making the place feel overwarm. She understood the necessity as a waitress passed her by wearing something more appropriate for a private bedroom than a dining hall.

The rest of the lodge was lined with tables and chairs. Patrons occupied every single seat. And all acted as if there wasn't a drought or famine or destitution in the land. While it looked as if they were filled with happiness, Gwen's heart broke for them. They had quit trying. Instead of finding their joy in hard work and an honest living, they drowned their woes in the frothy amber liquid being served by the woman behind the bar.

Gwen made her way to the lady to ask about her father.

The woman wore different clothes than the others in the tavern. She didn't show as much skin, but she still looked alluring. The woman had curly dark hair teased behind a red ribbon that tied at the nape. A white ruffled shirt slipped off one shoulder. Her apron knotted neatly around her waist. Her curves were rounded and soft. Missing was the gaunt look most had when trying to survive with little food.

She wiped her white towel over a glass mug with disinterest.

"If you're looking for work try the tavern on the other end of the street. We don't have any positions available." She turned away from the bar and placed the glass on the rack behind her.

"I'm not looking for work," Gwen glanced down at the varnished bar. "At least not yet."

"Oh?" the woman raised her eyebrows in interest. "What are you drinking then?"

Gwen pursed her lips and shook her head, reaching for the locket under her apron. "I'm not here for that either."

"I don't have all night miss. State your business, or…" she lifted her chin toward the door.

"I was wondering if you've seen this man." Gwen opened the necklace and showed her the picture of her father next to her mother.

"You his wife?"

"No," she sighed. "I'm his daughter."

"We don't tattle in this tavern. And you might want to put that thing away before someone sees and decides they'd like to have it for themselves."

"Its not genuine gold and it's not worth anything."

"It looks authentic enough so that wouldn't stop a thief."

Gwen tucked the locket back under her collar. "My father is home safe. I'm only searching for the tavern to see if he has a debt to settle."

The woman laughed loudly, drawing the attention of several patrons around her. Gwen pulled her head into her shoulders under the scrutiny.

"I've never heard of such a thing. Why would you come seeking to settle his debts?"

"He's my father and if he has a debt, I'm also responsible for it. He's taken care of me all these years why would I not care for him?"

The surrounding men had gone back to drinking and talking. "I'm Tilly." The woman reached out with her right hand to Gwen.

"Gwen," she said, taking the woman's hand and shaking it. "How do you keep this place running? I can barely find water enough for two."

Tilly nodded and went back to wiping the glasses. "The king supplies all taverns. Calls it essential business. I don't argue. *Essentially* I'm keeping the peace here." She nudged her chin towards Gwen. "Your father was in here. He settled his own tab."

The king was shrewd, keeping everyone too drunk to rebel.

"But where did Papa get the money for that?" she asked.

"Rumor has it that he sold something valuable to the king."

"We have nothing."

"You will find, Gwen, that what one thinks has no value is often just looking for the right price."

"I suppose he could have sold the mill to the king, but I didn't think His Highness made offers twice."

"He doesn't." The glass squeaked as she wiped it around the rim.

"Who's this, Tilly?" A tall man, who obviously hadn't been missing any meals, interrupted their conversation.

"She's leaving Rosco."

"Aw. But I just met her. You can't be going yet."

Gwen stood from her seat. "Yes. Actually, I need to be getting back. My father will be waiting for me."

Rosco took a step closer so that his belly, fortunately covered by a rough flannel shirt, rubbed along her forearm. Gwen stepped away, but bumped into another man almost as big, who had silently appeared behind her.

"Boys. You will not harass my customer." Tilly motioned with her head for the man Gwen followed in to come over.

"We just want to have a little talk. And besides she didn't buy no drinks, so she ain't a customer."

Gwen was tall, but these two were at least a foot taller than her. She peered up at them. "I really need to be getting home. Rosco. It was a pleasure meeting you." Gwen tried to slip between the men. Rosco placed a meaty hand on her shoulder.

"Not so fast Gwen. It's dangerous out there at night. My brother Rowdy and I will walk you home."

Gwen laughed nervously. "That's so nice and gentlemanly of you really. But I can handle myself." Her toes moved back marginally, poised for running.

Rosco opened his mouth to insist again when a palm wrapped over Gwen's wrist. She found herself behind a man wearing all black. His dark hair waved over the crown of his head, curled around one ear and tapered down his neck. The only thing that stood out against his attire were his eyes, which burned with the fire of a thousand suns.

"Gwen. Go now." He motioned with those eyes toward the door.

Gwen stumbled out without looking back at the men or Tilly. As she careened toward her house in the dark, a few thoughts crossed her mind.

Who was he? How did he know my name?

What did my father sell?

There's no way that old man would hire me as a cook after the meal I served him today.

* * *

When she returned home windblown and tired, her father had not budged from where she'd left him.

He snorted from the table. She went to his side and tried to shake him awake. He only snored louder. "Papa. We need to get you to bed." She shook him again. He didn't even twitch an eye.

She looked about the room, trying to figure out what to do with him. "How can I move you to bed?" she whispered.

Gwen brought her hand to her chin and tapped it in thought. "On second thought perhaps you deserve to sleep on the table. It will serve you right." Her voice bounced around the little cottage, causing the cat's eyes to open to slits. Finding nothing amiss, he went back to napping.

She stoked the fire but didn't add another log. Without it, the house would be unbearably cold, but wood was almost as scarce as grain. Though that wasn't the fault of the weather. The king had cleared forest after forest for his building projects. He paid well for the property, and landowners didn't often turn down a deal with him. No one aspired to be put out with the king.

As she placed her hand on the beam that separated her bedroom from the living area, she looked over her shoulder. A loud snore erupted from her father. Her chest rose and fell as she sighed and shook her head. "I can't leave him like that. He'll freeze."

She stomped back over to his chair and lifted her palm. It fell onto his face with a loud slap. The sting traveled from her fingers up to her elbow. Her father jumped only slightly and cracked open his eyes into an annoyed squint.

"You have to go to bed."

"You won't tell me what… ta do," he said. His words slurred together. Gwen crossed her arms and waited for him to get himself up. There was no other way to move him to bed. She lifted her hand to slap him again. The only way to pull him out of this chair was to make him mad.

But he didn't get mad. He lifted his arms to protect himself from her. And wept.

"Please don't hit me."

The cracking of her heart was almost unbearable, stealing her breath. His arms slowly lowered, and pure terror stared back at her through his emerald eyes. He was genuinely afraid. Her boots barely made a sound as she took a slow step backwards. How had it come to this so quickly?

Tears burned the back of her eyes, and she shook her head. "I'm sorry Papa." She rushed to his side. He flinched away, but that didn't deter her. "I'm sorry. I was just trying to move you to your warm bed. You can't stay here and catch cold. I can't carry you."

His eyes softened with each word, and inch by inch he relaxed, as if her words could help him remember who she was. She finally tugged on his arm.

"Come on. Let's get you to bed and we can forget all about this."

He hoisted himself from the chair at her insistence. In the course of the day, he seemed to have aged ten years. She lifted his arm around her shoulders again to support his weight as he shuffled to his bedroom. His words were barely audible, but she heard clearly. "I know it seems dreadful now, but I've got it all worked out."

"It doesn't seem terrible papa. It is terrible."

"No. I made it right." His voice broke.

Gwen groaned as Papa rested the weight of his body on her. "I have no idea what you are talking about," she said.

"At the tavern. There was a man."

"Usually."

He pursed his lips before saying, "No, I mean a special man."

Gwen almost lost her hold on him. "Father. What did you do?"

"Nothing any father doesn't have a right to do. I'm so proud that you are my daughter. I just had to tell him all about you."

"And what did you tell him?"

Papa smiled that smile she saw when she did something he admired. Like when she was six and stood up to a little girl who was picking on another girl. Papa had leaned against a tree watching the exchange. When it was over, he knelt before her and told her how proud he was of her.

"Oh. Only the best stuff."

Gwen grumbled. *So, I will be sold off to a household to work as a maid or servant of some sort.* It hadn't sounded so bad a few moments ago when she had thought of it herself, but now that it was about to be reality, she didn't like it.

"Don't be that way. I told him how beautiful you were. And what amazing soup you make," he said.

"Great papa. Maybe I'll make enough to send you some every once in a while."

"Oh no. He wasn't interested in you working for him. I told him how just like your mama you are."

"No one even knows Mama. I doubt that was very endearing."

She took another step, dragging him along. The stubble on his chin scraped against her sleeve.

"She was the best." His lips pulled back from his crooked teeth in a genuine smile filled with love.

"I know you miss her, Papa." She grunted and let him fall into bed.

"She would have been able to save you." Papa's eyelids slid shut.

Gwen tilted her head. "Us you mean?"

"No. I mean you," he said, reaching for her cheek in a moment of clarity. "You look just like her. If only you really had her magic."

Magic

Gwen took a step back from him. Any moisture left in her mouth dried up. Her eyelids fluttered. Magic? No one had magic. Not since before she was born. An invisible force swept through the land and wiped out all the magic wielders. Magic died everywhere except in the kingdom of the White Witch, Mystrim. The witch had erected a barrier between the dying lands of Aurum and her kingdom. No one in Aurum could explain the loss. Some magic users lost their magic and died after many months of sickness. Some didn't get sick at all.

She shook her head. Her father had to be mistaken. He had explained this himself many times and believed the death of magic in Aurum to be the reason for the drought.

He's drunk, she told herself. *He hardly knows where he is, much less anything about magic.*

Papa's lips fluttered. The slow whooshing of breath proved he had finally rested. Any moment and it would sound as if the mill had started again. She tugged at the old leather of his boots. They slipped free from his feet, revealing soiled, holey socks. She sighed. Another chore to add to the next day. Washing and mending, if they lived that long, and if she could find the water.

She left him snoring on his bed, fully clothed. She doubled over his blanket and wrapped it to his chin.

It had been a long, eventful evening. Gwen knew she should retire, but with her father tucked safely in, there was no longer a need to worry about when or if he might return. It was a perfect time to read the only book kept in the house. Her mother's diary.

"I've read this a hundred times and there's never any mention of magic," she whispered.

The only light in the small home came from the dying fire. The smell of smoke and soot that coated everything was barely noticeable. Anyone who visited would probably think differently. She slid a chair near the hearth, barely allowing it to scrape the floor. Her father wouldn't wake, but she cringed all the same. The sound grated on her.

"Let's see what Mama has to say." She turned page after yellowed page, reading the familiar words. From when she met Frederick, Gwen's papa, up to when she was about to give birth to Gwen. The entries cut off after that. The last page had a rough, jagged edge near the binding. A mystery since she had first read the diary. No one seemed to know anything about it.

Her mother didn't live long after giving birth. All her strength had gone into delivering a baby into the world, and there was nothing left to keep her going. Though Gwen often dreamt of her mother chasing her through a forest, laughing. Even in the dream, she could smell honeysuckle mixed with the earth musk of the forest floor. She always assumed her mother must smell of honey. It always ended with the golden light of the afternoon sun filtering through the trees. Her mother's carefree laughter turned to a stern warning. "Run!" Gwen woke up screaming night after night until she was a teenager. Then the dreams just stopped. Along with the terror of the dream, Gwen dreaded having children for fear of ending up like her mother. Dead.

But even after scouring the pages for mentions of magic, there was nothing that even came close to it. She needed to put this out of her mind. A whisper of magic or hiding anyone with it was enough for a treason charge. Gwen could only hope her father had said nothing about it in the tavern.

But even as she hoped it wasn't so, dread built in her chest as a whole new set of fears took over.

* * *

"Gwen!" her father screamed from the bedroom. Her body pitched forward, and eyes opened wide. Her breath immediately sped up. She realized she had fallen asleep. Her mother's diary lay closed, her thumb still on the page she was reading, when she let her eyes drift shut for a quick rest.

"Gwen!" Papa's voice was closer now.

"I'm here Papa," she said.

The sun hadn't quite made it over the horizon, but the morning light was enough to see by. The fire had died, and a chill had settled over the cabin. Goosebumps prickled along Gwen's arms and down her spine.

His eyes were full of fear and worry. The lines on his face seemed to have deepened overnight, and his shoulders were slightly more hunched. "Oh Gwen… What have I done?" He pressed his hands to the sides of his face.

"You went to the local tavern and sold me to the highest bidder," she said, with more anger than she felt. She knelt beside the fire. Ash floated into a single ray of sunlight when she stirred the coals and added another log barely the size of her arm to the fire. Her cheeks puffed as she blew the embers into bright red sparks until a small flame caught. She loved the crackle of wood. Keeping a fire wasn't always easy, and starting one could be challenging. The sound of the wood catching was victory.

Papa threw back the blankets and hopped off the bed. His hands gripped what little hair he had left on either side of his face. "I didn't… I didn't have a choi… I'm so sorry Gwen. I didn't know what…"

She held up a hand. "It's fine papa. I knew this day would come if you didn't find work. Why you turned down the king's offer to buy this place, I'll never understand."

"I didn't want to leave your mother then. But… this is bad." He paced from the bed to the hearth.

"I know things could always be worse. But perhaps its not as bad as it seems."

He knelt beside her, grabbed her hands and squeezed. "You must flee."

"What? Why? What are you talking about." She searched his eyes for remnants of the drunkenness of the night before. They were clear.

"I told everyone."

"Told them what?"

"What you are."

She pulled her hands away and stood. "I'm just a girl. A miller's daughter." She stepped beside him to start her tasks for the day. But he blocked her and took her shoulders in both hands.

"No! You are more. Your mother forbade me from talking about it, from telling you. But she's been gone for so long. It must be done. Gwen, you have magic."

She tried to shake him off. His fingers curled and dug into her bony flesh. Gwen winced at the pain it caused. "Stop it. Stop talking about magic. You know I don't have any such thing."

His eyes glistened while his eyebrows pressed up in the middle. "It doesn't matter now. You must run girl." He dropped his hands.

"What are you talking about?"

"The king's men will be here any moment to arrest you."

"Why would they?"

"I've sold you. You see. And I deeply regret it now. But I can't change it. You are to marry the prince as is your birthright."

"My birthright?! You must still be drunk. How can I? I am only a miller's daughter. A commoner."

"You're not. Your mother had magic, she was a…" he couldn't finish the sentence. Not that he didn't want to. It was more that it was physically impossible. He gave up and settled with, "And you have it too."

Gwen shook her head. "I don't understand."

His hands shook. "And I wish I had time to explain, but there is none. You must run." He grabbed her arm again, just above the elbow, and rushed her toward the door.

He stopped with hands on the wooden knob when hoofbeats now pounded out a rhythmic thud against the hard ground. The beats slowed even as Gwen's heart raced. Papa's mouth formed a grim line. He spoke nothing else, pushing her toward the back window and making her go. "Will I ever see you again?" she whispered.

He didn't say a word. Only shook his head. A glint of a tear in his eye as he hardened his features and turned away from her. The sharp knocks against the front door set her feet toward escape.

Sold

Gwen scurried over the field just behind their home. There was nowhere to hide. The fields were dead, and the trees had all been felled. But as she ran as fast as she could, she tripped over a mound of dirt someone had forgotten. Debris had piled around it. She hoped an animal hadn't made its home inside. No time to worry about that. She hid. Her curiosity couldn't be contained, though, so she peeked over the edge.

She was too close, but it was too late to run further. If the king's men saw her, they would arrest her for certain. It was best to wait it out and try to get away later. If only Papa had let her in on his little tryst earlier.

"Hello gentlemen. What brings you to my humble home?" Papa asked. He didn't bow or grovel. His words were friendly, but his tone hinted he wouldn't be cowed.

"We've come to collect what you've promised the king," the captain said. His slow steps the only sound disturbing the shaky peace of the morning. His eyes darted from one side of the cottage to the other in his obvious inspection for hiding spots.

Papa's eyes slid between the royal guards and the captain, who barely raised an eyebrow.

"Oh yes, that." He raised a finger in the air as if he were finally remembering. "Well, as you can see my daughter is not here. She's gone away. Been gone for days actually. I hadn't realized she went on a trip to see her cousins in Caerphilly. Perhaps if you head out now, you can catch up with her."

The captain tsked. "In fact, your daughter was seen in the tavern just last night. The prince himself rescued her from two rather rough looking fellows. You know the punishment for not living up to your promise to the king." His stance was wide and relaxed. Both gauntleted hands rested on the hilt of his sword.

"The prince?" Gwen whispered. She hadn't recognized him. She was sure most of the occupants of the tavern hadn't either.

Papa lifted his chin. "Yes. I'm aware."

"You are her father. You are in charge. If she is gone then you are responsible."

"Ha. That girl is as stubborn as they come. I can't be held responsible for her actions. Why do you think I sold her to you?"

It was true. He had sold her. Gwen's heart raced against her rib cage. Why had Papa done this? He had been rather drunk. Had his mouth run away with him? He said he didn't have a choice?

All excellent questions to which she would likely never have the answers. At least not answers she would like. *It doesn't matter now.* She thought. *What matters is surviving the next few moments.*

The captain and her father continued to argue. He was buying her time to escape. And all she could do was lie in the tall dead grass and hide.

She lifted herself onto her arms and knees, trying to stay low and crawl away.

"And where do you think you're going?" a rough voice said from behind her. She flipped around just in time to catch a boot in the chin. A dull ache filled her skull as her head bounced against the hard ground. Bright lights danced across her vision even as she was forming a somewhat coherent answer to the question.

"I was just coming home and saw the king's guard."

"So you thought to hide in the field?" he said.

"I thought it wise to wait."

"You thought wrong." His massive hand folded around her golden hair and yanked her up to standing. The metal plating of the gauntlet dug into her scalp. As her toes swiped against the dusty ground, she felt the sharp burn of a cut. A warm liquid slid down her neck onto the collar of the blouse.

The guard grabbed the reins of his horse. *How had I not heard him approach?*

She chastised herself silently.

Pushing her with one hand and leading his horse with the other, he made his way back to her house. She struggled against his grip. "I can walk on my own," she said, even though she wasn't sure she could.

"I can't have you running off again. I don't want this to take all day."

"No. We wouldn't want you to be away from the hole you crawled out of for longer than is necessary," she said.

He tightened his grip and pulled her close. He sniffed the air next to her ear. "It smells better than the one you live in," he whispered. She tried to pull away from the putrid stench of his mangled teeth, but his fist was like a vise.

In a few dreadful seconds, they reached the front of the house. He released her, letting her fall. Her hands scraped along the dry ground. Dirt filled the crevices. Sharp stings added to her list of aches. The soil covered her apron as she lifted her body to a kneeling position. Then, her foot moved forward. She placed both scraped and bleeding hands on her knee, giving herself leverage to push her body to standing.

"Gwen. It's such a surprise to see you back from your visit so soon." Papa smiled insincerely. "These men were just looking for you."

The man behind her growled a warning not to run. She dusted her hands over her apron, glaring over her shoulder. "Why would they care so much about finding me, Papa? I'm just a nobody."

The captain looked from her father to her. "You have been bought and paid for. You will put your talents to use in the castle."

Papa's eyes filled with terror, which quickly turned to anger. "You said she would be married to the king."

The captain drew his sword and pressed it to Papa's throat. "Once she proves she can do what you claimed she can do."

Papa's hands raised in defense, and he leaned away from the sword. "And if she can't do what I said she could do?"

The captain pressed the sword further until a small trickle of blood formed on the edge. "You wouldn't have lied to the king would you?" The captain whispered, his lips pulling into a sneer.

"No. No of course not." Papa's voice was weak. He barely formed a whispered rebuttal. His courage had run its course.

Gwen slipped out of the range of the guard behind her and placed a gentle hand on the captain's arm. "Put the sword down. I'll do it. Whatever it is. Just don't hurt him further."

The captain's smile grew wider, and he pushed Papa away. His fingers wrapped around her thin neck. "Do you even know what he promised?" he growled.

Gwen didn't look away or at her father. She met the captain's eyes. "Probably that I have magic." Her voice strained against the crushing of her windpipe.

The captain squeezed more. He could have easily broken her neck with a single hand, but she didn't allow herself to whimper. The captain's lips turned down. Deep lines marred his face on either side of his mouth, and dark stubble made him all the more menacing.

He released her with a growl.

He twirled his finger, and a powerful arm grabbed the back of her dress and placed her on a horse. She found herself in front of the guard who had captured her in the field. Struggling in his grasp, she turned to look at her father as they were riding away.

She couldn't convey how much she would miss him or that she was sorry she would never see him again. His face filled with sorrow. The guard adjusted herself on the horse, trying to keep her from looking backward, but she managed to see her father one last time as he fell to his knees. His eyes never left her as the captain knocked him on the head with the hilt of his sword. Dirt puffed up around him as his body hit the ground. The captain stepped over him and walked to his horse, leaving her father for dead.

The Castle

"Nooo," the word tore from her throat, burning on its way out.

The guard wrestled her and held her tight. "Quiet! And quit squirming or you'll end up with your head in the dirt too." He warned. His teeth ground together.

"He killed him." Tears spilled over the rims of her eyes and poured down her cheeks. A sob built in her throat. She hid her face in her hands. Against her will, her body relaxed into her captors. Her muscles were too weak to protest any longer.

"Don't worry. He's not likely dead, but he'll wake up with a nasty lump." His rough words bit through her grief.

"It doesn't matter," she said. Her voice was weak. "He'll be dead by morning if he's left there."

The guard grunted and leaned forward to speed up the horse. The giant black mare easily cantered, carrying two. Her bridle and reins jingled with each hoofbeat. Gwen allowed the cadence to lull her body into a numb acceptance. She relaxed into the guard's hold. If she fell from the horse, would it matter?

The sun had reached its peak by the time the king's men slowed, bringing the horses to a halt. The guard lowered her to the ground. It was the gentlest he had been. Gwen had sat uncomfortably in front of him. Even after the short ride, she was stiff. Her left leg had long ago gone numb. As the blood rushed into it, her gait was slow and uneven. She rubbed her thighs, willing the tingles to abate.

The captain tied his horse to a nearby tree and approached Gwen.

"Hold out your hands."

Gwen didn't move.

"Hold out your hands."

She refused to take her eyes off him as she raised them in front of her. Annoyance flashed across the captain's face at her slow pace. He grabbed her hands and moved them to shoulder level. He slipped a rope around her wrists.

"Worried I'll run away?" she asked.

"I'm hoping you're smarter than that," he said, wrapping another coil around her wrists. "But its been seven nights since I've slept in my own bed, and I don't want to delay that luxury any longer by hunting you down in the forest. This is a precaution."

She rolled her eyes.

The captain shoved her toward a nearby stump. "Rest up. We have several more hours of riding ahead of us."

Gwen barely held back a sneer, but took a seat on a felled tree.

The men went about feeding and watering the horses. Some even brought out grooming kits and wiped down their mounts. They removed the saddles and blankets and gave them a quick brush. It surprised Gwen how well they cared for the animals.

Another of the guards, a tall man with skin that hadn't wrinkled with age, pulled a satchel from his bags. He allowed himself a slight smile as he handed her a bit of dried meat.

"Thank you," she said as she grasped the morsel between her bound hands.

"Don't thank me yet. It's not the best, but it does well on long journeys such as this." His voice was not as low as the other guards. Gwen guessed he hadn't been employed by the king long enough to develop the gravel in his voice.

"Have you been traveling long?"

"Yes. We are required to carry out the king's business routinely. And this journey took us farther to the south than is normal."

"It is rare to see the King's guard in Sterling," Gwen agreed.

"Blum… tend to your horse," the captain barked the order.

Gwen lifted the dried meat to her lips and tore a piece with her teeth. It was the first bite she had eaten in two days. She wasn't sure what type of meat it was, but it was overly salted and required every drop of moisture in her mouth to swallow. Even so, she didn't dare ask for a drink. She dropped the rest into her apron pocket.

Once they had attended to the animals, the Captain stood in front of her. He pulled her up by her bound hands and dragged her to his horse. He unscrewed the lid of his canteen and lifted it to her lips. She desperately wanted to refuse, but her lips seemed to have a mind of their own.

"You'll ride astride behind me the rest of the way," he said as he pulled the water away.

Gwen flinched as if someone had hit her.

"I prefer not to sit with a murderer."

"None of my men are murderers. We carry out the king's justice swiftly."

She scoffed. "Whatever you have to tell yourself," she whispered.

The captain leaned into her space. She could feel his breath as he spoke. "You will ride behind me on my horse or be dragged. Which do you prefer?"

She squinted her eyes but said nothing. The captain backed away and mounted his horse with ease. He reached for Gwen. She placed her still-bound hands in his and allowed him to help her onto the steed. She wrapped her fingers into the back of his shirt to keep from falling off as he urged his charcoal horse back onto the road. If he hadn't belonged to the captain, she would have found the color unique for horses.

"Jones's horse caught a rock in her hoof. Carrying two isn't possible," he said.

"Too bad. I was just getting used to his awful smell."

The captain shook his head and continued on in silence.

* * *

They approached the castle just after the sun had sunk below the horizon. The torches threw shadows that danced against the bricks. Even in the dark, it was imposing. Built high on a hill, its silhouette loomed over the countryside.

It was a typical castle with turrets and towers made of rock. Gwen only noticed as they passed through the stone gate, which remained open most of the time. It was only closed during times of war or unrest. If the drought remained for much longer, they would be closed soon. Perhaps Tilly's tavern was part of the plan to keep it open. But Gwen and her papa were not the only ones to have had their last meal recently. When people went hungry, they got angry.

The royal guard wound its way through the cobblestone streets. An entire village had risen within the walls surrounding the castle. Small cottages built into hillsides and buildings on top of each other. Candles lit up narrow windows throughout the town.

Laundry hung to dry between the windows like tiny flags waving them on. It was quaint and quiet, as if nothing bad could ever happen here. Gwen knew better. Bad situations happened everywhere. The places where it seemed nothing evil could take place were usually where the worst things went on. Where you'd least expect it. Nothing all that awful had ever happened to her, until now, but she had heard stories from the local farm girls.

A stable boy approached and helped her off the horse. Hours of riding had taken their toll on her body, and she longed for a soothing bath.

"Don't think about running," the captain grumbled and nudged her toward the castle entrance.

"Where would I go?" she asked.

"Exactly."

She gathered her skirts the best she could and trudged up the steps. With each step, she wanted to swear that she would use whatever magic her father thought she had to punish those who had caused his death. But the truth was, she did not know what magic she had or how to manage it. She would never make a vow she didn't know if she could keep. And if she had magic, she would want to use it for good. In defense of people, rather than destroying in the name of her vengeance.

As she walked beside him through the castle doors and on its carpeted floors, she buried the anger. She needed to stay focused and be ready.

She hadn't expected them to keep their end of the bargain they had with her father. But here she was in the castle. For a few minutes at least. When they discovered she had no abilities, they'd throw her out, or worse. It was no longer anger that caused her hands to shake.

They walked through endless halls and finally stood before a guarded room with grand mahogany doors. Of course, Gwen couldn't be sure it was mahogany-she had never seen one- but it was large and thick and deep crimson. The captain untied the rope from her hands. She absently rubbed at her wrists where the binding had been. Fortunately, the skin was only slightly red. Much longer and she would have open wounds.

"Open the doors. We are expected," the captain said.

The guards didn't move. They stood like silly statues dressed in crisp black pants, shiny shoes, and bright red coats. Their coats had gold brocade draped from shoulder to hip. Gwen could barely see their eyes. They wore their tall cylinder helmets low on the brow and strapped below their chin.

The captain cleared his throat, waiting for them to comply with his directive. The guard on the right shifted from one foot to the other, showing his nervousness at ignoring the captain.

"Brody. Graden?" There was a question in his tone. Then he sighed.

"I'm assuming the king has reversed his decision and no longer wants to share a meal with his betrothed," the captain asked.

The one on the left cleared his throat. "We don't know. Only that he doesn't want to be disturbed."

The captain kept his annoyance on a tight leash, but it showed in the twitch of his lip. His chest rose and fell. Gwen stumbled after him when he yanked her by the elbow as he stomped away. His frown and the muscle ticking in his jaw betrayed him.

"Where are we to go now?" Gwen asked.

The captain didn't stop until he was down the hall and around the corner from the two guards. He stopped and put both hands on her shoulders. "I'm truly sorry for what is about to happen. This is not what you deserve."

The captain was gruff and intolerable in front of the guards. His men. What was so bad that the captain was apologizing beforehand? Or could it all be an act for those he was in charge of? Perhaps she had misjudged the captain. But it didn't matter. He had already killed her father. Probably.

She allowed herself to whimper only once. A small outlet for her anxiety. She was at their mercy, especially the captain's. When she couldn't produce the magic her father promised, she would be next.

The captain turned away from her. He ran his hand through his short dark hair, grabbing it at the end. "You were to have a meal before…"

"I'm not hungry…" she cut herself off as her stomach chose that moment to betray her. She had expected to starve to death, and with the day's events, her hunger hadn't registered.

"Right. Come with me."

He didn't touch her, just expected her to follow. She did. What else was she to do? She'd already gotten lost in the labyrinth of the unfamiliar castle.

After turning left and taking a few steps, they reached the end of the hallway. Each corner of the corridor was rounded with stones. Regal banners and tapestries hung from the ceiling. Red velvet curtains with golden tassels were tied back on either side of the wall in front of them. It was odd and ostentatious. But the captain disappeared behind the column on the right, leaving her alone. She tilted her head, trying to figure out the space and why it was so different.

The captain poked his nose out of the column and motioned for her to follow him. "We don't have all night," he grumbled.

"Just when I thought he was being nice to me," Gwen whispered. Remembering she was on her way to her destiny, which was probably death, she put one foot in front of the other and made it to the captain. The column hid a spiral staircase, which now opened before her. She and the captain would not fit together. An oil lantern nestled into a niche above every other step. The stone and plaster wall wound around the steps. There were no windows, so the lights were necessary. Gwen wondered if they were perpetually burning or if someone had to light them. She silently trudged down the steps behind the captain until the space opened to a bright and warm kitchen.

Gwen blinked in surprise. Great ovens lined the wall to the right. Two rows of prep counters stood between her and the ovens, and still she could feel the heat. It wasn't unpleasant, but stifling. One of the prep counters held baskets of vegetables. Carrots, leeks, cabbage, potatoes. The second was currently bare, but by the bloodstained butcher blocks and sharp knives that lay upon it, Gwen decided it was the meat prep area.

Opposite her were large sinks full of dishes. In front of them, a petite maid scrubbed away the dirt and grime. The rest of the staff sat at a large table eating their meal. The smell of which made Gwen's mouth water. Her stomach growled again.

The captain looked over his shoulder at her, a grumble escaping his throat. He took a step back and grabbed her upper arm, shoving her toward the table. All the kitchen staff had stopped eating and stared at her. Some with their utensil midway to their mouth with a bite of food.

The captain pulled out a chair and shoved her into it.

"Eat."

She looked around the table. Their eyes found other places to look. A large fist landed on the table, clattering the plates. Gwen wasn't the only one to jump.

"We don't have time for you to be shy." He grabbed an empty plate someone had left and piled food from the table onto it. A roll, a slice of ham, a couple of carrots. It was the most decadent meal she had in weeks.

With the plate in front of her, she could hold back her manners no longer. She shoveled the food into her mouth as politely as she could and pushed it aside. No one had looked at her the entire time and refused to speak in her presence. There wasn't much to say, anyway. She was likely to be dead in a few hours.

As Gwen rose from the table, so did the bile. She forced it to stay inside. She would not be sick in front of strangers, and most especially in front of the captain. He had taken a place nearby. Arms crossed over his chest, knee raised, foot resting against the wall. His sword hung freely at his side. His hands crossed over the hilt.

She stepped away from the table and took a step toward the stairs they had come down.

"Not that way," the captain said without moving. She froze, waiting for him to lead. He shoved away from the wall and started in the opposite direction.

She turned and followed him, but paused. Turning to the kitchen staff, she curtsied. "Thank you for allowing me to share your meal. I won't forget your kindness," she said and ran to catch up.

Descent

As they descended another hidden staircase, the hushed whispers reached her ears. "That's the miller's daughter."

"It's said she has magic."

She cringed. There would be no escaping it now. The entire kingdom thought she had magic, and when they found out she didn't, she would be ridiculed and driven out. There would be no recovering her reputation. Death was the least of her worries.

The descent continued, and goosebumps rose along Gwen's arms through her thin fabric. Dingy grey and bright green moss grew along the bottom of the liquid coated the walls. She barely held herself back from licking the walls. While the villages were struggling, water dripped along the walls here. Why had the drought not affected the castle?

She shook the question out of her mind. "Where are we going exactly?"

The captain didn't answer immediately, and she thought he wouldn't when he cleared his throat. "Somewhere you can… demonstrate your magic."

She sighed. "Oh good. I was beginning to think you were taking me to the dungeon."

He remained silent. After a few more steps, they reached the base of the staircase. The lamps still filled the niches in the wall, but the darkness felt as though it was pressing down on her. On the other side of the circular platform, stood a closed metal door. Huge rivets lined its edges, and in the center was a small opening with bars. What little light there was from the window was dim and tinted green.

"Oh," she whimpered, realizing he had taken her to the dungeon.

He produced a key and shoved it into the lock. She was too preoccupied with her new fate that she hadn't noticed where it came from.

The door swung toward them, and she backed up a little, looking over her shoulder at the stairs. For a moment she contemplated escaping up them, but how would she make it up without being overrun by the captain, and where would she go when she reached the top? Would that be better than dying in the damp dungeon?

She turned toward the cells and lifted her chin. If she were to die, she would do it with dignity. Not running from her fate.

She stepped through the opening. "May I ask a favor?"

The captain didn't respond. The only sounds were their footsteps as they walked down the narrow corridor, passing black metal doors every few feet.

"If I die please don't leave my body to be eaten by rats."

"There are no rats in our dungeons," he replied after another long silence.

"Oh? That's good. I'm glad I can mark that off my list of worries," she said. Her voice, barely above a whisper.

He finally stopped at the only open cell door. She hadn't seen or heard another prisoner during this entire journey.

"Why are the other prisoners so quiet?"

"There is a sound suppression spell on the cells so that the sounds don't carry up to the ears of the royal household."

Gwen's mouth opened in shock. Magic died years ago. How could a spell still be active?

He held up a hand, anticipating her unspoken question. "Don't ask me how it works. It was in place long before magic died."

He stood outside the door and motioned her in. Nothing could have prepared her for what she stepped into. She turned to run out as quickly as she could, but the captain blocked the exit.

She pushed against his broad chest but couldn't make it past him. After three attempts, she took two steps back, heaving deep breaths of stale air. "Where did you get all this straw?" she asked between breaths.

"It doesn't matter. You are to spin it into gold."

Gwen laughed. Of all her tasks at the mill, spinning had never been one of them. Surely this was the work of some dark fate playing games with her life.

"You think I can spin straw into gold?"

He continued to fill the doorway with his feet apart, hand on his weapon as if she might bolt at any moment. "No. But the king was told and convinced you can. He paid a hefty sum for your ability. He is expecting a return on his investment."

"Families are starving. Animals are starving and yet you have straw sitting around in warehouses ready for the impossible task of being spun into gold?" Infuriated, she stepped up to the captain, inches from his nose. She had to look up into his eyes, but that did not squelch the fire in her own. Still, he did not budge.

"Your only concern with this straw is whether it becomes gold. You have until morning. Survive that task and you may well be able to do something about its further use."

He shoved her back, and the heavy metal door slammed into place.

The lock clicked. There was no sound of his retreat. The sound suppression spell wouldn't allow it, she supposed.

She collapsed where she stood. Her skirts billowed around her, and she caught her head in her hands. Hot tears spilled onto her burning cheeks. The heat of her anger drained away and left her cold and shivering. Her breath became visible before her. Even if she could spin, her fingers would be too frozen to do the job.

"They really are making this more difficult than necessary," she said, but no one could hear her.

Dungeon

"By the way, I can't be in a room full of straw without suffocating to death," she said to no one. She truly would be dead by morning. Was starving to death a better way to go?

Her skin was already itching with what were sure to be red welts. In the next few minutes, her eyes would become bloodshot, watery, and puffy. After that, her nose would be stuffed up and runny simultaneously. However, that worked. It wouldn't be an hour before her windpipe was closing.

Weeping into her hands wasn't helping the situation. She sat near the door, but they had filled the cell floor to ceiling with bales of straw. There was barely space for the spinning wheel.

She wished for some water or something to dampen the cloth of her apron, but of course, even with the abundance of water in the castle, the cell was dry. Dusty material would have to do. She pulled the bottom toward her nose and mouth.

She didn't really know what she was aiming for. Either she died from anaphylactic shock or from an executioner's blade. For a few moments, she longed for the blade. It would be quicker and less painful. Here she would suffer. Had her father known this would be her fate? Dying. Alone in a dungeon. Her stomach churned as heat flushed her face. Why had he done this? A question she would never get the answer to, and her anger would only make the problem worse. If he had known, he wouldn't have deserved a moment more of her thoughts. But what if he truly believed she could do this?

As she pulled her apron up, the card from the strange old man tumbled out and twirled to the ground at her feet. She snatched it up and read the name out loud. "Woolworth," she said. Liquid in her eyes spilled over. Her body's way of protecting her from the onslaught of foreign microparticles.

She groaned. "I will not rub them. I will not rub them," she chanted, knowing that would only make it worse. Once she started pressing her palm into her eye to get relief, she would never stop.

There was no use in calling for anyone to take her to the executioner now. Her cries would die at the door. "I have to at least give the gold spinning a try. Maybe Papa knew something I don't."

Perhaps she could unlock some latent magic everyone seemed to think she possessed. The king's men were certainly more than a little skeptical. She wished to prove them wrong.

"I'll use my apron as a mask. But I need my hands free if I'm going to do this." Her fingers were so stiff the knots were difficult to manage. After several attempts, the apron slipped free, and she wrapped it over her head, covering her nose and mouth, then secured it with another knot. Hopefully, it would filter out some of the allergens, or simply prolong her suffering. Her shoulders wanted to slump at the thought, but she wouldn't let them. It wasn't the first time things had looked bleak, so she resolved to hope. *"If I accomplish this task, somehow, perhaps the king will let me go home and check on Papa."* She nodded, agreeing with her own delusion.

The room was lit with oil lamps, the same as the stairway. They were in the niches on the wall and covered by clear panes. At least she could see and not risk burning to death.

"I'll try the spinning wheel first I guess."

She sat at the wheel and placed her foot on the pedal. A piece of straw could be fed into the maidens, but there was no way to stretch it into thread over the wheel without magic. Turning it to gold would take exceptional power.

After a few tries, she actually made it spin. She almost cheered at her accomplishment, but remembered that it was only the first step in her impossible task.

She plucked a stray piece of straw from the floor using the edge of her dress, careful not to let it touch any part of her skin. She held it on the wheel and spun. Nothing happened.

"I don't have magic!" she screamed to the ceiling.

"But I do," a voice from behind her said.

She jumped up, nearly knocking over the wheel, and held out a fist in front of her. She wasn't good at fighting, but she would do her best to defend herself.

A young man leaned against the closed cell door. He wore a fitted white shirt; the sleeves rolled to his forearms, and black trousers. A dark brocade waistcoat lined with silver buttons covered his torso. His dark hair was short on the sides, longer on top. Peculiar pointed ears protruded from each side of his head. She might have called him handsome if she wasn't actively worried about her life. How had she gotten here, fighting to live on multiple fronts? Just hours ago, she was prepared to starve to death.

"Who are you and how did you get in here?" she asked, willing the quiver out of her voice.

"You used my calling card so I don't think you are entirely clueless as to who I am. And as I said, I have magic." His arms rested on his chest.

Gwen squinted her eyes. "You are Mr. Woolworth? The old man who visited my home just yesterday."

He rubbed his fingernails against his brocade. "I'm taking over the family business so to speak. You can call me Aurius."

Before she could think on it further, she coughed violently. The apron was doing very little.

The man didn't seem to notice or care that the straw was about to kill her one way or another. He continued his leaning against the cell door with no urgency.

"What services are you requesting exactly?" he asked.

She bent over, holding her hand to her chest, and resting the other against the wall of the cell. Between gasps for air, she managed to explain her task. "I'm to turn this straw to gold."

The corner of his lip lifted in a half grin. If she was noticing, Gwen might have said that he was even more handsome when he smiled. "I hadn't realized how greedy the king had become. Using an innocent maiden to build his wealth."

"It doesn't matter." Her voice strained. "I can't spin straw into gold and I have an allergy to straw," she wheezed. "Either way I'll… be dead… by morning."

"Yes, I understand your predicament." He pushed himself off the door. "Well, let's discuss the details of payment."

"You can see… I have nothing sir… Perhaps a spool of gold… once its spun?" Black dotted the edges of her eyes.

He stalked toward her. There was nowhere for her to go. He lifted his hand and gently tugged her apron down from her face. His dark hair didn't move when he tilted his head to the side and leaned in. What little light there was glinted on a few strands. His closeness brought a fresh reprieve from the sharp scent of earth and hay.

She thought he meant to kiss her. Perhaps that was what he wanted as payment. Her heart rate ticked up a notch.

But at the last second, his hand slid to her neck. He hooked a finger under the chain that still hung there. The locket tickled her collarbone as he gently tugged it from under her tunic. "This will do." A ruthless smile followed the statement.

"As I told your father. It's only value is to me," she whispered.

His eyes flicked from the gleaming gold to the soft sea-foam green of her irises. "And is it worth your life?" he asked.

Gwen paused, then nodded.

"Then it is a prize indeed," he said.

Her fingers trembled as she lifted them to the clasp, releasing it from her neck. She placed it in his waiting hands, letting the golden chain gather over the top of the locket and dangle in his grasp. She held the clasp for a few more seconds. "I will get this back," she said through clenched teeth.

His mouth moved up into a hint of a smile. "I look forward to it." His silky voice held a promise of more. Of what she wasn't sure, but as she met his brown eyes, she knew this wouldn't be the last she saw of him.

As soon as she let the necklace go, he wrapped his fingers around it, depositing it in the pocket of his black waistcoat.

From the other pocket, he pulled a long tube with a sharp point at the end. In one smooth motion, he drew her closer and pressed it into her leg through the layers of fabric of her dress and undergarments. As soon as the point pierced her skin, he pressed a button at the top. After just a few seconds, he released her and placed the vial back where it came from.

She was so shocked that she didn't react until he let her go. She took one step away. "What was that?"

"Medicine. For the…" he wiggled his fingers and waved them around her face. "To keep you alive a bit longer. It would hardly be fitting to save you from one fate, just to lose you to another."

He reached up. This time, she flinched and blocked him from coming near her again. "I need a strand of your golden hair to perform the magic of turning this straw into gold."

He waited for a few moments and lifted his hand again. "Forgive me. It's been so long since we've had a catalyst. I forgot that I must ask permission." He paused. "May I?" he asked.

She watched him with wary eyes, but nodded.

He took a strand of hair in his fingers with gentle grace. The prick of pain was slight, but she lifted her hand to it and rubbed the modest itch it produced.

The man said nothing else. He turned and immediately sat at the spinning wheel, threaded the strand of her hair through the maidens, around the wheel, and onto the bobbins. He began feeding straw into the whirring machine.

She crept to a position where she could see his process. If she had magic, as her father insisted, perhaps she could learn to use it.

The corner of Mr. Woolworth's mouth quirked into a sly grin as he noticed her watching the machine. "The gold is an illusion," he said.

Gwen's head popped up, and she leaned away. She felt the heat creep up her neck. This time, it had nothing to do with her allergy.

"Illusion magic is rare magic." The machine creaked as he pressed the pedal. His hand danced over the fibers as they passed the bit of hair she contributed. A soft yellow glow flowed around each portion as he fed it into the machine, and it stretched into shiny metal.

"If it is an illusion why not just wave a hand instead of doing the work of spinning?"

He shrugged. "I could. It would easily fool you and I could be off. But that is not what we agreed." He stopped spinning for just a moment to meet her eye. "I must weave the illusion into each piece for it to hold."

Gwen reached to touch the piece of gold thread. Mr. Woolworth slapped it away. She pulled it to her chest and rubbed the itchy sting away.

"So it doesn't actually turn into gold?"

He ignored her question, having already answered it.

"It would require much more than spinning to rearrange the properties of straw into the properties of gold. It's impossible. But," he shrugged his shoulders. "People see what they want to see and are easily fooled by the magic."

"So if I take a lamp from its niche and throw it into the gold…"

His eyes narrowed and met hers again. "I suggest you keep flames away from the spun gold."

She held her hands in front of her in defense. "I don't have a death wish."

"Hmmfph," was his only answer.

They fell into a comfortable silence. The sound of the wheel and the scent of damp earth lulled her. She allowed her eyes to close. Even her shivering could not keep her awake. Upon completing his task, the man slipped his card back into her apron, gently stroking her cheek with the back of his hand. The tumbler in the lock rolled over, and he disappeared into the shadows of her cell.

The Prince

Gwen fell backwards and landed on a pair of pristine shoes. The gloss nearly blinded her. She hadn't heard him approach, unlock the door, and wrench it open.

The ride and the previous day's blood matted her hair. Her face was red and splotchy, eyes swollen, fingers frozen. She couldn't tell if the stench was coming from her or the floor she lay on. Likely both.

The man knelt and placed a gentle palm on her shoulder. He smelled of fresh linen and cedar. Creases and sharp points were evident in his clothing, freshly laundered. It was a welcome change from the damp, musty smell of the cell.

He took her hand and helped her to sit up. Familiar blue eyes roved over her face as muscular fingers lifted the dirty, blood-matted strands of hair.

"Who did this to you?" he asked. His voice was low and possessive. But they had only just met. Without waiting for a reply, his eyes flicked to the captain standing behind him, who did not meet his gaze. He stood and pulled her with him.

"Do you treat all prisoners in this manner?" The question was directed behind him, but his gaze landed on Gwen.

The captain's dark eyes shifted from Gwen. "Only those that try to run your highness," the captain responded.

Gwen whimpered at the confirmation of who stood before her. She tried to step backward, to bow, but he had her firmly in his grasp.

The prince turned his attention back to Gwen. He put a thumb just below her lip and ducked his head to meet her eyes. "You tried to run from the royal guard?" He tilted his head as he studied her face.

She searched him for a hint of cruelty. When she found none, she gave him the truth. "My father woke and regretted his decision to *sell* me to the king. I did as he bade me, but I only got as far as the dead field behind my house. I waited to see why the royal guard had come."

The prince examined her face, looking for the untruth. She held his gaze until he broke it to look expectantly at the captain.

"Jones was overzealous," the captain admitted. He had enough conscience to duck his head and shuffle his feet. "I will speak with him." The captain, who had always been headstrong and proud to the point of cruelty, was now reluctant.

The prince took one step back and curled his hand into a fist. "No," he growled. "I will speak with him about touching my betrothed."

"Ryland, be reasonable. It is unnecessary for his royal highness to deal with a guard. I will handle the matter." The captain dared to argue with the prince.

"And yet, I feel it entirely necessary to protect what is mine." The gravel in his voice rolled over the last word.

Gwen wanted to whimper at the threat, but tried to stay as quiet as possible. Perhaps they would forget she was there. Her eyes flicked between the captain and the prince. She probably should have kept them pointed toward the floor, but she couldn't help it. No one had cared about what became of her two days ago, and now the prince was calling her his betrothed.

"That is yet to be determined," the captain reminded him.

Anger flashed in the prince's eyes. "She is mine and she will not be touched again. Do I make myself clear?"

The captain's eyes rounded. His boot tapped the floor as he stepped back. A brief expression crossed the captain's face as if the prince had slapped him. He bent slightly at the hips. "Yes. Your highness."

The prince met her eyes again. There was something familiar about them, but she knew she had never met the prince before. She was lowborn and had never been to court. The captain had said the prince rescued her at the tavern, but he was rarely seen at all and never outside the castle. She blinked the familiarity away and dismissed it.

The captain cleared his throat. "Should we determine if she accomplished the task?"

She had fallen asleep while Mr. Woolworth worked, so she hadn't seen the finished product herself. She was keen to learn her fate.

Prince Ryland released her, and the air whooshed back into her lungs. He motioned for her to enter first. Her boot hit the stone floor of the cell.

What was before her was breathtaking, but she dared not breathe a sigh of relief. Not a single speck of straw remained in the cell. On the far side of the room, in neat little rows, were spool after spool of spun gold.

Not wanting to give away how surprised she was herself, she stepped away and allowed the captain and the prince into the room.

Each of their expressions shared her awe.

The prince approached the nearest spool. He unraveled a small length of gold and broke it. Gwen half expected it to turn back into straw, but it remained.

The prince twisted it until it formed a ring. He stepped over to Gwen and took her hand, which was still almost frozen. He slipped it onto the third finger of her left hand. Then, he hooked his forefinger under her chin. "Gwen Miller. Thank you for being who you said you are."

She tried to interrupt…"I never said…" but the prince wouldn't allow her to speak.

"Please let me finish," he swallowed. "We will be wed by the end of the week."

"What?" she and the captain spoke simultaneously.

"That was the bargain. I would marry the miller's daughter if she was who she claimed to be. If she had magic. Magic that can save this kingdom from the white witch."

"The bargain was that she would marry the king," the captain argued.

Gwen's eyes shifted between the two men again.

"The king has abdicated his responsibility in this to me."

The captain rolled his eyes. He lowered his voice. "His abdication goes well beyond this." If the prince heard it, he ignored the blatant act of treason.

Gwen ignored it as well, along with many other things. "How can spinning straw into gold save the kingdom from the white witch?" Gwen asked.

"It is much needed to fund the impending war, of course. She has magic, but no one in Aurum has had magic in years. The drought, the loss of magic was probably all her doing. But you will be a symbol of hope. And hope is a powerful tool."

It wasn't true. Speaking of magic was forbidden. She doubted that the people would accept her. But perhaps the prince didn't know his kingdom's rules, or he didn't care.

The hope he spoke about lit up his eyes and his words. It was difficult for her to deny him. She opened her mouth again to disclaim having any magic at all, when the prince continued.

"Of course if you hadn't made good on your claim you would be executed, but I'm so grateful that your father was true to his word."

And Gwen found the will to keep her mouth shut. As long as she never had to do it again, she would never have to reveal the truth about where the magic had originated.

The silence didn't linger much longer. The prince turned to the captain. "Take her to our joined suites. Bath, breakfast and new clothes. Do not tell the king about the gold until those things have been done."

The captain bowed. "Yes, Prince Ryland."

The prince left immediately, and Gwen's eyes followed him. "Where is he going?" she wondered.

The captain grabbed her by the elbow and shoved her through the door into the chilled hallway. It was only slightly warmer than the cell. "You have earned your way out of the dungeon, but if you think for a second you are out of danger you are mistaken."

He locked the door of the cell behind them. "I don't know how you managed that, but I don't believe you have that kind of magic."

Gwen lifted her chin. "Why not?"

"I saw the hovel you crawled out of. The squalor your family lived in. You are starving to death." He paused at the black door, left open by the prince. "If you could spin straw to gold why wouldn't you have done it to save your family? Why would your father want to sell you to the king?"

"Perhaps I just needed a cold cell and proper motivation to activate my magic."

The captain stepped in close. He was no longer wearing his metal armor. This morning, his attire comprised a less formal version of the guard's uniform from the day before. Black pants, a red fitted shirt, and a steel blade hung at his hip. He pressed his lips to her ear and lowered his voice. "If you betray the prince or this kingdom, I will slice off your head myself."

The captain stepped away, closed the dungeon door with a creak, and stomped up the steps to the corridor. Gwen swallowed hard once and followed him back the way they had come just the night before.

Aurius

The young prince bowed before his queen, waiting for her to address him. "Stand, Sir Aurius. You know there's no need for this formality." She waved a dismissive hand.

He lifted himself from the floor. The Queen's suite was lavish. Four rooms adorned with elegant gilded wallpaper, each a different shade of white with a hint of floral design. The dining room, sitting room, great room, and foyer. Behind these rooms, where the Queen met with her court, were her private quarters, which included two bedrooms and a bathing room. The castle had a larger dining room for formal meals or the Queen's breakfast she held twice a month. Sensible decor adorned each room. Nothing too fancy, but a little fancier than everyone else.

Elaborate woven rugs covered her stone floors. It was one of the easiest places to kneel. The queen never let his formalities last long. "You are my queen and I will treat you as such."

The queen ignored him and focused on her task of threading an elaborate tapestry on canvas. "Do you have news?" Her voice trilled with the question.

"Yes, your majesty."

"Have you found her?" The purple thread made a dull ripping sound as it passed through the canvas.

"I believe I have."

She turned to him for the first time since he had entered her suite, raising her eyebrows. "You are not sure?"

"She has the magic we discussed she would have, but she is not titled."

The queen returned to her task and stabbed the needle through the fabric with more fervor.

"Liora protected her well. It has taken us ages to find even a hint of the child's existence. I was certain she would have hidden her within the court at least."

"The girl was raised as a miller's daughter, which explains why we haven't been able to find her after all this time."

"Why has the king brought her to court? Does he know of her lineage?"

Aurius folded his arms over his chest and leaned against a nearby column. "Her father blabbed at the tavern that she had magic and could turn straw into gold."

The queen scoffed. "That's ridiculous. Only goblins can turn straw to gold."

"Yes."

"And you are the only goblin left in existence."

"Half-goblin. That we know of," the prince corrected her.

"Does the king believe the miller's proclamation?"

Aurius nodded. "The king bought her. He would have married her himself, but changed his mind and put her in a dungeon cell. She used my calling card. I helped her. Now he has proof of her magic. Prince Ryland plans to marry her by week's end."

The Queen pursed her lips and stopped her embroidery, but did not look at him. "Prince Aurius. I told you to watch from a distance. This complicates matters for all of us but for you especially."

"There is no way to tell someone has magic from afar. I followed my instincts. Instincts you trust."

The queen released a heavy sigh and looked at him. "So the King of Aurum now has a room full of gold."

He nodded, satisfied the queen did not know the true secret to the gold illusion. He had surprised himself when he had shared it with Gwen, but chose not to examine it further. "There's more," he said.

The queen remained silent, awaiting further bad news.

"The king was cursed with greed. He won't stop until all the straw in the kingdom has been turned to gold and..." He paused, waiting for the queen to draw her own conclusions.

"He'll imprison her until he's gotten everything he can out of her. Including an heir," she said.

He nodded.

There was a long silence as she returned to her hobby, contemplating the news.

"It was a mistake to help her," her voice echoed in the room.

"If I didn't she would be dead, my queen."

"That might be a better fate for her." The queen looked sad. Sad for the princess, maybe, or sad that the world had come to this. Prince Aurius was never good at guessing by the look on people's faces. He often wished people would speak their minds.

"If Prince Ryland is on the throne would she be safe?" she asked.

"I don't think much of Ryland, but he is perhaps better than his father…"

"Stepfather."

"I beg your pardon your majesty. Stepfather. I do believe the prince will shield her if only to spite the king."

"But Prince Ryland thinks me a villain too. He has named me the white witch and calls for my execution. He believes my death will restore magic and end the drought." The queen looked tired suddenly, as if running a kingdom was too much to bear.

"No doubt his mind has been poisoned by the king," Aurius said.

"Maybe."

"What are your orders my queen?"

The queen lifted her chin and squared her shoulders. All traces of sadness faded and were replaced by cruel resolve. "Continue to help the girl and keep her alive. Whatever that means. Try to limit the damage it causes this kingdom. If she truly is the catalyst, we need her."

"Yes, your majesty." Aurius bowed again. "Should I retrieve her if the opportunity arises?"

"Only if her life is in danger. I want the king to think he has a pawn. His arrogance will be his weakness. Now leave me, please. I'm tired."

Aurius bowed and left the queen's chambers, walking to his own. He pushed the door and sealed it with his magic. When he was sure it was safe, he pulled the locket from his black waistcoat and gently pressed the clasp. The portrait had to have been made with magic. It was too perfect to be a painting. The edges of the thick paper had curled. If he were right, the image was over twenty years old. The woman looked just like Gwen, though, and it was difficult not to separate the woman in the portrait from the one he rescued in the dungeon. This was the proof he needed, but he wasn't ready to tell the queen. If she knew, she would steal her away, and he wanted to keep her to himself for a little longer. And there was the contract to consider. A secret agreement he had shared only with a few trusted advisors, of whom the queen was not one. It was only a slip of paper, but it weighed on him, leading him headlong into his fate.

He curled his fingers around the oval trinket given to him by Gwen. And squeezed.

"AAAH" he slammed it down onto his wooden workbench. He suddenly wanted nothing more than to destroy it. To forget about the innocent little girl stuck in the dungeon, forced to do something she had no business doing. Complicated magic. It took years of study and at least a thimble of goblin blood in her veins to learn.

"There is no doubt I will be back there soon. The king is greedy."

Aurius could not forget her. Not even if he wished it. She was no one's pawn, and he had a powerful urge to rescue her out of Aurum and away from the queen as well. He could take her to Holtavium. They could live in the forest for years.

But it was a struggle to disobey his queen. She had been kind and taken him in long ago when… he sighed. He pushed those thoughts aside. He hated thinking about that time.

He pulled down the mortar and pestle. His hand hovered over the glass jars, deciding which would be best. The one with dark red organs. He took it from the shelf and twisted the tin cap. She would need another dose when he saw her again. He hoped they would feed her. She needed the energy. The catalyst's power never waned. It kept going. Reused again and again. It would keep her young, and she would live longer than any other human.

Perhaps the allergy had drained her? It was a risk he wouldn't take again. If they hadn't fed her, he would have to. He planned to visit the kitchens after this task was complete and procure a meal. He stretched his fingers apart, opening the space near his workbench. In front of others, he would just make things appear or disappear, but here in his rooms he could leave the space between planes open longer. He placed a few items in his inventory to be accessed when he needed them. He was just a few years old when Rumpelstiltskin appeared to him, spending several days teaching him goblin tricks.

"Why am I thinking of my father again?" He took a few deep, cleansing breaths. His father was the one who started all this. He did not want to think about it. He avoided pondering it at all costs. It only caused pain and anguish.

To avoid his thoughts, he murmured his actions, telling himself what to do next. "Grind the kidneys." He ground the kidney into powder. "Add to the pot." He poured the dark red dust into the boiling pot in the fireplace near the door. The concoction did not need magic. He found the recipe in the castle library among the medicinal grimoires.

Of course, he didn't look like a goblin - he could thank his human mother for that; he assumed, so it caught people off guard. That was another mystery that might never reveal itself. Though he had tried and failed for many years to discern who she was. He knew only that at a few weeks old, Queen Helen had taken him in. He was likely a changeling, but he never pushed the issue with the queen.

He knew little about how his magic worked. Much of it was instinctive. He had learned during his time with the fairies to trust his instincts. Some knowledge came from extensive research.

"Did someone curse her?" he wondered about Gwen aloud. He had seen the concoction and how to administer the previous morning. The preparation was complete before she even requested his help, prepared for his inevitable second visit to save the princess.

The King

A warm bath goes a long way in giving one a new perspective on life. And as far as baths were concerned, the one in the prince's suite was the best.

Two maids, one tall and slender, the other short and portly, laid out clothes and promised to be close by to help her dress. No one had helped her dress since she was a child. After seeing what she was required to wear for the day, she could understand why she would need it.

There were layers of fabric, all of which had to be laced and tightened in the back. The first layer was, of course, undergarments. They were light, airy, and soft. She had felt nothing so delicate against her skin. It almost made her want to sink into the fabric and never come out of the room. If only she could wear these clothes all day. But that would be scandalous and no way for a maiden to act, let alone the betrothed… She didn't let herself think it. Not yet. There wasn't any way she could be engaged to the Prince of Aurum. She was a nobody from nowhere.

Then she stepped into the next layer of fabric, a golden gauzy chiffon. It's iridescence, providing a mystical aura around her body. It wouldn't last though, because the layers were not finished. She didn't know how she would walk with the weight of it all, but fortunately until this point, the fabrics had been light. Around her waist, the maids placed a boned device that laced in the back. They pulled until her ribs almost cracked in her chest. "If I survived the dungeons, I can survive this," she thought, but with each pull, her determination faltered. When she finally let out a whimper, they relented their assault and tied off the laces.

The short maid lifted her arms while the tall one slid the golden brocade over her head. A strapless bodice fit perfectly, hiding her gaunt frame, and accentuated her waist and hips. The golden lace binding around the edge formed a V at her navel and flared out around the skirt. She picked at the off-white pearls sewn into each peak of the lace. Gwen wondered if she might be able to keep the dress. Not to wear. She would sell the fabric and feed her village for a month, probably more.

The maids again laced the bodice in the back, though loosely this time. One of them slipped sleeves of the same material over the chiffon, hiding most of it and causing it to puff at the shoulders and gather at her wrists. The sleeves had a few relief cuts through them that allowed her movement of arms in the stiff fabric.

And while it couldn't have been true, it seemed the dress was made for her. Every layer impeccably matched the golden color of her hair.

Gwen slid her toes into very sensible slippers that also coordinated with the color of the gown. The tall maid picked up her old, raggedy clothes with the end of a broom handle. She scrunched up her nose and held the broom as far away as possible. "I'll just make sure these are laundered Miss."

"Wait one moment please." Gwen ran toward her as fast as her new attire would allow. When she took the apron from the broom, the maid lifted her top lip in disgust. Gwen could tell she wanted to make a bigger fuss, but held her tongue. Now that she had had a bath and new fresh clothes, she could smell the reason. A day of travel and a night on the floor of the dung... well, they didn't call it a dungeon for nothing. No wonder the prince had sent her up to bathe right away. But it wasn't the clothes she wanted or the reminder of her days as the miller's daughter. Turning her back to the maid, she fished her hand inside her apron and pulled out the golden calling card. Gwen hoped she wouldn't need it again, but she knew greed when she saw it.

She handed the rags back to the young woman standing across from her. "Thank you so much for your kindness. I won't forget your help today." The maid took it between two fingers, careful not to touch it more than necessary. "No need to launder that. Just burn it. Hopefully I won't require it again."

The maids both curtsied and left giggling through the servant's entrance at the side of the room. No wonder the castle seemed empty.

As the prince had ordered, breakfast sat upon a nearby table. She ate alone. Thankfully. The food was rich and decadent. Only a few bites filled her.

It hadn't occurred to her that she would be in the prince's suite and what that implied. Her thoughts didn't extend beyond whether she would die. She had come so close. If Mr. Woolworth hadn't shown up… she shoved all thoughts aside about the night before. About his handsome face and his broad shoulders.

Gwen stood abruptly to clear her mind of all that had happened. She would never see him again, could never speak of him.

Instead, she focused on the tapestries on the wall and the lovely furniture.

It wasn't long before the door opened and in strode the captain, this time with a young girl.

"Your presence has been requested in the throne room," he announced.

The girl slipped past him. She couldn't have been older than nineteen. A year or two younger than Gwen. "You should address her with her title now, Drake." She gave the captain a withering stare.

"Your Highness, *she* doesn't have a title." His eyes were cold when he looked at Gwen.

Gwen's eyes rounded, and she stooped into a deep curtsy. "Your Highness." She kept her gaze pointed toward the floor.

"Please call me Avonlea. I wouldn't have it any other way," the princess, the real one, said.

"I wouldn't dare address Your Highness without her title."

Avonlea turned to the captain, her lips pulled into a slight smile. "See she has manners," she teased.

"Yes, your highness, but *she* is yet to become a lady."

"After today she will be. You can rise. There is no need for all the formality. We will be sisters soon and you'll be a princess with me!"

The captain stepped between them and quirked an eyebrow at Avonlea. "So she can drop your title, but I have to address her with one she hasn't yet earned?" His tone was light and playful. Gwen never would have imagined the captain could be anything other than gruff and mean.

Avonlea giggled at the captain's question and swatted him on the arm. "Oh, Drake. You know titles aren't earned."

The captain, Drake, turned his lips down. "She has still to meet the king. We do not know what the day holds. So let's not get ahead of ourselves."

The princess reached around the captain and took her by the arm, leading her away.

"Don't worry. My brother will be able to talk him around."

Gwen looked at the captain. "The king or the captain? Why should I worry? Hasn't my bargain been fulfilled?"

The princess and the captain exchanged a glance that she couldn't interpret. Avonlea patted her hand. "There's no talking the captain around. Whatever grudge he has against you, you will never be able to change his mind." She paused. "My brother may be able to sway his opinion. We'll see how it unfolds."

Gwen's eyes shifted to Drake. But if she wasn't talking about him, then Avonlea must be talking about the king. Gwen's hands trembled. Another night in the dungeon? Surely she wouldn't survive twice.

"As I said don't worry," Avonlea said. Leading her out of the sanctuary of the prince's suite.

The walk to the throne room seemed to be over in a few seconds. Gwen nodded along as Avonlea chattered on about the court and how everyone was buzzing with gossip about her betrothal to the prince. She even gave some pointers about how to act when standing before the king, but nothing could have prepared her. Two days ago, she was making her last meal and expected to die with her father at the mill. Now she was bowing before the dais of the King of Aurum.

The prince stood silently near the throne, but not on the dais with his father. As they had entered, the princess and the captain took places beside him. He wouldn't meet her eyes. Of course, they had just met. He had been kind, but perhaps her humble appearance had changed his mind about marrying her. As she waited for the king to allow her to rise, she looked at the ring on her left hand. It was a gift. A gift that had cost the giver nothing.

And nothing was exactly what she had expected. But he had fed her, bathed and clothed her, so at least that was something.

"Rise." There was no lilt to the king's voice, only monotone boredom.

She stood and remained silent. Gwen had no experience at court, so she waited until addressed. She fidgeted with the ring on her finger. The king's eyes shifted to the movement. Not that she had wanted to draw his attention to it, but the skin around the accoutrements had started to itch. Gwen knew the gold to be an illusion, but removing the ring might seem disrespectful to the prince.

"You are responsible for the spools of gold in the dungeon cell?" the king asked.

"Yes, Your Highness," she responded. Thankfully, she didn't need to lie. Indirectly, she was responsible for it.

"Your ROYAL Highness," someone corrected her.

"Excuse me. Your Royal Highness."

The king ignored it. He leaned forward on his throne. His belly protruded with movement. "You have magic?" he asked with a greedy glint in his eye.

"There seems to be a bit in here somewhere." Gwen smiled. Though the throne room was the largest room she had ever been in, the walls seemed to move toward her.

"My son thinks you are our savior and wants to make you his bride."

"I can't presume to say what will become of us. I know that wars are expensive and I believe this was the deal struck with my father."

"We are hoping you have more than this one ability," the king replied.

"I am young."

"You don't know your own power?"

"I've only just discovered that I had any magical abilities and with no one to show me I don't know how to practice any ability I might have or what to do to make it manifest." The lie had come so easily it shocked her. She had never lied, but with her life on the line, it was easy.

The king leaned back and stroked his beard. "I see."

"Father, I…"

The king held up his hand, and the prince snapped his jaw shut. "And what happened to allow you to perform the feat you managed last night?"

"Well, truly I didn't even know if I could, but my father," her voice caught at the thought of Papa laying in the dirt in front of their cottage. She took a moment to swallow the lump in her throat. "Said I could. In his memory I thought I should at least try."

"Is your father dead girl?"

Gwen realized her mistake a moment too late. If her father were dead, there would be no need to honor their agreement. She stuttered, not knowing for certain, and looked at the prince, who shook his head ever so slightly. She was sure the king couldn't have seen. Her eyes found the captain, who stared above the heads of everyone in the room.

"I'm not positive Your Royal Highness. The last I saw he was laying face down in the dirt. So perhaps he is. But if it is so, his contracts transfer to me his only daughter and heir," she said without a hint of the emotion she felt.

The prince cut his eyes toward the captain with a glare so sharp it could sever glass.

The king clapped his hands and folded them together as he leaned forward. "Well, the good news is that you found your magic. If you can do it once you can do it again."

"Sire I…"

"Are you interrupting me?"

"No sir. I didn't mean to. I just…"

He shook his head as if everyone around him were imbeciles. "Go on. What is so important that you disrespect your king?"

"I meant no offense. It's just that all the straw was used. There was none left in the cell."

The king leaned back and grabbed his belly. His deep laugh filled the chamber. Everyone looked uncomfortable, including Avonlea, whose gaze never lifted from the ground.

The king pinned Gwen with a glare. She froze under his scrutiny. "The prince has negotiated for your removal from the dungeons." A cruel smile crept across his face. "You will be given a room on the first floor of the castle."

The look from the prince said she probably shouldn't be happy about that, but she internally rejoiced. She didn't think another cold night on the dungeon floor would be fun or helpful.

"You will be given more straw, a spinning wheel and other necessary supplies. I want to see it spun to gold by morning."

"But.."

He held up a finger. "If you interrupt me again your father's blood will be on your hands. And your head will be on spire in front of the castle."

She hadn't seen any heads on the castle gate, but she wasn't about to take chances. She pressed her lips together, and satisfaction smoothed the king's harsh features.

"I'm not sure that I trust that you do have the ability to complete this task. I will need to see it for myself. If you do not complete your task by the morning you will likely…" He made a gesture with his finger along his neck and chuckled cruelly.

Gwen tilted her head to the side, wondering why he would want to murder the only person who had magic in twenty years. Deciding it would be best to keep her mouth shut, she didn't utter her question aloud.

Princess Avonlea floated to the king's side. "Father, may I make a request?"

The king didn't look pleased. But his voice was sweet with his only daughter. "Anything for my daughter."

The princess cleared her throat and proceeded. "In all the old books it mentions that magic wielders often need time to recharge when their magic has been used. It might be beneficial to everyone if Gwen has a few days to refresh from her stay in the dungeon."

Gwen found Avonlea's eyes. Did she know Gwen's secret? If this were true, shouldn't Gwen have known this? Perhaps everyone would chalk it up to her lack of knowledge about her own magic.

"I should have burned all the books!" the king growled through his teeth.

"Father you know they have their uses," the princess said as if she was joking with an old friend. "Perhaps we could host a banquet in your honor and show off your newest asset."

The king lifted his chin and narrowed his eyes. Gwen didn't even flinch at being called an asset rather than a person. Certainly if this was true, even Mr. Woolworth would need time before he might help her again.

After several agonizing minutes, the king spoke again. "We will have a feast in honor of our new lady of magic." A flicker of hope burned in her chest. Perhaps he had changed his mind about her. "Tomorrow evening, after the feast you will be put to the test." The flicker died before it could become a raging inferno.

The king lifted his hand and twitched his first two fingers. A valet appeared from behind a curtain, leaned over as the king whispered into his ear, nodded and stepped away.

A cruel smile swept across the king's face. His eyes cut to his son as he addressed Gwen. "You will be given the suite in Gelding hall until after the banquet."

The princess's eyes rounded in shock, and Prince Ryland balled his hands into fists. The captain remained stoic as ever.

"Ryland see her to her rooms. She is not to leave without an escort."

King Aric snapped his fingers. Prince Ryland, Princess Avonlea and the Captain all bowed. Gwen thought it best to curtsy. The captain hooked his calloused fingers under her elbow. She stumbled over her feet as he led her out of the throne room. The prince and princess were close behind them.

Once they were out of hearing of others, the captain dropped her elbow and whirled around on the prince.

"What were you thinking?" he whisper-yelled.

The prince crossed his arms over his chest. "I was thinking that I would negotiate my marriage and save my betrothed a night in the dungeon."

"He would have killed you in a second. Don't ever put your life on the line like that again."

"And sacrifice the only person in this kingdom with any ability to defeat the white witch?" The prince scoffed. "Not on your life."

"The only thing you did was put a bigger target on her back. Your father loves to torture you by torturing those you lo…. express interest in. Putting her in Gelding hall." He pressed his lips together and paced two steps before he turned again.

"Don't call him my father, you know he's not. And I am well aware of my own torment," the prince said softly.

The captain grabbed Gwen again and began walking down the corridor. He dragged her more than escorted her. The prince grabbed the captain's shoulder.

"Take your hands off her."

The captain let go of her arm after a few seconds. "We all have to pretend don't we?"

Gwen tried to make herself smaller so that they wouldn't remember she was there. It wasn't as if they were trying to be discreet in their argument, but it felt like she was eavesdropping on the royal's personal lives, and the less she knew, the more likely she was to survive.

The prince ground his teeth until the captain relented. "Fine. Your stepfather, not that it makes a bit of difference. He is the king and he will torture you."

"He makes himself fat on the backs of my people. I can only hope that he will die from his gluttony and soon."

"Stop it. Stepfather will not die of gluttony," Avonlea chimed in, the happiness in her tone contrasting the statement.

Everyone stopped and stared at her. She wound her arm through Gwen's. "He will die with a knife to his villainous throat," she said without a hint of emotion. It sounded as though they would all love to see the king dead.

As they approached the end of a corridor, a stone formed in the pit of Gwen's stomach. The trio's voices had become background noise as the weight of her fate pressed down. Her steps slowed. She clutched the princess's arm just a little tighter.

"Oh poor dear. Don't worry. We are not conspiring. The king will get what's coming to him, but not by our hands."

She thought she might have caught the captain and the prince briefly exchanging a look that said Avonlea was mistaken. It wouldn't matter, though, if she didn't make it through the next few hours.

"Come on we have to find you a dress for the banquet," Avonlea said. The princess pulled her toward a camouflaged door.

"But I thought… the king said."

Avonlea winked. "He ordered you escorted to your room. He didn't say how long it should take to get there."

The Dress

The town around the castle was busier than she had expected. A couple walked past them, cheeks glowing with health. They smiled at each other as they swung their arms, hand in hand.

"You wouldn't think there was a lack of water at all," Gwen said. She didn't mean for it to be a whisper. But as they walked the cobbled streets, there wasn't anything that said their kingdom was experiencing the worst disaster in centuries. Gwen didn't know how to account for it.

"What was that?" Avonlea asked.

"Nothing. That couple just looked so happy. It's a rare sight," Gwen said.

"Oh. Yes. Romance. Love at first sight." She waved a dismissive hand.

"You don't believe in love?"

"For me? Love is as scarce as water."

"What about Drake? It looked like you two were more than friendly."

"Drake and I are friends. And we like to flirt, but..." Avonlea shrugged her shoulders.

The conversation died, and they arrived on a road aptly named Merchant Row. The street wound around and intersected with other curved pathways that continued up hills, and she felt certain that she would immediately get lost if she came here alone.

The trio walked past a bookshop that looked interesting and quaint. She had loved reading when she was younger, but had little time for it after she took over the household duties.

There was an apothecary with what they called potions. Bunches of herbs and flowers hung upside down in the windows to dry. As the door opened in front of them, the lovely floral smell wafted to them. She wanted more than anything to wander through the aisles. They might have a cure for her reaction to straw. Perhaps something similar to Mr. Woolworth's. If she could purchase something and keep it with her, there would be less need to worry. She looked at her hands. The only things valuable she had were the two rings that adorned her slender fingers. The golden engagement wire the prince had given her that very morning. It had cost her one of her most valuable possessions. Perhaps the value was equal. On the other hand, her mother's signet ring. It had no intricacies. It was only a letter M inlaid into an oval set atop wide sides that tapered as they circled her finger. The letter stood for her mother's maiden name.

Before she could decide to bargain away her earthly possessions, the princess clutched her arm and dragged her forward. "Come now. The dress shop is just a few doors down."

Gwen sighed. It was for the best, probably. She couldn't shake the nervous feeling in the pit of her stomach, unsure if she was prepared to disclose her secret just yet.

Avonlea stopped in front of a shop that looked like all the others. Two windows to display what one might find inside and in between the entrance. Above this area, the outer walls were layered with siding, shingles darkened by weather and time. Two smaller paned windows allowed in the light to the upper floor. Likely where the shop owners lived.

As the prince approached the door, Avonlea tugged her along, but it felt as if her feet had sprouted rocks and had become too heavy to lift.

"I can't buy a dress."

"Of course you can. You are the new lady of magic, betrothed to the prince. And you spin straw into gold. You make money."

"Titles do not give me money."

Avonlea laughed. "That is exactly what they give you. The prince set up the account himself, in your name, just this morning. Before his visit to our stepfather."

Gwen's mouth dropped open as the prince looked around the street to avoid meeting her eyes.

"You have more than enough money to live comfortably as a royal," Avonlea said.

"But why?"

The prince stepped next to her and took her left hand. "You are my betrothed and you will be taken care of."

She tried to pull it away. The last thing she needed was for the prince to notice the red welts on her finger from his engagement band. "But I can't accept money from you."

"It is not a gift. It is a payment for the service you performed. And only a fraction of what you deserve after all you have endured."

"I don't think the king would…"

"It's not the king's money. I inherited it from my mother. It is mine and he has no say what I do with it."

He lifted her hand to his lips. Gwen found herself caught in a social dilemma. Pull away and risk offending the prince, or allow his royal lips to brush her swollen, red fingers. She opted for the latter. He didn't notice the state of her hand, fortunately, but he held it tight and pressed it to his chest.

"But why not use it to feed the people?" she asked.

"There are still limits bound by law, unfortunately, and the people seem quite well fed. But it is in your account under your name, now, so you can do with it as you will."

Gwen narrowed her eyes, her held tilted even as she squeezed his hand. It was the most anyone had ever done for her, but she got the feeling he didn't know his people were starving. Had he not noticed how thin she was?

"Thank you," she said. Her voice, breathy with shock.

He looked down at their joined hands. Gwen knew the minute he noticed her ailment. He dropped her hand and stepped away.

"What has happened?"

Gwen stretched her fingers out before her and frowned. The red welts had spread across the back of her hand. "I'm allergic…"

She barely had the words out of her mouth before he unwrapped the ring from her finger and tossed it to the ground. "How can you be allergic to gold? The ring on your other hand is fine."

Avonlea put a gentle hand on her brother's forearm. "Don't embarrass her brother," she whispered with a stern look of warning.

The prince looked as bewildered as Gwen felt, so Avonlea continued. "The other ring is likely not made of pure gold."

Prince Ryland's shoulders sagged briefly before he lifted himself to his full height. "I apologize. It's just you live in a kingdom named for gold. You can spin straw into gold and yet you are allergic to the very thing you have an ability for?"

Gwen's mouth opened and closed as she searched for words to explain that it wasn't the gold she was allergic to. "It is I that owe you an apology. You have been noble and kind, and I have hidden this from you. Really, it is only a mild allergy," she lied, remembering it had nearly killed her the night before. "I had hoped I could find a cure at the apothecary."

"Why wear the ring if you knew of your allergy?"

Gwen met his eyes and searched for an answer. She couldn't reveal the illusion. She gave him the only one she had. "It was a gift. From you. How could I part with it?"

A small smile formed on his lips. He stepped closer and took her hand in his, placing it near his heart. His hands were rough from training, but they somehow soothed her ailing skin. "It's not enough."

She swallowed the thick lump that had formed. "It is for me."

Avonlea cleared her throat. "Let's get started and then I'll visit the apothecary for you Gwen."

She nodded and followed Avonlea into the dress shop.

"Unfortunately, we don't have time for our dress maker to make you a custom dress, but I'm sure Uncle George can adjust something for you from his pre-made options."

Gwen looked down at her dress. "Surely what I'm wearing now will do for a banquet."

Avonlea looked over her shoulder and down her nose. "You look lovely but that is not a dinner dress. And we need something that will wow everyone."

The prince stepped away and took a seat on a plush velvet couch near a platform and a trio of mirrors. He placed both arms on the back of the couch, looking completely at home, waiting for his sister. Gwen wondered how many women had come here with him. How many women had he brought to this shop to lavish them with extravagant dresses?

"Did I hear something about wowing everyone?" A tall, smartly dressed man floated in from behind a wall. He wore thick, dark-rimmed spectacles and a measuring tape as if it were an accessory around his neck. Uncle George grabbed the princess by the shoulders and pulled her into a hug. He bunched his lips together and pressed his cheek to each side of her face. She did the same. "Hello darling. Its been a while."

"You know how stepfather is. It's difficult to leave the prison... I mean the castle." It was obvious her slip was on purpose.

"Oh darling. I'm just glad to get any moment I can with my two favorite people."

Avonlea released the tailor and looked over at Gwen. "Don't look so shocked. Uncle George was our mother's best friend. He was practically a brother to her." She sat beside the prince on the deep blue velvet couch. "Of course the king replaced all of Mother's old friends when he took over after her death."

The prince wrapped his arm around Avonlea, who looked so forlorn that Gwen almost cried. The tailor clapped his hands twice, and the moment passed.

"What brings you lovelies in today?"

The prince released his sister and took over the explanations. "My betrothed is in need of a dress for tomorrow night's banquet. There isn't time for a custom so Avonlea thought a visit was in order."

George clasped his hands together and batted his eyes at Gwen. "Your betrothed. Oh how lovely." He took a step toward Gwen and put a hand on each of her shoulders. "Let me look at you dear." He examined her from head to toe, released her and motioned for her to twirl. "You are beautiful dear. A bit thin but I'm sure Rufus will fatten you right up." He paused and looked over his shoulder at the royal siblings. "Is the cook still employed?"

The prince and princess nodded.

"Yes, of course he is. He was always very pragmatic." He unwound his tape measure and began to take measurements while he prattled on. "When is the big day?"

"Oh well. I have to prove myself to the king first or it's…" Gwen drew a line across her neck with her forefinger.

"You seem oddly ok with that."

"I've lived two days longer than I thought and I'm engaged to the prince, so I'm decently happy with my current situation."

"You are just the cutest." He booped her on the nose. "I have the perfect dress for you. Come with me and we'll get you into a dressing room."

She looked at the Prince and Avonlea, who both nodded their encouragement, then followed George to a small suite behind the mirrors. He pulled away a heavy white drape and pushed her through the space. "Just stay here for a few seconds, I'll be right back with a new dress. Nissy will be by to help you disrobe."

"Disrobe?"

"How else are we to know if my creation fits?"

"Yes of course, it's just that it took forever to get into this thing."

"I'm sure it did plus two or three maids to lace you up. But don't worry I have something more simple in mind."

Nissy poked her head around the corner. "Don't worry miss. I'll help you."

Gwen nodded, and Nissy entered the tiny room. It barely held her, the girl, and her current dress. But Nissy got right to work unlacing the golden gown.

After several minutes, the borrowed dress pooled around her feet, leaving her standing in her undergarments. She crossed her arms over her chest as she waited for the new apparel.

When it arrived, it did not have billowing skirts and yards of fabric. It wasn't golden. She hung the hanger on the hook near the curtain.

"You'll need to completely undress and you won't require help dressing with this gown. Just step into it and slip it up over your hips and torso. Mr. Barrister will make adjustments when you emerge." Nissy didn't even wait to hear if she had any questions. She retreated before Gwen could object.

"Well she took my other dress, so what choice do I have." She examined the new arrival. It was scandalous. There was barely enough fabric to cover her thin frame, yet it hung to the floor. She pulled it off the hanger and lowered it in front of her.

After a few minutes, she heard Uncle George calling for her from the showcase.

"Come out darling, everyone is waiting."

Gwen hid behind the curtain.

"I can't wear this," she called.

"We have to see it to make adjustments dear."

"Is the prince still here?"

"Yes."

Gwen tilted her head toward the ceiling and groaned. Was George doing this on purpose? She wouldn't need to face the executioner. She was going to die of embarrassment before the banquet.

"We haven't much time and this is the only dress I have that is near fitting you."

She sighed. "Fine."

Gwen stepped around the wall and took the three steps to the platform. She searched for the princess to plead for help, but the princess was nowhere to be found. However, the prince was still very much present. His jaw unhinged and hung open. A hungry gleam quickly replaced the shock, and culminated in a terrifying scowl of rage; the transformation happened in seconds.

"What are you thinking George? She can't wear that!"

"Why ever not?"

"She looks…"

George raised his eyebrows. "Desirable? Hmm?"

Gwen's eyebrows shot up in surprise. Of all the descriptions she had heard of herself, desirable was never one of them.

"Too desirable." The prince agreed.

Gwen let out a small gasp. Too quiet for the prince to hear, but George must have caught it because he pulled his lips back into a satisfied smile. It was shocking to hear the prince agree with George's description.

She had been too nervous to look in the mirror, but with these proclamations, she had to see what they were talking about.

Slowly, she turned toward the mirror. Behind her, she heard the prince groan, but the smile stayed on the tailor's face. Stretchy black material gathered just below her breasts in the front, where it met a grey swath of gauzy material, which was darker at the bottom and faded toward the top. The black wrapped around the grey and crisscrossed behind her neck. The entire back was open, exposing her from the neck to just above her hipbones. She imagined her spine must be protruding. Maybe that had caused the prince's disdain. As the stretch of black material reached around her hips in the front, it split into three sections. Two slits allowed her legs to peep through. The black faded into a light grey to match the top of the dress.

She agreed with Uncle George, but more than just desirable, she looked powerful. Like the sorceress everyone thought she was.

But she knew better. She didn't have power. A dress was only window dressing. A facade hiding her secret. She couldn't do what the prince, the king, said she must.

George stepped behind her and put his hands on her shoulders again. His eyes met hers in the reflection. "It is armor. And where you're going. You will need it."

"It's not protecting much."

"It's protecting your image."

"My image?"

"Do you think I don't know, the entire kingdom doesn't know by now, about the miller's daughter who can turn straw to gold?"

"But I…"

He held up a finger and whispered, "However it was done, it is done. You must hold your head high and play the part." George didn't believe her. He met her eyes again with a knowing glare. Then the prince was behind her.

"Please remove your hands from my betrothed George."

George let her go, stepped aside, and bowed. "Of course your highness."

"Don't you have anything more modest for her?" he asked.

"I'm afraid nothing that may be sized down before the banquet your highness. But I can perhaps add…"

George looked around. Having found what he was looking for, he scurried across the shop and came back with a studded black belt with thin yards of tool draped along the bottom. He wrapped it around her waist and overlapped it in the front. With a press of his fingers, it snapped together and rested just below her navel.

"That's hardly better."

George pursed his lips. "Her legs are less visible."

"I'll take it." Gwen blurted out.

Both George and Prince Ryland snapped their heads toward her.

"You gave me an account. Do you have to approve my purchases?" Gwen honestly didn't know how it worked.

The color drained from the prince's face. He wiped a hand down his cheek and around the back of his neck. "After tomorrow night, you will never wear this dress again."

Gwen looked up through her lashes. Feeling a little bold, she asked, "Is that a threat your highness?"

"It's going to take every bit of willpower I possess not to rip the eyes out of each man that looks upon you. I told you once that you are mine. Don't forget it." The prince's face inched closer to hers. She thought he might kiss her then and there, but as quickly as the moment began, he growled and walked away.

George cleared his throat and pointed toward the steps. "Why don't you get changed. I'll wrap this up for you and have it sent to the palace."

"Thank you George. You can bill my account." She smiled.

The trip back to the castle was uneventful and oddly quiet. The prince brooded. Gwen worried she had made him angry, but couldn't bring herself to apologize. This might be the last night she had. George had been right. The dress was stunning, and everyone would believe she was exactly who she was pretending to be — a powerful magic wielder.

Her heart wilted only slightly with the thought that it was a lie. And only slightly more that her relationship with the prince was contingent upon that lie.

She sighed as her thoughts grew darker. *I'll likely be dead soon, and the prince will move on to another.*

Prince Ryland led her to a new wing in the castle. As her hand fit perfectly in the crook of his elbow, she smiled at how their lives were now woven together.

This part of the castle smelled bright and fresh. It matched the lighting. This was the happiest place she had visited so far. Red carpets gave way to a pale brocade floor, and airy sheer panels replaced the wall tapestries. Sconces remained extinguished. The sky light spires, provided ample light to the area.

"You're smiling."

The prince's sudden words startled her back to reality.

"It's so different than other parts of the castle."

"Yes. This was designed by my great grandmother. She loved the natural light."

"This is itself magic."

The prince's smile faded. "She did have some magical abilities. I'm glad she passed before magic died here."

"I'm so sorry. Did you know her well?"

"No. I was very young. But I know her through her work and her legacy."

They stopped in front of a pair of ornate doors.

"We've arrived at your suite."

"My suite?"

"Yes. Your dress will arrive here if it is not already. My suite is adjoined to yours."

"How is that possible? Your hall looks nothing like this one."

He pushed the doors open. The maids were still busy preparing the room, fluffing pillows and dusting trinkets. He guided her just inside the double doors.

"My suite shares a wall with yours, though the entrance is on a different wing. It was built in preparation for my bride. It's remained empty until today."

"Empty?"

"Yes. You are the first to sleep in the room. And you will be the last."

"Don't limit yourself. When I'm gone you will need to find a new bride."

He stopped inside the door. "Why do you doubt you'll be successful?"

Her shoulders slumped as much as her corset would allow. "I guess I've defaulted to live day to day. I can barely believe I've lived the past few hours at all."

She hesitated to remove her hand from his arm. "The captain seemed to think this was a way to torture you."

The prince's lips turned down. He didn't meet her eyes. His throat bobbed as he swallowed. "It's a reminder to me of what can happen when you cross the king."

The muscles in his jaw ticked. "Will turning the straw to gold cause an allergic reaction?" he asked, changing the topic.

"Dear brother it is time for us to prepare for the evening." Avonlea pushed past them both and saved Gwen from answering. Each of them took a step back from each other to allow her through. "You will have your fiance all to yourself when you've been wed." She clasped her hands together as her skirts swished around her ankles. "Thank goodness there were maids in here or we would have a scandal." Avonlea winked at Gwen as if she were a conspirator in on the joke.

The prince held Gwen's gaze. He didn't smile or move, and for a moment, Gwen was lost in his eyes. She wanted to step into his arms and let him hold her and shield her from all that was to come.

"Go Brother. Shoo. We've doubled the guards on this wing. Stepfather is trying to isolate her, but we will be fine." Avonlea's insistence broke the moment. Prince Ryland bowed without a smile to each of them and unceremoniously left the room. Avonlea turned to the maids. "You can go too. I will help the lady prepare for the evening."

Each of the maids curtsied and left the room. When the door clicked shut, Avonlea shifted to Gwen. "Girl… You've got it bad."

"What do I have?"

The princess took out a tub, opened the lid and scooped some cream onto the back of Gwen's hand. Gwen almost melted with relief.

"You like the prince."

"What? No. I can't like the prince. Maybe after tomorrow, but no. Not now."

Avonlea danced and twirled around the room. "More importantly he likes you."

"That can't be true. We barely know each other."

"That doesn't matter. There's vibes." Avonlea wiggled her fingers at Gwen.

"Vibes?"

"Like soul mate magic," Avonlea answered.

"Magic doesn't… work that way." Gwen almost slipped and admitted that it didn't work at all.

"Oh fine. You are no fun."

Avonlea

"What are you doing?" Gwen whispered. A warm glow had begun just outside her window, but the sky was still dark and the birds had not begun to chirp their morning song.

Avonlea held a finger to her lips. "Sssh. You aren't supposed to leave the room, but I'm taking you on an adventure today. I've ordered the maids away while you rest." She wiggled two fingers on each hand when she said the word rest. "Here put this robe on."

"Where we're going doesn't require fancy clothes?"

"No. We can just be plain Janes today." The princess smiled and shrugged. "One of my favorite days."

Gwen wiggled her toes into a pair of slippers by the bed and threw the satin robe around her shoulders. An adventure where they didn't have to pretend they were someone else thrilled Gwen out of her morning grogginess. She was immediately alert.

Avonlea took her hand and pulled her toward the back of her suite. On the wall next to the lavish wardrobe, Avonlea pulled a sconce. Gwen shielded her ears against the scraping sound as the floor lowered in front of them, revealing a dark pit. Steps appeared as tiny lights inset into the wall lit the path downward. It appeared to be a chain reaction, with one lighting the next.

She took a step back from the entrance. Her hands trembled. Her eyes widened, and all the moisture in her mouth dried up. "I'm not going back to the dungeon, Avonlea. Take me to the executioner now, because I can't go there."

Avonlea's head popped up in surprise. Genuine sorrow contorted her face. "Oh heavens. We aren't going to the dungeon. That is on the other side of the castle. I promise this is safe. I won't leave your side."

Gwen searched her eyes for a sign of cruelty. Avonlea had been kind up to this point. She looked back at the warm bed.

Curiosity was a weakness. "What are we going to see?"

"The thing your heart desires most."

Gwen huffed a quiet laugh and shook her head, backing away from the princess.

Avonlea grabbed her hand again. "I promise you will love this."

If the princess had a cruel plan, Gwen supposed it couldn't be much worse than the last few days. Fear wouldn't get the best of her. She sighed and steeled her nerves. She nodded and let Avonlea pull her by the hand again, leading her down the steps.

The descent was shorter than her trip to the dungeon. Gwen let shallow breaths into her lungs as they reached the landing.

An opening from the stairs spread into an enormous cavern.

A cavern lake lapped over smooth stones, producing a tiny tinkling sound.

The blue glow of the water lit Avonlea's face, which held the brightest smile she had ever seen her wear. The lights from the stairs continued around the lake.

What little breath Gwen had left her. "You have more water here than I've seen in my life. Why don't you share it?"

"It is a secret. And if you haven't noticed, the king doesn't share well. My brother is beginning to pick up some of his habits."

"Is it safe to drink?"

"Yes, of course."

Gwen knelt beside the pool, allowing the slick stones to wet her dress. The cool lake rippled under her trembling touch. Her reflection distorted in the tiny waves.

"What makes it glow?"

"There are tiny creatures that produce the light." Avonlea stooped beside her. "What is your village like?" she asked.

"My village? Is nothing like this place. Before the captain kidnapped me,"

"Kidnapped?" Avonlea interrupted.

Gwen pursed her lips. "Before my father sold me."

Avonlea pursed her lips but didn't interrupt further.

"I had made our last meal. We had a few vegetables in the cellar and one pot of water. The fields dried up two years ago. Our numbers started dwindling. No one brought grain to be milled any more. But apparently the taverns are well stocked. So no worries about the locals storming the castle. Although if they knew this was here, they probably would."

"I guess it is a good idea to keep it secret."

"Secret is fine. The location is fine, but not using it is huge mistake."

"Who says that we're not using it?" Avonlea asked.

"I can see that those that live in town are well fed, but perhaps some relief could be directed toward the outer villages."

Avonlea sighed. "I'll speak to Stepfather about it. I don't think it will do much good. My powers of persuasion only go so far."

Her lips turned down as she swirled a finger in the water. "Can I tell you a secret?"

Gwen shrugged. "As long as I won't lose my head if I hear it."

Avonlea giggled. Something, Gwen noticed, she did when she was nervous. "You probably won't if you don't tell anyone."

Gwen smiled. "I won't tell."

"This is where I meet Drake sometimes." She pointed behind her, and Gwen turned, noticing for the first time several sets of stairs. "Those stairs lead to his office." She moved her raised finger slightly to the right. "And those go to the forbidden courtyard."

Gwen squeezed her eyebrows together and turned back to the lake. "What do you do when you meet?"

"Oh nothing improper. He's barely held my hand. Drake has always been like a brother to me. He came to live here when we were all children. But lately, I've felt something more. And I hate it."

"Why?"

"Because I can't marry him. My marriage will be advantageous to the crown and nothing more."

Gwen wrapped her fingers between Avonlea's and squeezed. "I'm sorry."

Avonlea's lips thinned. "Me too."

They sat in silence for a few more moments until the princess broke it. "Ok. No more moping." She stood and started disrobing. "Do you want to go for a swim?"

Gwen's eyes rounded as wide as saucers. She nearly toppled over at the suggestion. "I can't swim."

"Come on, you'll be fine. We won't go deeper than you can stand. And it's perfectly safe. There are no creatures other than the glowing ones."

Gwen lifted herself from the ground with measured timidity.

"It's best if you don't let your gown weigh you down." Avonlea was already in her undergarments and wading into the lake.

Gwen took off her robe and laid it beside the other garments that had piled on the dry walkway away from the water.

She carefully followed Avonlea into the water. She had expected it to be freezing, and though it was cool as it flowed over her ankles, it was not unpleasant. When the water finally reached her hips, her foot hit a slick spot. Liquid covered her body, and she immediately began thrashing. But Avonlea grabbed one of her flailing hands and pulled her to standing.

Gwen came out of the water, gasping for air. Her hair hung dripping over her face.

Avonlea slapped her on the back as Gwen coughed. "I won't let you drown," she said.

Once she caught her breath, Gwen stooped in the water for a bit longer, while the princess shared gossip from the court. Gwen finally relaxed and enjoyed the sensation of liquid flowing over her body, but a chill that ran up her spine as she looked into the vast darkness of the cave.

A rock formation — Avonlea had called it shelfstone — made a ledge with a smaller pool on the other side of the lake. "What is that?" she asked.

"Are you ready to go further?"

"What? I thought you weren't going to make me swim?"

"It's not deep. You can walk the whole way."

Gwen hesitated to take another slippery step on the limestone bottom.

Avonlea tilted her head. "What? You didn't think this was your heart's desire did you?"

Gwen raised her eyebrows. "A secret cavernous lake is absolutely my heart's desire."

Avonlea shook her head. "Don't make me blackmail you into going to the pool with me."

Gwen sighed and held out her hand to the princess, who took it readily.

The pair made it across the lake and to the small pool. The water in this pool had dripped from a pointed spike on the ceiling of the cavern. As Gwen looked into the crystal clear water, a droplet plopped into the pool, making it ripple. Through the ripples, Mr. Woolworth's reflection appeared behind her. Her mouth dropped open as she turned to see if he was there, covering herself with her arm.

But the space behind her was empty.

"What did you see?"

She looked back into the pool. The only reflection behind her was the ceiling of the cave. "This is supposed to show your heart's desire?"

"Yes."

"What did you see?" Gwen asked.

"Drake of course." She huffed. "The same thing I always see."

Gwen jumped from the rocks into the water. The water whooshed around her and echoed through the cavern. "It's time to go back to the room and get ready for the banquet."

"It will not take all day to get ready for the banquet." Silence as she waited a beat for Gwen to answer. "Gwen, what did you see?"

"Nothing," she called back, trudging through the water.

"You're lying."

Gwen stopped her movement. "I'm sorry. I'm… It's just all too much."

Avonlea caught up with her. "That's fair, but what did you see that frightened you?"

"It's broken. I didn't…"

"Do not say you didn't see anything… I know you did. You looked as frightened as a lamb."

"Ok. I saw Ryland. I thought he was standing right behind me so it scared me."

Avonlea laughed. "Oh. I can see why that would give you a fright."

Gwen rolled her eyes. "It's time to get ready for the banquet," she said again. She stepped over the slippery rocks and back onto the embankment with their clothes. She dressed quickly and waited for Avonlea to make her way out of the water. Avonlea didn't push her to give a clearer answer, and they returned to her room in silence.

The princess offered a quiet goodnight and clicked the door closed behind her. Gwen tucked her feet into the satin sheets, trying not to think about the lies that were mounting.

The Banquet

The savory scent of roasted fowl filled the banquet hall and wrapped itself around Gwen. Drool threatened to slip over her lips. A winter chill crept along the edges of the windows, creating a mosaic of designs. But the cold didn't reach beyond the casement. Roaring fires lit in enormous fireplaces warmed the room from each end. Servers wound their way through throngs of people with trays of dark red liquid. Already a few of the guests' faces were flushed with the heat and wine.

Despite Avonlea's efforts to prepare her for the banquet, there was no grand entrance for the new Lady of Magic. The herald quietly announced her and seated her at the table farthest from the king's seat.

As the server presented each course, Gwen ate silently, enjoying the soft music and the murmur of the crowd. She had suspected Prince Ryland of hiding her from the court until he appeared before her with his hand out and bowed. "Shall we dance?"

"I don't know all the steps," she said, her voice quiet. "I'm afraid I'll just embarrass you."

"You could never embarrass me, except by refusing. Or leaving me standing here with my hand out while you decide." His eyes darted to the others around the room, who had turned their attention toward them. His alluring smile remained in place, while a twinge of panic flashed in his eyes.

Gwen smiled and tilted her head at the thought. "Very well, we can't have that." She placed her napkin on the table in front of her and stood, putting her delicate hand in Prince Ryland's firm grip.

Gwen let the prince lead her to the polished floor in front of the ring of banquet tables. They were alone on the floor. She felt every eye turn to her as they trekked through the room. The prince hadn't made any attempts to yank them out yet, but as he gripped her hand even tighter, she feared he might not be far from doing just that. Gwen would have been happy to continue sitting at her place at the banquet table. It had been the prince to ask her for this display, so why should he be jealous? And yet his control was on edge.

The music turned somber as they reached the space for dancing. Other couples, allowing the prince to set the example, finally followed them and took their places. The prince pulled her closer. Intimate, but leaving distance to maintain propriety. His clean scent of freshly pressed linen drifted around them.

The prince lifted Gwen's arm and twirled her. He leaned in close. "Follow me as much as you can. I promise not to step on your toes," he whispered. Gwen smiled up at him. There was no way he was that clumsy.

"I learned a few steps this afternoon, but I'm afraid I'm no expert." Avonlea had insisted there would be dancing tonight and that she needed to know at least the basics.

A rumble came from the prince's chest as he lifted her right hand and placed her left on his shoulder. His was warm as it rested against the small of her back. His thumb barely grazed her exposed skin there. Goosebumps arose along her bare arms at the sudden and surprising contact. She didn't dare say a thing. The prince had already warned her that the dress was scandalous. Now he was proving just how much.

The others on the dance floor disappeared as the music wafted over them. At least in Gwen's mind, it was only her and the prince. He moved them around the floor with the practiced grace of a royal. Gwen became lost in the steps of the dance, the movement of the music, and Prince Ryland's blue eyes.

Gwen tilted her head. She had seen those eyes before, but before she could discern where, the prince pulled her in close. "I'm glad your father has a big mouth," he said. The sound of his low voice caressed her ear.

Gwen pressed her brows together in confusion. "Why are you concerned with my father's mouth?"

They turned as the dance demanded. "I'm just glad he told everyone about your abilities. I never would have found you otherwise. You are the answer to our prayers."

"I'm nothing. A nobody. I'm not even a princess."

"You have magic Gwen. The first person in twenty years to have magic in this kingdom. And we can use it to defeat the White Witch in the North." He twirled her away as the musicians began another song and pulled her back toward him. "Just get through the next few hours. We'll be married and you will be a princess."

She didn't want to say the words out loud. It was trouble enough to think about them. She wasn't magical at all. The magic came from a mysterious man who had appeared in her cell. He had done all the work. He had saved her from death. It was his magic they wanted. But admitting that would get her killed, and the man imprisoned.

She lifted her chin, decision made. He would not be involved anymore. She would solve her own problems even if her solution led to her death.

The prince smiled at her and ran his forefinger along her jawline. "I see strength in you. And we need it, Gwen. Me most of all."

She wanted to be strong. In that moment when he was asking for her strength, she wanted to be able to give it to him, but unless she turned straw into gold in the next few hours, strength wouldn't matter.

The music faded, and the turning stopped. The prince escorted her back to her seat and turned to the lord occupying the seat next to hers.

"Move, Lord Devaro."

The chair screeched along the floor in Lord Devaro's haste to obey the prince. Gwen fought the urge to cringe. He bowed to both of them and disappeared into the crowd.

The night wore on as Prince Ryland entertained her with stories of his childhood. She laughed along with him as they watched other couples turn around the dance floor. For a few brief moments, Gwen forgot why she was at the banquet. She forgot the danger she was in. A few days ago, she was preparing her final meal. This too could be her last. But that was forgotten in Prince Ryland's smile. His accidental caress as she reached for her glass. His stories of heroic feats by the captain of the guard. How he held his friend in high regard. For those few priceless minutes, she didn't worry about her life and what she might lose. She relished in the moment of everything she had gained.

One more meal. One more day. Tomorrow, it could all change again.

Power

The king clapped his hands and sent the musicians away. The banquet ended, but most of the attendees still milled about the hall. Low murmurs took the place of the musicians, filling the hall was anxious expectation. Gwen didn't blame them. She might not have wanted to leave either if there was a promise of magic for the first time in twenty-two years.

It was time for Gwen to prove her worth. Again. But thankfully, it wouldn't be on display here in the banquet hall.

The prince walked her through the winding corridors to yet another wing of the castle. Well away from their adjoining suite. They stopped in front of enormous plain double doors.

"I'll order food brought up. Perhaps you will need it to perform this service to the crown. This room has an opening here for servants to deliver items to you." The prince pointed to a cabinet in the wall. "The two sides can't be opened simultaneously, I'm afraid, so no escaping."

She looked around him and back into his eyes. "Oh I wasn't thinking of..."

The prince smiled, and she lost all train of thought. "I was only joking," he said.

Gwen dropped her arm and walked away from the prince without another word. He took a broad step into her space and tilted her head toward his with the bend of his forefinger. Her breathing nearly stopped as he looked down at her through his dark lashes. He pulled his lips back into a bright smile, which revealed his dimples she hadn't noticed before. She almost lost her balance and leaned forward, but kept herself upright and managed not to embarrass herself.

"I'm sorry we must delay our marriage for a few more days."

"Well, we only just met a day or so ago. What is a few more?"

"They will be the longest days I've ever waited."

Gwen's lips flattened.

"That was corny wasn't it?"

She laughed. "A little your highness."

"Please call me Ryland."

"Ryland. Thank you for your kindness."

"I wish I were able to help you more."

She stepped back to take a breath of fresh air. "There is one thing your… Ryland."

Prince Ryland raised an eyebrow. "Anything Gwen Miller."

"If I don't make it out of this room," she looked at the daunting doors, "will you find my father and tell him I did my best? That I love him and I forgive him."

The prince placed one hand over his chest and bowed at his waist. "It would be my honor." He lifted his torso. "But I'm confident you will be successful."

She nodded and stepped around him. He offered his elbow again, which she gladly took to help her steady herself.

The prince pushed down the brushed bronze handle and nudged open the doors of the room.

Her jaw dropped. The king had his servants stack the straw from floor to twenty-foot ceiling. Light filtered in through two windows, but with straw stacked in front, it was dim. It created an eerie aura throughout the room, fed by the flickering light of the fireplaces.

Ryland had a similar reaction, but soon his features turned from shock to anger. "You were right to question how my father acquired all this straw. It surely would be put to better use in the stables."

"Gold has it's uses too. Perhaps it can be used to buy food from neighboring kingdoms less affected by the drought."

Ryland looked at her with curiosity. "You are a marvel." He cupped her cheek in his palm and, for the second time in just a few minutes, she thought he might kiss her. He lowered his head toward hers until his breath tickled her cheek. "I will vow that the gold you make for this kingdom will go to help the people."

Her sea-foam green eyes locked with his. She could see the honesty he held. "Thank you Ryland." His eyes landed on her lips as she said his name.

He ran his thumb along her bottom lip. "I like the sound of my name on your lips," he whispered. His eyes examined the soft lines of her face and met her eyes again. For a few seconds, she forgot all of her problems and got lost in his gaze, the minty smell of his breath, and the rough touch of his calloused thumb on her face.

From behind her, someone cleared his throat, and the moment was over. She took a large step back from the prince, giving herself space to breathe.

"Pardon the interruption your highness." The poor servant bowed. "The door was open so I thought it might be better than using the delivery hatch."

The prince looked around her. "It's fine. You can set the tray over there in the corner please."

Once they delivered the food and the staff left, he returned his attention to her. "Is there any way I may stay and help you?"

Her eyes widened in surprise. "What?" she laughed nervously.

"Can I assist you?" he asked again.

"That is a very kind offer, but I don't think there is much you can do. Unless you want to go on the run with me."

He smiled kindly. "Trust me you don't want to run from my stepfather. His resources reach far and wide. Perhaps I might keep you company?"

"No. No. That's ok. I need to…" she looked around the room and fiddled with the fabric of her skirts, "concentrate really hard to make this happen and it wouldn't do either of us any good. And you probably have a million tasks to take care of. You would be bored."

"An evening with you would never bore me."

"How do you know?"

The prince grinned. "I just have a feeling my life got a lot more exciting."

A smile touched Gwen's lips as she considered the impact she had. It wouldn't matter, though. She would likely die in a few hours, just as she had thought she would yesterday. It was getting quite mundane to be in so many life-threatening situations in such a short amount of time.

"There's nothing you can do for me here. I will see you in the morning."

He turned to go but paused in the entryway, looking more than a little dejected. "I apologize if I made you uncomfortable."

She rushed toward him and took his hand. "No Ryland. You haven't made me uncomfortable at all. I'm just not sure how to handle all of this. Two days ago I was a miller's daughter with no magic, preparing our last meal. And now I can turn straw to gold. I'm still learning and I don't want to do anything to hurt you."

It wasn't a complete lie. He didn't need to watch as she died. She was uncertain of his affection being sincere, but it might not be a pretty sight to see a girl suffocate to death.

"Gwen."

She lifted her eyes to meet his in answer.

The rough skin of a calloused thumb moved over her cheek again. "Stay alive one more day. I promise I will make my stepfather allow us to wed."

All she was able to do was nod.

He slipped through the door without another word. It shut with a loud bang, and the lock clicked into place. There was no escaping now. Red welts had already formed on her arms. Perhaps she should have told him the truth. Maybe he could have helped her. But while he was affectionate and protective, she still wasn't sure she could trust him.

As Gwen paced the large suite, she noticed a wardrobe near the door opposite the food cabinet pass through. She pulled back the wooden doors. A few simple dresses hung in a neat row. "How long do they expect me to remain in this room?" she wondered. Still, she was grateful to have something else to wear.

She pulled her evening gown off and replaced it quickly with the simple blue dress she found at the end. The red welts had spread, but she dared not look at them. The black dress went on a hanger and into the wardrobe.

Her pacing began again, trying to stay as far from the straw as possible, thankful to be out of the cell, but not in a much better position. The door remained tightly locked. Absentmindedly, her hand moved to her neck where she slid the sharp points of her fingernails over the welts that popped up there.

She chewed her thumb as the boots she now wore clacked against the stone floor. The fire roared in the massive fireplace, creating such heat in the room that sweat poured from her brow. A barred window existed on the other side of the straw. At least she was permitted to see the sky.

A four-poster bed stood in the back corner of the room. Gwen couldn't imagine why they hadn't removed it to stuff in more straw. She longed to lie down. The stones of the dungeon had been freezing and hard, and sleep hadn't come easily in the prince's adjoining suite either. Comfort is not a concern for the poor, though. But every time she sat on the soft and luxurious cushions, she hopped right back up. How was she capable of sleeping at such a time? Her life was on the line, as if the first night hadn't been enough. Now, the greedy king wanted more.

She slid down the door, determined not to call on Mr. Woolworth. Attempting to spin the straw would only make her ailment worse. Tears wet her cheeks. In the morning, the straw would still be straw, and she would be headless. While she didn't want him to be captured, she wanted someone to talk to. Another person who shared her secret and understood before she died. Perhaps she could call him a friend. The only one who knew the whole truth.

She palmed the golden card she had fished from her shoe, where she had shoved it before the banquet. Flipping it over. Waiting. Flipping it again.

The hissing of the fire filled the room, its warm glow casting flickering shadows. The smell of burning wood mingled with the damp straw as sparks danced upwards.

Her resolve crumbled. She stood and walked closer to the bed. "Mr. Woolworth," she whispered.

She nearly jumped out of her skin when a man's deep voice came from behind her.

"It looks as if I was right after all."

The swelling affected her face and eyes, but she did her best to squint. "No one likes a know-it-all."

"And I got here just in time."

"I don't want to make another bargain with you, I just wanted a friend to talk to about this," Gwen said.

Mr. Woolworth's head tilted to the right. His eyes narrowed. "I don't do friendships." His rough voice somehow dipped lower.

"I just wanted someone to talk to before I die."

He remained silent, unrelenting.

"Fine. If I bargain with you will you stay and talk."

He crossed a leg over the other in a step to inspect her, reminding her of a cat on the prowl. Gwen swallowed as she suddenly felt Mr. Woolworth might not be as safe as she once thought. His black skin-tight pants slid over the corded muscles in his thighs. A predator ready to pounce. Black leather boots rose to his knees and matched the leather coat that hung to his mid-thigh. He appeared slightly more weathered than their last encounter, with a faint scent of earthiness clinging to him. After finishing his inspection, he spread his hands to either side as if to say, I'm listening.

"It doesn't look as if you have a choice," he said.

"What do you want?"

"What everyone wants."

Gwen raised her brows, encouraging him to continue.

"Power," he said.

"I have no power to give. I have nothing. I'm going to die. Either here or on the executioner's block."

"You have more than you realize," he mumbled. His next words were louder. "Fine. What is your most valuable possession?"

"All I have left is this signet ring. It was my mother's."

It was difficult to twist off over her swollen knuckles, but she slipped it from her trembling fingers and placed it into his hands. He held it between his forefinger and thumb. His hands weren't soft, but they didn't have the calluses that fighting men had from sword work. He looked to be strong and muscular from another vocation. More like her father's hands from mill work, not the idle hands of those who relied only on magic to do their bidding.

He held the ring to the light to inspect it. Turning it one way and then another, causing the gold to gleam. "It will do," he said. He caught the ring with a swipe of his hand and pushed the token into his pocket.

She blew out a breath in relief until his hand moved toward her face.

"May I?" he asked.

She nodded, and he plucked a single strand of hair from the top of her head. Gwen rubbed where it pricked her. He handed her a sharp device, took off his coat, and sat at the spinning wheel. His flowing white shirt hung loosely over his masculine frame.

"What are you doing?"

"Saving your life? If we're to be friends, it will be much longer than a single night." He nodded at the device in her hand. "That goes in your leg and then press the top. You will start feeling better."

Hope rose in Gwen's heart. If he was here already and willing, she might as well let him. Her courage allowed her to go farther.

"Teach me to use magic?"

"I'm not a teacher," he grumbled.

"Then show me the trick to turn the straw to gold."

He bowed his head. "You may attempt to pick up my techniques if you can."

This time, instead of sleeping while he worked. She watched. Even with her allergy, she should at least try to learn. But she soon realized she would never have this ability. She doubted she could even spin wool into yarn. So instead, she peppered him with questions until she couldn't hold her eyes open any longer.

At least this time, she had a bed to lie in. She had dozed off about two-thirds of the way through the bales of straw. "She lasted longer this time than the before," he whispered to himself. Still, he worried; something could be off with her magic. Maybe living in Aurum for so long had corrupted it?

He ran the back of his hand along her jaw and moved a strand of hair out of her face. He debated taking a lock. The greedy goblin part of him longed to possess the power it contained, but he refrained. It wouldn't have worked, anyway. Her magic couldn't be taken. "Don't worry Gwen. I'll be back tomorrow. No one will force you to give up your power again," he promised. He pressed his finger to his fleshy pink lips. A single incisor poked over the bottom. He couldn't help it. As part goblin, he had some peculiar features. He pushed his finger to Gwen's lips and sealed his promise, and probably his fate.

"Goodbye Gwen."

As she stirred under his touch, he spun away and faded out of sight.

Defiance

Gwen touched her delicate fingers to her own lips. Her brows pressed together in confusion. She looked around the room for Mr. Woolworth, but he was absent again.

She fell back against the pillows. "I did it again," she groaned. "How could I have fallen asleep?"

She had wanted to learn magic. But she supposed there was a price to pay for the knowledge. "And I doubt a tiny signet ring would do the job."

A knock interrupted her thoughts. "Yes, come in," she said cheerily.

A head of perfectly coiffed curls poked through. "You look exhausted!" Avonlea pushed the rest of her body through the door.

"Thanks?"

"I mean, of course you are because you stayed up all night doing this." She held her arms out wide and did a tiny circle, her mouth agape. Gwen followed her gaze to the spools of gold that had replaced the straw.

Laughing nervously, "I had to prove my worth," she said.

Avonlea clucked her tongue like a mother hen. "Your value has nothing to do with your ability to fill my stepfather's coffers." Her eyes widened. "But now you can marry my brother!" She took Gwen's hands in hers and squealed. "We will be sisters!"

Gwen giggled at Avonlea's excitement. It would be nice to have a sister. Just as she was pondering the implications, the prince pushed the door wider and stood in the doorway. He caught her eye and didn't break his gaze for a long moment. To dilute the uncomfortable attention, Gwen dropped her chin and bent into a shallow curtsy.

Avonlea nudged her over. "You don't have to bow to him. He's your betrothed."

Gwen merely smiled and moved a strand of hair behind her ear.

Prince Ryland stepped into the room. His crisp white pants and a formal blue jacket rustled with each step as he stopped beside Gwen. "I'm glad you've endured through the night and accomplished your task."

Gwen sighed. "I hope your father is satisfied with the outcome."

Just as the words left her mouth, a few men entered the room and began loading the spools into boxes.

The prince turned to them. "What are you doing?"

A short man with a scruffy beard addressed the prince. "We are moving these to the treasury."

Ryland's lips pressed together as his head turned at the pace of a glacier. Gwen could feel the tension rippling off of him. "You will not touch them until the king has had a chance to inspect them."

The men looked uncomfortably at each other and shifted from foot to foot. "We have been ordered to do this."

Prince Ryland took a step toward them. "I am overriding your orders."

"They can't be overridden. The orders are directly from the king."

The muscles in Ryland's jaw tensed and released a few times. He paced angrily from the spools and back to Gwen. A huff escaped through his nose. "He is doing this on purpose. I can't believe he would do this."

Gwen's eyes shifted between Avonlea and Ryland. "Do what?"

Avonlea grabbed her hand and squeezed. "He is having the gold moved from the room before he can see it. He'll be able to deny that it happened."

"Why?" Gwen's voice broke. "Why would he do that?"

As Prince Ryland paced and watched the men remove the spools of gold, Avonlea answered Gwen's questions. "There are a multitude of reasons. He's greedy, trying to intimidate you, manipulating the prince."

"But I am nobody. How could this be used to manipulate him?"

Avonlea's head tilted and her lips pressed down into a slight frown. But no matter what face she pulled, it didn't detract from her beauty. Ryland stopped his pacing for two seconds to share a look with his sister, but gave her a shake of his head.

He began pacing again with a faraway look, trying to work through plausible scenarios to convince the king to stop the madness. The tap of his dress shoes on the stone floor kept pace with her heart.

Gwen stepped into Ryland's path, causing him to halt abruptly in front of her. He dropped his hand and stared down at her. She tilted her head back to meet his eyes. For a few moments, they held each other's gaze. Gwen tried to comfort without words.

She took his hand. "It's ok. I don't know that I can do this again, but I've been resigned to my death for a long while."

He was quiet for longer than Gwen expected him to be. He lifted a hand to her cheek. His thumb swept across her rosy skin. "I just found you. I can't... I won't lose you now."

Then, he was gone. Marching through the door where the spools of gold were quickly disappearing. The sight left Gwen speechless and breathless. What was that supposed to mean? She assumed it was the fact that she had magic. The prince had said exactly that just hours ago. He had been looking for a magician for a while. She tried not to be disappointed and hoped he wouldn't spend too much effort on her. Especially since magic wasn't really something she could help with.

Avonlea took his place. "Don't worry. It's going to be more difficult for the king to dismiss this now. Too many people have seen the result."

Gwen swallowed the lump that had formed in her throat. She wanted to tell Avonlea everything. That it wasn't she who had spun the straw to gold. She had no special abilities. If she had thought for a moment they would let her go home, she would absolutely have shared the truth with her new friend.

She knew better. This had gone too far. No one would let her go back to her father or the mill. This was her new life, and it would probably be short. Her lungs filled with a cleansing breath as she cleared her thoughts.

"I have lived from day to day all my life. This is no different. No one is guaranteed tomorrow so let's make the best of today."

Avonlea looped her arm through Gwen's. "Well said sister." She tugged her toward the door with a giggle.

"What are we doing?"

"I'm taking you to breakfast. I noticed that you haven't touched much of your meals that were delivered and as amazing as you looked in that dress. We need to put a little meat on your bones."

Gwen laughed. "Lead the way."

"Then we'll order you some new dresses. We'll have to use the castle seamstress because Uncle George had to leave town abruptly."

"Oh? I hope he is alright," Gwen said with genuine concern.

"There was something about making the Prince's betrothed a scandalous gown," she tried and failed to hide her smirk, but Gwen stopped short. Her hand flew to her mouth in her concern.

"Oh no. I would never want him to be troubled because of me."

Avonlea pursed her lips and patted her hand. "Uncle George will be fine. He'll let all this blow over and be back in no time. It's us you should be concerned about. We have to put up with Edwina."

"Edwina?"

"The official dressmaker of the crown. And she'll let you know it too."

They had made it five steps outside of the door before a scowling captain of the guard joined them.

"I'm sorry to deliver bad news ladies. I am to be your escort today."

"Will Prince Ryland be joining us?" Gwen asked, her face lit with hope. He had just left, but she had a strange desire to see him again. Their brief morning interaction had not been enough to calm the tumult that formed in her belly when he was around.

"Prince Ryland is currently preoccupied." The captain's eyes shifted briefly to Avonlea's. Gwen sighed. There was obviously an unspoken conversation between them. Their ability to speak without words was becoming annoying, but Gwen didn't think it polite to pry, so she let it go.

Avonlea quickly wiped the concern from her face and pasted on a smile. Something Gwen was sure she would need to learn to do if she were to navigate court life in the future. That fate was still in the air, so she didn't let the weight of it buckle her knees, though they threatened to do just that.

"I'm afraid it will be quite a boring day Captain. Just fitting for new dresses. Her wardrobe is lacking."

"Yes. She is a poor miller's daughter. I imagine she doesn't have much." The captain kept in step with them.

Avonlea turned on her heel. "Isn't there something better you should be doing with your time?"

"My orders are to stay with her."

"Surely a captain of the guard can delegate this matter?"

"Why are you so opposed to my accompanying you?"

"This is girl time and you are encroaching and you are being rude," the princess said bluntly. The captain stepped away with his leather-gloved hands held defensively in front of him.

"Orders are orders Your Highness," he said.

Avonlea rolled her eyes and wound her hand back through Gwen's arm. She took a step before looking over her shoulder. "Fine, but keep your distance. You are not part of the entourage today."

"Yes, Your Highness." He bowed slightly. There was no hint of hurt in his voice. Gwen would have been heartbroken at being reminded of her place so easily, but it seemed the Captain didn't take it personally. She doubted he wanted to follow them around any more than Avonlea wanted him to. She looked over her shoulder as the captain waited for them to get an appropriate distance away before following. Then again, maybe he didn't mind so much. Even though he was harsh with Gwen, he indulged the princess.

Avonlea guided them around hallways while chatting about the courtiers. Gwen listened intently, but there was no way she would remember their names. Avonlea knew every courtier, their children, and their relationships. Listening to the princess exhausted Gwen.

The suites in this wing had become more store front than living area, and she guessed this was where all the work took place. Sure enough, they stopped in front of an elegant door with a black and white awning over it. It was out-of-place inside the castle. There was a thin window on each side of the door. The sign on the door read couturier. They had arrived at the seamstress.

"I thought we were getting breakfast first?" Gwen asked.

"Oh! This was on the way. I'll have something brought up."

The princess didn't bother to knock. She simply opened it and pulled Gwen through. The captain entered a few steps after and leaned against a wall as he was so good at doing.

She hadn't seen movement through the windows, but women lined the foyer, waiting their turn. Champagne-colored brocade, embossed with gold magnolia flowers, covered the cushioned sofas. Though Gwen couldn't see much of the fabric through the women blocking it. The wooden arms, legs and camel back were also foiled with gold trim. A fresh linen scent lingered about the room, and even though women sat shoulder to shoulder, it was as if they had entered a sacred space. They barely breathed to keep from disturbing the silence.

The room was dimly lit, but the area beyond was stunningly bright. In the middle of it, there was a pedestal with a faceless mannequin. The round room allowed viewing of the display from every direction. Velvet ropes kept patron's hands away.

Natural light that seemed to beam from the open sky lit the display. Gwen realized someone had positioned a skylight directly over the mannequin. The round room was plain other than the display. Nothing to distract from the main attraction. And it caused Gwen's jaw to drop.

It was her dress. The one she wore to the banquet. The first dress she had ever bought with her own money. Well, money from the prince. Had someone stolen it and given it to the couturier to display?

Avonlea leaned over and whispered, "It was requested that you loan the dress for display. You will get it back I promise."

A tear almost slipped from the corner of her eye. She waved away Avonlea's concern. "It's fine. I just don't want George's creation to be mishandled."

Avonlea's lips thinned. "It's best not to say anything," she whispered.

Gwen nodded. She understood. It could endanger George further.

A stout woman zigzagged through the display room and entered the waiting room. She appeared disheveled, with tangled hair pulled into a hasty bun. She adjusted her crisp clothes that kept riding up over her belly with each step she took. Her eyes were tired, darting around frantically. "Oh dear. Oh dear," she huffed. As she reached the entrance to the lounge, she looked up from the paper in her hand.

The blood drained from her face when she saw the princess. "She is not going to like this." The woman turned and went back in the direction she came.

After a few more minutes of waiting, a couple of women had offered to let them sit, but Avonlea had pointedly declined. As princess and soon to be princess, they were apparently entitled to skip the line. Gwen had quietly protested, but Avonlea insisted and indicated she would explain later.

Finally, a tall, thin woman with a pinched face, as if her breakfast had been lemons, made her way around the display to the lounge.

She curtsied enough to show respect, but her black pencil skirt only allowed so much movement. "Your Highness. What a great surprise."

"Surely you expected to be dressing the Prince's betrothed."

"Betrothed? I haven't heard an announcement."

"The King is being a bit stubborn," Avonlea admitted. "But he had already proposed. Rest assured Gwen will be my sister sooner than you think."

The seamstress pulled her ruby-red lips into a pretentious smile and lifted her nose. "Of course we will do what we can. I'm sure you must have left most of your clothing behind when the captain retrieved you from the mill."

Gwen flinched as the memory flared to life. It was not a moment she wanted to relive. But she guessed they couldn't have kept it a secret. Gwen looked around the room. None of the courtiers waiting would meet her eyes. The captain didn't move from the wall. He was keeping his promise not to interfere with their day. Avonlea opened her mouth to defend her, but Gwen beat her to it. "You're right. My relocation to the castle was quite abrupt. But I was able to commission this lovely dress just yesterday. Now I think I need a few things that are more practical for court life."

Gwen could feel the women's attention shift to her.

"Well, let's get you to a room then. Shall we?" Edwina motioned for them to follow her.

The captain pushed himself off the wall. But the couturier stopped him.

"Sorry no men beyond this point."

"The princess and the prince's betrothed are under the protection of the crown. I will wait outside the dressing room for propriety's sake."

The women waiting gasped at the captain's admission, establishing Gwen's betrothal to the prince. Every courtier in the kingdom would know about it by nightfall. Avonlea folded her arms over her chest and pulled a corner of her lips. She shared a satisfied look with the captain. Even the king would have a difficult time denying it now.

"Very well." The woman lifted her chin and straightened her pleated jacket. "Ladies. I'm afraid you will need to come back this afternoon." The women's faces fell, and they shuffled through the door. They looked more dejected that they weren't in on the court gossip than that she rescheduled their fittings.

Once they found the room, she turned to the portly woman. "Gertrude, once everyone is out, please lock the door and draw the curtains. We will reopen later this afternoon. Notify the others," she said, clearly annoyed.

"Yes. Madam."

Avonlea turned toward Gertrude. "And breakfast should be brought to our fitting room immediately."

Edwina huffed and pulled her lips into an insincere smile. "Princess you know food is not allowed in the fitting rooms."

The princess lifted her nose into the air. "Today you will make an exception."

Though Gwen hadn't known the princess to be stuck-up, she was rethinking her use of power to manipulate.

"I think you've given me quite enough orders for the day," the dressmaker snapped.

"I am the Princess, so I think I've given the appropriate amount of orders."

Edwina leaned in close and lowered her voice. "For today… princess." She looked over her nose at Avonlea. "Soon you'll be the one…"

"The one what Edwina? The one you come to to get favors from the queen?"

Edwina straightened. Her smile didn't falter. "We'll see." She lifted her chin and walked past the ladies.

Black doors lined a long hallway like soldiers. Each had a covered window in the middle of them. Gwen wondered how many women occupied those rooms. For now, the couturier was giving them her full attention. The captain kept his word and remained outside as the assistant ushered the ladies down the hall and into a private room.

Avonlea took a seat near the door while Gwen went further into the room. It was larger than Uncle George's changing room. Five or six people could fit into the room easily.

"You'll need to undress behind that screen." She pointed to the folded divider across the room.

Two women helped her into a new dress with a bodice that was surprisingly comfortable. She said as much.

A young woman with hair the color of a mouse spoke. "It's a new design that follows fashion norms while allowing the wearer comfort. The ribbing is made from a flexible material that allows movement instead of bone that is rigid."

"How industrious," Gwen commented. "Where did you learn this technique?"

Edwina interrupted as she stepped into the dressing room. "I invented it," she said boldly, but her eyes shifted to Avonlea, daring her to challenge the statement. When the princess didn't take the bait, she quickly transitioned to another topic.

Several more women brought in an array of fabrics and laid them in front of Gwen. "Please choose the color and texture you would like."

"We'll have several dresses made," Avonlea declared.

"Of course. Will they be the same style in different colors or different styles same color? Or a mixture of both?"

"Gwen what is your favorite color?"Avonlea asked.

"I don't have a favorite."

She turned back to the couturier. "Different colors different gowns."

The seamstress bowed her head. "Of course."

"Gwen which of the fabrics do you like?"

Gwen ran her hands over the textiles. A deep green with gold inlay caught her attention. She ran her hands over the weave. Her palm immediately stung. Pulling her hand away, she noticed red welts forming. She slipped her hand inside her skirt pocket to hide the reaction.

"What is this made of?" she asked.

"Actually that is a special blended weave. We've used a special thread the king acquired recently to create the gold inlay. It is a rare fabric and precious."

Avonlea's mouth dropped open. "Why on Earth... ouch."

Gwen stomped her toe.

"That does sound very rare indeed. Can you tell me about the other fabrics?"

"The burgundy is an import from a nearby kingdom, and the plum is also custom made in house, though it lacks the gold inlay."

"I like the plum. No need for the gold inlay."

Avonlea turned to the seamstress. "She'll take two dresses, different styles, in each of the fabrics you presented."

"Three dress in the burgundy and plum," Gwen corrected. "I've decided I don't like green at all."

"You must have a cool shade to break the monotony," Edwina insisted.

"Fine. Do you have any other fabric in a cool tone? Blue perhaps?"

"Yes. We have similar textiles in a royal blue."

"I'll take dresses in that color then. And of course you will be paid for your time and expertise."

Edwina lifted her nose and straightened her shoulders. "The crown pays my salary. Your money is not wanted."

Gwen squinted her eyes back at the woman.

"I have all the measurements I need from the gown you stole from the..."

"Stole? I paid for that work of art." Heat crept into Gwen's face as she defended herself against the accusations.

"The work of art that now adorns my lobby? That will be considered by all, my creation? If it ever leaves this establishment it will be in rags."

Gwen lifted her hand to slap the woman, but as her hand fell, Avonlea swooped in to intercept the blow. The look in her eyes, pleading for Gwen to understand, allowed her to regain her composure.

Edwina clapped twice. "You have seen the styles I'll prepare. Now take off that dress and redress in your other rags."

Avonlea flipped around to face Edwina. "You are talking to a future queen of this realm. Mind your tongue."

Edwina sneered. "It is not my tongue you should be worried about Princess. This peasant will never be queen."

Gratitude

The captain wrapped his arm around Avonlea's waist just as she lunged at the seamstress. How had he known to come to their aid? Gwen would never figure that out. He pulled Avonlea out of the dress shop before she threw a punch and ruined her reputation at court. He had to throw her over his shoulder.

He set her on her feet and looked into her eyes. "I'm going to let you go. Can you control yourself?"

She squinted her eyes at him and ground her teeth. "No, I want to tear that woman limb from limb."

The captain smiled. "As much as I'd like to see that, Scrappy, we still have to be prudent." He held her shoulders. "Take a deep breath."

Avonlea pulled her eyes from the shop doors toward the captain. "Let it go," he coaxed.

"She threatened my brother."

The captain looked back at Gwen, then back at the princess. "Ok. Don't, but bury it deep. So deep that no one can see it. And when the time is right you can pull that anger back up and use it when it's most helpful. That's not today. Not now."

Avonlea pulled her shoulder away from him, grabbed her skirts and stomped into the corridor. They swished and ruffled around her as moved on a mission to appease her need for vengeance.

The captain followed a few paces away, but Gwen caught up with her.

"Can we visit the kitchens?" she asked.

Avonlea stopped abruptly. "The kitchens? Whatever for?"

"I would like to thank them for all the lovely meals they've made. And we never received our breakfast."

The princess forced a laugh and looked over her shoulder at the captain.

"It will be fine," he said, answering her unasked question. "I need to drop by my office anyway for some paperwork."

The princess continued her march through the corridors. "I suppose we can stop by on our way back to the East wing."

After traveling through several winding staircases and twisting through hallways, the captain stopped in front of a door. He pointed down a familiar hallway. "The kitchens are twenty steps in that direction. Do not take a step out of them until I arrive to escort you."

Avonlea lifted her lips in a wry smile. "You better make it quick. I'm not sure how long it takes to say thank you."

"Avonlea. I'm not asking. Do not leave without me." His tone brooked no argument, though Gwen doubted that would stop the princess.

She turned, saying nothing more. The captain didn't follow or argue, and when Gwen looked over her shoulder, he had vanished.

"Honestly, I don't think I've ever been down here," Avonlea said. She stepped over the threshold into the sweltering room. The scent of the afternoon's meals assaulted them immediately.

"I have when we first arrived. There is actually a shortcut through here to the dungeons," Gwen said.

The princess shuddered. "Well, let's not find our way back there."

"No, it was not a pleasant stay." She hid the tremor of her hand in her skirt.

Avonlea grabbed her hand and met her eyes. "I'm so sorry the captain did that to you."

Gwen offered a small smile. "He just follows orders. And no one knew me then."

"How do you do it?" Avonlea asked.

Gwen tilted her head. "Do what?"

"Find ways to be so forgiving?"

"I'm not all that forgiving. I prefer to place the blame where it lies."

The kitchen staff stopped as the ladies walked in.

"Hello," Gwen said with a wave. "I wanted to stop by and thank you for all you have done for me. Each meal has been lovely. Please let me know if there is anything I can do in return."

A rotund woman sat beside the table, pulled her boot off, and placed her foot on the table with a loud thud. The utensils shook with its weight. "How 'bout a foot massage. My Laaaady," she said. The laugh that followed was coarse and caused a coughing fit afterwards. Her lips stretched away from four blackened teeth.

A man flapped a small towel at her. "Shut up Deborah. She's the first lady to thank us for our work and you treat her like that. No wonder no one wants to come down here." The tall cook with a white poofy hat lambasted the overweight woman.

He had a kind smile. "And get your foot off the table. No one wants to eat where your stinky feet have been." He turned to Gwen. "Lady Gwen, what has been your favorite dish?"

"She's no lady," she mumbled, hobbling back to the prep tables. Everyone ignored her.

"It's hard to choose just one. They've all been so delicious. But if I had to, it would be those amazing cream cheese danishes you serve for breakfast."

The chef smiled and bowed slightly. "It was my grandmother's specialty."

Gwen's face lit up with genuine delight. "I'm so delighted she shared her recipe with you." A young lady brought a basket without a word. When Gwen pulled back the napkin that covered it, it was full of the very danishes. She pulled a danish nestled in the middle and took a bite. The soft bread melted on her tongue and gave way to a burst of tart gel. The bite finished with a bit of sweet cream, leaving her wanting to taste more.

"Thank you. May I take these with me?" Gwen asked the young maid.

"Of course, Lady Gwen. We are delighted you enjoy them."

Gwen folded the napkin over the danishes and rested the handle on her forearm.

The chef folded his arms across his chest. "Could I be so bold as to invite the Lady and her retinue to a personal dinner prepared by my staff and myself?"

"That would be amazing! I accept," Gwen said.

Avonlea grabbed her by the shoulder and turned her away. "The lady thanks you for your invitation. We will check her schedule and decide the best time to attend the dinner."

He bowed as they left the room. "Of course Princess, we look forward to your communication."

When the two were out of sight and within earshot of the kitchen, Avonlea turned and slapped her arm. "How could you accept his invitation?"

Gwen flinched and absentmindedly rubbed the offended spot on her arm. "He was nice to me and it would be rude not to."

"Accepting might get you killed."

Gwen scoffed. "The chef is not going to kill me."

"No. But the king might. The chef is the finest in the kingdom, but he's never invited the king to a personal dinner."

"Can't he order a personal dinner."

"It's complicated. But you can't accept that invitation. It's dangerous that it was made to begin with."

Gwen shrugged. "Maybe the king doesn't have to know."

Avonlea paced in little circles in the small hallway. "I guarantee word is traveling to his ear right now."

Gwen's smile fell. "I… I apologize," she stammered. "Honestly, I didn't realize this was a political issue. I was just trying to be nice. We didn't have much at the mill and I'm so grateful for warm meals."

Avonlea rubbed her forehead and sighed. "At court, everything is a political issue." She paced back and forth a step. "We'll ignore it for now and hope for the best." She wrapped her arm around Gwen's. "There's at least one bit of good news."

"What's that?" Gwen allowed herself to be pulled forward.

"We know the chef is with us."

The captain stepped through his office door.

"Come along. Let's get you back to the safety of your room," Avonlea said, pulling Gwen behind her.

Escape

Gwen didn't think she could endure another moment of court life. Avonlea navigated it beautifully with a kind word here and a nasty one there, and everyone fell at her feet. Gwen's thoughts ran away with her. "It's Avonlea who should be queen. Not me, a peasant from the outskirts of the kingdom."

Though the words were under her breath, the princess responded. "I cannot rule," she said. She walked across the room and lowered herself onto the bench beside the window. There was no balcony here. But the windows opened to a bright view of the courtyard. The gauzy fabrics from the hall adorned the glass panes. "Prince Ryland will inherit the throne. And seeing all that he must endure, I know that I do not want it."

"But you are so amazing at court."

Avonlea shook her head. "I'll be married off to a noble of a far away land to the advantage of the kingdom. And I will leave my brother. If I've done my job well, you will be here to help him and support him."

Gwen's shoulders fell. How could she support a prince and future king? She could barely save herself.

"Do you love him?" Avonlea asked.

Gwen ignored the question and looked out the window. She watched a fawn jumping through a brook.

Avonlea joined her by the window. "The blight of magic hasn't touched the inner sanctum. It is why no one is allowed to go into the courtyard. We managed to slow the progression. As you heard our grandmother had magic and created this portion of the palace. Her body lies just there." She pointed to a mound on the other side of the courtyard. "We think she keeps the area lush and green even in death."

"She must have been very powerful."

There was a long moment of silence between them.

Gwen sighed. "I am fond of your brother."

"But you do not love him."

"I enjoy being around him. I wish for him to be here now. If I'm truly honest I yearn for his lips to brush against mine. But is that love?"

"It is the seed I believe."

"And what of the prince? Does he love me?"

"He has gone further with Stepfather than he ever has."

"That is love?" Gwen asked.

"For men? It is. They will battle to protect those they love."

"And yet I remain here, with death looming over my head."

Avonlea patted her hand. "Patience. The battle is not yet won, but he fights on."

"Perhaps its best for Ryland if there is no battle at all."

"What are you saying?"

"If he were to denounce me as his bride and send me back to my father there would be no need for a fight."

Avonlea rolled her eyes and went back to gazing out the window. "Men thrive on war. Whether or not you were his bride, he would have a battle to fight."

"Then how does the battle prove his love for me?"

"He's willing to start a war with Stepfather for you. He was willing to sacrifice Uncle George for you. He was willing to give our mother's inheritance to you. Just because men thrive in battle doesn't mean they don't choose them wisely or with purpose." Avonlea looked Gwen up and down. "Or in this case maybe not so wisely."

The princess's abrupt turn in attitude startled Gwen. It was the first time Avonlea had turned her sharp tongue on Gwen. And she would be lying to herself if it didn't hurt a little. It served as a reminder that while the princess acted as her friend, she could trust no one.

Gwen backed away from the window. "Thank you for your help today. Your instruction has been most appreciated."

Avonlea stood as well. "I apologize for my harsh words." She took Gwen's hands. "I just want my brother to be successful and the only way is with a strong woman by his side."

"Then he has chosen poorly indeed."

Avonlea pulled her close and wrapped her in a hug. "I don't think so, but it will be up to you."

The princess released her and walked toward the door. "It's been an exhausting day and we will be expected for dinner. I'll let the staff know to help you dress. Please get some rest until then."

She watched the princess leave and then fell into a nearby chair. The satin skirts of her gown billowed up around her, and her hands sank into it. "How did I get here?" she wondered. This was the first moment she had to herself since she had arrived. Even in the dungeons, the magician had appeared.

Now she had a minute to reflect on the past few days. They seemed extraordinary. They took her from her home; possibly killed her father; placed her in the dungeon; she attended a banquet with royalty, danced with the prince, and went dress shopping with a princess. All the while assuming each moment could be her last.

She shook her head. "This is too much."

Gwen stood again and crossed to the window. She had noticed a latch earlier. Did she dare to hope it was unlocked and unprotected? *Only one way to find out,* she thought.

She stepped onto the bench where Avonlea had been sitting just moments before. The latch was very high on the tall window. She stretched her body, using the windowsill for support with one hand, as she lifted the other. She pushed herself onto her toes. The tip of her finger brushed the brass latch.

"Come on," she whispered. "Just. a. little…"

She heard a rattle of the doorknob to her rooms, and she retracted her hand as if the latch had been a snake. She thought she would have more time. Her feet hit the floor just in time for the maids to walk through. She heard a male voice from the hallway. Her heart fluttered at the sound. Could the prince have come back to see her so soon?

The maids performed a shallow curtsy to Gwen. She had learned from Avonlea that she was not to curtsy back. She was the betrothed of the Prince, and her status was above theirs now. The only way to ease the uncomfortable tension of that status was to provide a little bow to them. It had only been days ago that she had hoped to be in their position.

The maids did not move as a tall figure strode through the door. Again, Gwen's heart pounded as she waited for him to reveal himself. And it immediately fell as the captain performed a shallow bow.

She let the momentary disappointment pass. "Well, isn't this a change," Gwen said, as she stepped toward him. "You bowing to me instead of throwing me to your men."

The captain didn't ignore the barb. "The princess has sharpened your tongue, I see." He crossed his wrists over the hilt of his sword and stood relaxed yet ready to strike at a second's notice. "I am to escort you to dinner."

"I have not dressed."

The captain turned toward the door. "Yes. It so happens that I ran into the couturier on the way here. She seemed to have gotten lost in the castle and I offered to bring your order to you." He swept his arm, and three servants brought four dresses each. "This should fill your wardrobe for a couple of weeks at least."

Gwen looked them over as the team paraded through her room to the wardrobe. "These dresses should last a lifetime."

"Definitely not. By this time next year, your belly will be round with the Prince's heir."

Gwen gasped. "Captain. How scandalous! There will be no talk of heirs until the marriage has taken place."

The captain bent slightly at the waist. "I apologize. That was rather crass. I only meant that you will need to make nice with the couturier as more dresses will indeed be required."

Gwen took a deep breath at the thought. The dressmaker had already threatened her today. She did not know how to win her over. "Perhaps you can wait in the hall while I dress," she said to the captain, motioning to the door.

His eyes followed her hand, which was covered in dust.

"Have the maids not dusted this room?" He looked around the impeccably clean space.

Gwen hid her hand behind her back. "No they've done a fine job. I must have just found the one place they missed."

"I'll report this to the master of servants. They will be dismissed immediately."

Gwen stepped into his path. "No, please don't. It is not their fault. This room hasn't been used in years. How could they know every place that gathers dust?"

The captain's eyes narrowed. He was much more difficult to manage when Avonlea wasn't nearby to get her way.

"Fine. I'll allow this one infraction. But if anything else goes wrong I will submit my report and dismiss them from their duties."

Gwen nodded. "I understand. Thank you for your discretion."

"And no. I will not be waiting in the hall. I'll be sitting here, facing the door."

Her mouth dropped open. "This is inappropriate." She scoffed.

He lifted the right side of his lips into a smile that was anything but innocent. He leaned into her personal space and whispered. "I suggest you dress quickly. Before I get bored." Gwen swallowed and wondered when he had gotten so close. She nodded and tried to parse the ideas she had about the captain together. It had seemed that he and Avonlea were in a relationship of some sort. She had assumed, but perhaps that wasn't what had happened.

He turned from his spot, grabbed a chair and drug it to the doorway of her suite.

He sat and crossed his legs in the way that men do.

"Tick Tock... *princess.*" He threw the title as if it were an insult. "Use all that powerful magic you have."

She rolled her eyes and motioned for the maids to help her. She was relieved to see the same ones that had helped after her night in the dungeon.

They ran promptly to her side. One poured water into a bowl, wet a cloth and wiped her hands. They escorted her to the wardrobe so that she could choose her attire for the evening. The evening gowns were more revealing than she had hoped and much less flattering.

"Don't choose anything like the monstrosity you wore to the banquet. If you want my advice. That will get you killed," the captain offered.

"Wouldn't you like that?"

"It would take a great deal of stress off my hands," he agreed.

The captain had pulled out his sword, and he twirled it in his hand. Then, she ran a finger up and down the smooth side of the blades. "But then I would have to console the prince."

"I doubt the prince would need all that much consoling. He's only known me for a few days. And I've barely seen him."

She stood before the twelve dresses, trying to decide which to wear for the evening. The hangers produced a scraping sound as she slid them from left to right. At least Edwina hadn't decided to make her look hideous, but nothing was as beautiful as the one George had created. As the last hanger scraped the rack, a tag fell from the last dress. *Wear this one.* It read.

Had someone slipped her a special dress? Who could it have been? There were a few suspects: George, Avonlea, the prince himself. It might have even been the magician. She doubted it was the captain. But there was no way to tell.

The maids helped her slip out of her billowing skirts and into the midnight blue evening dress. They stood on either side and pulled it up her body. One side of the dress had no sleeve, while the other cupped her neck and came to a point over the back of her hand. The fabric was stretchy, and there were no adornments. It was difficult to tell whether the color was blue or black until the light hit it just right and revealed a bit of sparkle. It was as if the night sky draped her. Fabric hugged her body in the front. The ribbing in the back formed a boundary, exposing the entirety of her back again. The maids zipped the dress to just below the flat of her back, her pale skin on display for all to see. Rather than billowing at the waist as most dresses did, this one fitted over her thighs to her knees. The skirt released into a flare around her lower leg. Her feet would be on display as she walked.

The maids pulled out a pair of gold shoes with sharp points at the end. They shimmered in the light. She slipped her feet into them. They were so comfortable she almost groaned.

She stepped from behind the wardrobe just as the captain was standing. Her eyes met his and narrowed.

He shrugged. "Well it looks as though you chose to make my job easier."

He crossed to the window and sat. He placed a black boot over one knee and rested his hands on the hilt of his sword. The captain looked into the lush courtyard.

"Perhaps I should call Princess Avonlea to cheer you up."

"She wouldn't come. It seems someone reminded her today that she is to marry a noble in a far off land."

Gwen shifted in her seat toward the captain. "Is that what you're upset about? I'll have you know she reminded herself. There's no need to take it out on me."

"I'll take it out on whomever I like. And since you are my charge, you get the job."

Gwen turned back to her mirror, letting the maids pile her golden hair on top of her head. They created a ring of hair around the mass as a makeshift crown. Pale powder, then light pink blush, was applied to her face. Her eyelashes received black cream, and her lips were painted with waxy crimson. They pressed dangling gold gems through the flesh of her ears with metal points. It happened so quickly; it was practically painless. Though the maids promised to help her treat the wounds after dinner.

By the time her preparations were finished, the sky had grown dark and Captain Drake had moved to lean casually at the door. She rose from her vanity table and met him there.

"Finally. Let's go meet your fate." He offered her his arm. She took it, but noticed it was not as comfortable as Prince Ryland.

"Why is the prince not to escort me?"

"I will deliver you safely into his hands. After that who knows what your destiny is to be."

The pair stepped through the doorway into the starlit hall.

Test

As they entered the dining hall, all eyes were on her. Again. They had invited everyone from the court and beyond. Every single invite had been answered. Not one noble had wanted to miss seeing their new mistress of magic.

She spotted the prince across the room just as his eyes met hers. Goosebumps rose down her back as he lifted himself from his chair and stepped toward her. It seemed an eternity for him to reach her. She barely registered that the captain had dropped her arm and moved aside. But as her hand fell, the Prince was there to scoop it up and place it in the crook of his arm.

He silently escorted her to her seat. His smile brought butterflies to life in her stomach, but not from the excitement of being near the prince. Something was wrong, but she couldn't pinpoint why dread was building in her chest.

He left her and sat five seats down on the same side. She wouldn't be able to watch him for cues. Avonlea was three places away and not in plain view, either. Gwen grimaced, hoping she wouldn't embarrass herself too much.

She lifted her chin. Not all was lost. She could look at those around her and follow their lead. But as she tried to meet their eyes, it seemed they all had more interesting conversations to attend to. Gwen wondered if this was the king's purpose. Could he want to embarrass and expose her poor upbringing? The king removed all who could aid her. Maybe it was a simple test or punishment for accepting an invitation from the chef?

She sat quietly as the servants brought the soup. A course all the others seemed to finish. She thanked the servers for their help. Steam rose from the bowl of creamy broth with bits of white meat, vegetables, and pasta. The smell of the spices made her mouth water. As the liquid touched her tongue, the flavors exploded. She had trouble keeping a groan of appreciation from escaping, but she avoided embarrassment. As she poked at a vegetable that had popped up in the wake of her spoon, she wondered again how she could convince the king to share the water under the castle. Living at the castle for a week, Gwen thought she had imagined the drought in the land that caused her father's desperate deal.

The meal went on without incident until the last course. When a woman Gwen had never seen before spoke loudly from a few seats down. "Would the new mistress of magic give us a demonstration?"

The morsel of food headed toward Gwen's mouth, stopped over her plate and fell. Her head popped up in surprise at being addressed. She quietly placed her fork next to her plate to hide the quiver of her hand.

"I…" She clasped her hand under the table to keep it from shaking. No one spoke. She searched the eyes of those around her. She did not find a single friendly face. They wanted a demonstration in front of everyone? Surely, this had been her last meal.

"Of course our mistress will demonstrate," the king bellowed from the end of the table. He lowered his chin and frowned, daring her to decline.

Gwen bowed her head, eyes closed. She took a deep breath and lifted her chin. When she opened them again, a smile spread across her crimson lips. Her options were not great. Confess and die, or try to perform magic, fail, and die.

"Of course, Your Royal Highness. I would be delighted."

The king twirled his finger, and servants moved at one end of the hall. A small set of doors opened, and four men carried a heavy contraption toward the center of the room. Everyone was curious to see what it was, but Gwen knew. They were bringing the spinning wheel.

She rose from her seat and placed the cloth used to clean her hands on the table.

This was the moment she had resigned herself, when the entire kingdom discovered her secret, and she lost her head.

She took measured steps toward the contraption that now called her to her death. As she passed their seats, she hoped to convey how grateful she had been for the past few days to the prince and princess. Neither of them moved or spoke. They did not meet her eyes. Had they known?

It was time to prove herself. And she had nothing.

Her body shook as she approached the center of the room. Her downfall would be on display for all to see. She looked about as she sat at the wheel. Putting her fear aside, she lifted her chin and turned toward the king. "And where is the straw I am to spin into gold?"

He did not respond but raised his other hand. Another door opened before a servant carrying a bushel of straw. The last in the kingdom, Gwen guessed. She watched it bounce on the shoulders of the servant, above the heads of those in the crowd. The man approached and lowered it to the floor at her feet.

The item of her death lay before her. She stared at it as if it were a viper ready to strike, trying her best to hold her breath. The people had turned in their chairs to see the spectacle. She tried to find the prince's eyes, but he refused to look at her. He sat stoically and looked only at the window, abandoning her to fate. In his stepfather's presence, he didn't seem willing to fight his battle.

A tear filled her eye. She reached with her covered hand to pick up a bit of straw. The fabric would cover the welts that would form on contact. She lifted the piece and fed it through the device. All eyes were on her - aside from the prince - so no one noticed a dark figure in the back of the room. But as she raised her head, Gwen saw him.

He blended with the shadows as he had in her cell, but she could make out his features. He lifted his hand to his lips, motioning for her to keep quiet, then gestured for her to take a piece of her hair.

She followed his motioned instructions and began spinning the wheel. His fingers danced. She took a shallow breath, but as the items wound through the device and onto the spool, they sparkled into gold filament.

The crowd gasped. One woman might have fainted. The man in the shadows smiled and disappeared.

A chair scraping against the floor broke the heavy silence as the prince stood. "Enough. You have had your show. Gwen will be my bride. Tomorrow."

The king's wide smile revealed the molars on his top teeth. "Very well. You may marry the maiden. Tomorrow at noon."

Murmurs turned into eager whispers, but Gwen struggled to catch her breath. She could feel the heat, the itchy marks, traveling up her arm. She needed to be out of this room in thirty seconds or her salvation would be short-lived.

She searched for the man in the shadows but found only darkness. The prince stepped into view and dropped to his knees. "Gwen, I'm so sorry. It was the only way to stop the charade and force him to acknowledge your gift."

"You planned this."

"Yes. I'm sorry I couldn't warn you. Will you still have me?"

She forced a smile. "Of course," she choked out. What else could she have said?

"Gwen? What's wrong?"

"I need." Her unclothed hand grasped at her neck. "Air."

He placed a muscular arm around her waist. "I'll get you out of here." Everyone had left their chairs and was milling around them. Someone kicked the bushel of straw. Particles flew into Gwen's face.

Her eyes widened. Even though she had passed the test, the court could still realize she had no magic.

The prince grasped her hand and pulled her through the crowd. She stumbled behind him, hardly noticing as Avonlea and the captain flanked either side.

The four of them spilled into the hallway.

Gwen sucked in a deep breath but immediately began choking.

The prince turned to her. "Have you been poisoned?"

She shook her head.

"Cursed?"

"No." She managed through clenched teeth. "Allergic."

The prince's face contorted from worry into resigned action. He scooped her into his arms, finally remembering her confession from a few days ago.

"Drake, go to the med office. Find something to counteract this. Meet us in her suite."

"Yes, sir." It was the quickest she had ever seen the captain move. Surely, he couldn't care if she died, but he was loyal to Prince Ryland.

The prince turned to his sister. "Avonlea you're on crowd control, they'll all be clamoring after her in a few seconds."

"Of course. It's my best skill." She pasted a smile on her face and swept back into the ballroom. The cacophony of the crowd rose and died with the swinging doors.

The prince carried Gwen as if she were a feather. He was silent. His lips flattened into a pursed line. As she closed her eyes, she couldn't tell whether he was worried or angry.

"Gwen, do not close your eyes. Wake up," he pleaded.

He arrived at her suite and kicked through the door. He laid her on her bed. The man in the shadows stepped forward.

The prince jumped into a fighting stance, pulled his sword, and pointed it at him.

Mr. Woolworth raised his hands. "Relax, I'm just here to help."

"Who are you and how did you get in here?" the prince growled.

"Would you like me to answer questions or save your fiance's life?"

"The captain will be here momentarily."

"There is no medicine in your infirmary to cure her."

"How do you know that?"

The man's lips pulled into a wide grin. "I've been curing her since you brought her here."

That earned the man a sword at his throat. "You've been near her? With magic."

The man from the shadows swallowed. "I did mention I saved her life. Magic had a little to do with it." He held his thumb and forefinger slightly apart.

The prince looked back at Gwen, whose face was turning a pale shade of violet.

Mr. Woolworth's eyes shifted toward her. His lips formed a thin line. "She is on the verge of death now. Trusting me won't make it worse."

"Perhaps you are the one who cursed her," the prince accused.

"This is not a curse." Mr. Woolworth countered.

The man lifted his finger to the prince's head. The prince collapsed in a heap at his feet. Rendered unconscious. He stepped over him toward Gwen's bed.

"Now where were we princess?"

He pressed the pointed metal into her chest, delivering the concoction straight to her heart. He stood over her, whispering words until Gwen's eyes popped open, her torso lifted off the bed, and she gasped for air. It rushed into her lungs, and she fell back against the bed.

Mr. Woolworth knelt beside her, placing a gentle palm on the side of her hand. "You have a choice Gwen. You can come with me now and save yourself or stay here and continue to suffer."

Gwen looked at the prince collapsed on the floor. "What have you done to him?"

A loud bang interrupted their conversation.

"Ryland open up. I have something I think will help." The captain had returned faster than Gwen had imagined, but it still might have been too late.

Mr. Woolworth held out his hand to Gwen. "You aren't ready, but we've run out of time. The king's greed and the Prince's lack of backbone has forced us to rescue you."

Gwen ignored his hand. The prince began to stir. The captain banged on the door again.

Mr. Woolworth grunted his displeasure and stepped into the shadow. "Meet me in the center of the courtyard at midnight," he said, as his form faded from view.

Gwen rubbed her head. The fabric slid against her skin and irritated the itchy rash she already had there. She stood on wobbly legs. Grasping the furniture, she supported herself until she fell toward the door. Taking a moment to catch her breath, she then twisted the handle and collapsed against the captain.

He caught her and helped her to stand. "Gwen? What's happened? Where is the prince?"

"Here." Prince Ryland sat on the floor beside her with his forearms resting against his knees. He shook his head back and forth as if clearing it.

The captain shoved Gwen back into the bed and knelt beside the prince.

"It's time to confess, Gwen."

Confession

The captain, satisfied the prince was fine, stood abruptly and placed his sword at Gwen's throat.

"Confess," he yelled.

Avonlea entered the room and slammed the door behind her.

"Drake, what are you doing?"

"I came here to deliver the medicine I found. Ryland was unconscious on the floor and she fell into my arms at the door. She couldn't even walk a few minutes ago. This is all an act. If she can spin straw to gold, why does it nearly kill her? Are you working with the king?"

The prince rose to his feet. "Remove your sword, Drake."

The fierceness in his eyes only grew darker. "She's dangerous."

"Remove. Your. Sword." The prince lowered his voice and placed a hand on his sword's hilt. "Before I draw mine."

The captain's eyes shifted to Ryland's. Taking a breath, he stepped back, but did not put his sword in the scabbard.

"Gwen didn't harm me. It was the dark prince. He came to…" the prince rubbed his temple where Mr. Woolworth had touched him.

"To what?"

The prince's jaw flexed and relaxed. "Save her."

Gwen looked between the three of them. "Who is the dark prince?"

"It has been long rumored that he still lives," Avonlea mentioned in a hushed tone, indirectly ignoring Gwen's question.

Drake put his sword away. "But he hasn't been seen in twenty years."

The prince sat in a nearby chair, resting his elbows on his knees and running his hands through his chestnut hair. "His death supposedly caused the chasm and the loss of magic," he said. "According to a letter left to me from my grandmother."

"Who is the dark prince?" Gwen asked again.

"Rumpelstiltskin," the three responded in unison.

Gwen laughed. "That's a children's story."

No one laughed with her, and it died in her throat. "Wait, you think the story is true?"

"It is true," Ryland said.

"And you think this man that helped us tonight is a character from a children's story?"

The prince shrugged. "It's the only thing that makes sense. The only question is, why is he interested in you?"

Gwen hoped the hurt she felt in her heart didn't show on her face. "I suppose the same as anyone else. He heard I had magic."

Prince Ryland lifted an eyebrow, but Gwen didn't dare share further than that. She couldn't let her possible feelings for the prince cloud her judgment. No one could save her from the secret that she actually didn't have any magic.

"There must be more to it than that. He hasn't been seen in over twenty years," Drake said.

"Well, if there is, he hasn't shared his thoughts with me. I don't even know who he is," she said.

"You've never seen him before?" Of course, it was a question Drake, the captain of the guard, would ask. No one got to that rank by being stupid. There was no escaping his suspicion.

Three pairs of expectant eyes waited for her answer. Gwen leaned against her pillows and swallowed hard. "I have once or twice. Though I didn't know who he was. He told me his name was Mr. Woolworth."

Prince Ryland knelt beside her and grabbed her hands in his. His lips met her long, slender fingers. "I am determined to do everything to keep you safe. Tomorrow we will be married. These petty tasks to prove your gift are done. And you'll have my protection."

Gwen nodded.

"About that," Drake started, earning him a glare from the prince. "What? It needs to be asked."

The prince was in his face in a second. "No, it does not."

"We need to know whether or not she has magic."

"We have seen her do it herself. There is no other evidence."

"How is it possible if she is allergic to the very material she's spinning? Ryland, if she doesn't have magic we need to know. Our plans depend on it."

Gwen cleared her throat and opened her mouth to speak.

Prince Ryland did not take his eyes off of Drake as he spoke. "Gwen, you do not have to answer these accusations."

"It's ok. I've always been allergic to straw. My father kept me away from the mill and any straw nearby. It was difficult but we managed. You may even recall me telling you that I didn't have magic and I couldn't spin straw to gold. It wasn't until I tried in the dungeon that I was able to complete the task."

"Straw?" Prince Ryland asked. "You told me at Uncle George's shop you were allergic to gold."

"No, you assumed it was gold. It seemed trivial at the time to correct you. I barely knew you."

"So even after the straw has been turned to gold you still get an allergic reaction?" Avonlea asked.

"It seems so. I'm sorry I misled you. I didn't think it would make a difference."

Drake stepped around Prince Ryland. "And how did you manage your allergy at each of the other trials?"

"I didn't manage it. It was Mr. Woolworth who has arrived each time to administer his concoction and save my life."

Prince Ryland took a deep breath. "He has saved your life three times now?"

"Yes."

He threw his head back and groaned. The trio exchanged glances that worried Gwen. "What does that mean?"

"It means.." Drake began.

"Nothing. You will be married to me tomorrow so it means nothing."

Gwen looked between the men. She didn't push the matter further. Prince Ryland seemed to think their nuptials would solve all their problems.

Avonlea finally spoke. "It's been a long day and a longer evening. Shall we all retreat and get some rest?"

The prince knelt beside her again and squeezed her fingers. "Remember what I told you about this room?" Ryland asked.

Gwen nodded again.

"We'll post guards at the doors as well."

Her eyes slipped to the underground passage unbidden. Avonlea pursed her lips and shifted her head in warning. "Don't reveal her secret." She conveyed clearly, without words.

The captain scoffed. "As if that will help."

"You will be as safe as I can make it until tomorrow."

Her eyes turned toward her hands, and she swallowed against the lump in her throat. "I trust you." The words were easy to say, but was there any truth to them?

As the three prepared to leave the chamber, there was a knock at the door. Everyone looked at each other.

Ryland and Drake lifted their swords. Avonlea went to answer. "Who is it?"

"The wedding gown has arrived."

After checking with each of the men and receiving a nod, she opened the door. The seamstress's assistants carried it inside.

The train was twelve feet long and took up most of the clothing nook at the back of the room. The dress itself used yards of golden fabric. It sparkled in the light from the chandeliers. Its sleeves poofed to orbs the size of her head at the shoulder. A satin bodice narrowed at the waist before it expanded to twice its width at the hips. Intricate embroidered designs arranged in lines down the front as if the thread were marching over the satin. The thread was the same color as the fabric, but the designs dulled the shimmering fabric to make it appear regal. These designs ran the full length of the skirt, which was cut to ribbons, revealing beneath the finest ivory silk skirt Gwen had ever seen. She was drawn to the fabric, but her hands were slapped away when she lifted them to feel it.

"No touching until tomorrow. We wouldn't want to damage it."

Properly chastised, Gwen backed away from the dress and turned her attention toward Avonlea.

"This was made very quickly," Gwen said.

"Almost too quickly." Avonlea looked at Drake. "How much do we trust the seamstress?"

The captain met her eyes as if having a silent conversation. Avonlea only pursed her lips in response.

"Lady Edwina started on it as soon as you left the shop. But she has been working on this creation for many years. She simply adjusted it to Lady Gwen's measurements."

"Thank you, Mila. That will be all." Avonlea said.

"Very well, I'll attend to the many other matters that are required by a hasty royal wedding," the maid chided.

Gwen snatched her hand, to the surprise of almost everyone. "Thank you for your help."

The servant curtsied with a slight smile. "It is my pleasure." She left without meeting the eyes of any others.

Gwen let out a deep breath. "I thought the couturier said I would never wed the prince."

"No. She said you would never be queen," Avonlea scoffed.

"That is a threat if I ever heard one," Drake said.

Avonlea inspected the dress from every angle. She lifted the delicate fabric, careful to touch very much of it. She stood and shook her head, having found nothing wrong.

She shrugged. "The seamstress is a favorite of the king so we can't accuse her without evidence," Avonlea argued.

"As soon as I am king, that will no longer be the case," Prince Ryland declared.

"Well, you better move quick, or you may not have Gwen as your queen.

I'm not sure what Edwina has up her sleeve, but she seemed very sure that Gwen wouldn't make it to the wedding."

"We've done everything we can to protect her. We can't wrap her in a bubble," Drake said.

"Perhaps her magic will aid her," Ryland said, placing his sword in his sheath. He took her hand in his. "We leave you now to rest. I will see you tomorrow at our wedding." The prince kissed her forehead and swept out of the room.

Drake bowed without a word and backed out. Avonlea moved to follow him silently. She turned when she reached the door and offered a small, reassuring smile. Before Gwen knew it, the princess's skirts swished as she exited, pulling the door closed behind her.

Gwen stood after she was sure no one would return. Whatever Mr. Woolworth - she wasn't prepared to call him Rumpelstiltskin - had given her worked quickly. Her legs didn't wobble at all, and she wasn't the least bit tired. She felt as if she could run home to the mill and back.

Thinking of the mill brought a pang to her chest. She rubbed the bone that covered her heart absently, as if that could relieve the pain she felt. More than anything, she wanted to see her father and ensure he was alive and well. There wasn't much time for missing her home while also trying to survive. But on the eve of her nuptials to the prince, she wished her father could be there with her.

In a land without magic, wishing never amounted to anything.

Gwen paced from the bed to the window. Her skirts dragged along the floor. Fortunately, the stone was well swept. She didn't want to ruin the fine dresses from the seamstress shop, no matter how awful the maker was.

She tapped her forefinger on her lip. Everyone had seen her spin straw into gold. No one would challenge her ability to do it again. The problem would be that they expected it to be done easily on a whim. Now the question was, how did she do it? Gwen knew she had no magical talent. She couldn't even stay awake when Mr. Woolworth appeared to help her.

Mr. Woolworth was a problem. Gwen stopped her pacing. Did he help her spin the gold tonight? She had never spun the gold before. It was always his doing. Was it his ministrations that caused the change? Could he do such a thing without touching the spinning wheel?

"He's the real catch." Gwen decided. "And if they do, there is no telling what might happen to either of us."

She began her pacing anew. "He said to meet him in the courtyard at midnight." She looked at the wall sconce. The one leading to the lake. "I must warn him never to return for both our sakes."

Midnight

It was torture waiting for the dark skies to indicate it was time to leave. No one had bothered her or even checked in to see if she was still breathing. She imagined the wedding preparations would occupy their time.

Just before midnight, she pulled the sconce. She made her way down the staircase Avonlea had showed her during their adventure and up the steps leading to the garden. Pushing up on a wooden door, she exited just past the outer wall of the castle. She could see the large window of her suite as she crouched in the darkness cast by the stone walls.

She scurried past the French doors that opened from the hallway below her suite. Two guards turned to face the garden just as she melted into the shadow of the balcony. She stiffened and willed them to look past her. It felt like hours, but they finally turned their gazes away from her hiding spot.

The magic of the garden zinged around her, and the midnight roses lifted their heads to greet her as she wandered past them. Other flowers glowed when she touched them. Every plant seemed pleased by her visit and turned to her as she drew near, as if an unseen force were drawing them to her. With no visitors in years, the enchanted garden was happy for some attention.

She hardly noticed as she approached the middle of the garden. Waiting for Mr. Woolworth to appear and looking for any sign she had been caught.

"I didn't think you would come." His voice was low.

Gwen gasped and spun in his direction.

"It's not yet midnight," he said.

She sighed in relief at the sight of Mr. Woolworth leaning against the dark obelisk in the middle of the garden. "Oh Mr. Woolworth, I'm so glad it was you."

He pushed himself off the object and stepped toward her. "I'm relieved to hear it. Shall we go?" he said, with an outstretched hand.

"I.. I didn't meet you so that I could leave with you," she stumbled and stammered over her words.

He remained silent, so she surged forward. "I came to warn you. You can't come back. My life is already forfeit, if they capture you there is no telling what they will be able to do."

He dropped his hand. "I don't understand."

"I can't go with you. I must stay and wed the prince. Then we'll be safe."

He pressed his lips together. "I understand you are besotted with him, but that will pass in time. You can't marry him."

"I know we've only just met, but I do believe he cares for me."

"That would be quite a feat for the prince."

"I'm only trying to protect you. I've been prepared to die for many days now. But I don't want anything to happen to you. You have shown me kindness and have saved me from death. But if they capture you…"

"I'm not so easy to catch." His calm demeanor did not put Gwen at ease. He failed to recognize the urgency of her warning.

"Please… I don't want to see you tortured for your power."

"What power do you think I have?"

"I've seen your magic. Obviously you can spin gold. But I suspect you have much more."

He tilted his head back, considering her words. "Who did your prince tell you I was?"

She wrung her hands before admitting, "Rumpelstiltskin?"

Mr. Woolworth pulled up the right side of his lips in a sly smile. It made him more handsome, if that were possible.

"Do you deny it?" she asked.

He ignored the question. "Gwen. You are in danger. I am not. If you stay I have no doubt you will die. If not from your allergy, or the executioner's block, the land itself will kill you."

"I know. I've prepared for it."

He shook his head and grabbed her hand. "I can't let that happen."

She pulled it away. "Why do you care?"

"I can't explain here." He reached for her hand again, but Gwen took a step back. "Gwen. You need to come with me. If you don't, terrible things will happen to both of us."

"I'm trying to prevent that."

"You can't understand. Come with me and we'll figure it out."

Gwen shifted her eyes toward the doors. Unfortunately, Mr. Woolworth was standing between her and them. There was no way around him or of avoiding the shadows that he could obviously travel through.

She stepped to the side. "You've saved me so often. Please allow me to return the favor."

"Gwen."

"I hope not to see you again."

She sprinted toward the doors, careful to stay in the moonlight and avoid shadows. She banged against the glass until one of the guards moved from his post and opened the door. Gwen slipped between the frame and the guard, looking over her shoulder at the obelisk. There was no one behind her. Mr. Woolworth was gone. He had taken her advice at last. She breathed a sigh of relief as she slipped past the guard and into the hallway.

She was jerked back as he grabbed her wrist.

"Ow. That hurts."

"Why were you in the garden? It is off limits to everyone." Both guards converged on her.

She lifted her chin in her best impression of Avonlea. "The flowers were so beautiful and they called to me. I leaned over to look and fell out of my upstairs window."

"The gardens are off limits to everyone," they repeated.

"The prince gave me special permission. After all they are his grandmother's gardens and he can do what he likes. And I am the lady of magic."

The guard leaned back, but didn't release her hand. "That's right your the miller's daughter. I heard about you."

"Then you've also heard I'm engaged to the prince."

"I did hear that. But why should he have you all to himself?" he laughed.

"We're engaged."

"Yes you said that. But if you can spin straw to gold, why didn't you save your father? Why weren't you the richest girl in the country?"

A familiar voice entered the conversation. "A question I would like answered as well." Drake sauntered to the enclave.

He crowded near the guards without breaking eye contact with Gwen. "Unhand the princess."

"But she came from the garden."

His eyes shifted from Gwen to the guard who spoke, and his voice dropped an octave. "If Prince Ryland catches you with your hand on his betrothed, he will have your head. As it is, you will both receive thirty lashes for daring to touch what belongs to him."

Gwen placed her delicate fingers on the captain's forearm. He shifted his attention from the guard to her hand, to her face. She retracted her hand as she said, "Please, they were doing their duty. Don't punish them for performing the task you gave them."

Drake's dark stubble enhanced his menacing features. "If you keep talking, princess, you will receive their lashes, instead."

She lifted her chin. "I will gladly take them."

Drake growled. "Add ten lashes for the princess's insolence."

Both guards groaned. Gwen opened her mouth to defend them again. Drake raised his eyebrows. The other guard interrupted. "Thank you, sir we will take our lashes. We have learned our lesson. In the future, we will notify you instead of apprehending the lady of magic ourselves."

The words spilled rapidly from his mouth. With a glare from Drake, it snapped shut.

"You will not speak of this to anyone, unless you want to spar with me in the ring."

The guards swallowed. "Yes sir." They said in unison.

"Good."

Drake tugged Gwen in front of him and pushed her toward the stairs. "I'll escort you to the safety of your room."

Gwen lifted her skirts slightly in the front to traverse the stairs without slipping.

Once they reached her suite, he opened the door for her. He scanned the area for intruders. His eyes stopped at the open window.

Drake stepped back into the hallway and looked both ways. He pulled Gwen into the room but left the door open.

"What were you doing down there?"

Gwen weighed her words. The lies were stacking up, and she knew they would haunt her, so she tried for vague truth. "It called to me. And it was so beautiful I had to see it. And as I said, I fell."

Drake put his head in his hand and squeezed his temples. "You are going to be the death of this kingdom."

"Then turn me in and be rid of me."

Drake stalked to the door. "I might do just that." He paused before walking through it. "I have a better idea" His face brightened at the thought and stalked back toward her. "Perhaps you should disappear." His words came out in a growl. Gwen held her breath, ready for the blow he was about to give.

She squeezed her eyes shut. "Do it quickly. But please tell Ryland I lo…"

Drake laughed. "That you love him?" He was so close she could smell the crisp linen of his uniform. "We both know that's a lie." His voice was a whisper. "I'm not going to kill you Miller."

She opened her eyes one at a time, pressing eyebrows together. How could he know she didn't love the prince?

He smiled as his plan clicked into place in his mind. "No. There won't be guards posted at your door. No locks will deter you. You can escape like I know you long to do. Go back to your father in the village. I heard he was drinking away all the gold the king paid him," he said with a sneer.

Without another word or a look back, the captain was gone. She stood as still as a statue, wondering if she had just imagined that the captain had let her go. True to his word, the door remained open, and the guards on her door were gone.

Laughter bubbled out of her. "I'm free." She looked over her shoulder at the lavish room and the overflow of golden fabric in the room's corner. "My father is alive and I'm free."

Friends

Gwen opened the door and ran down the hall but stopped short at the first intersecting hallway. She twisted her hands over each other. "Perhaps I should have just gone with Mr. Woolworth. But I wanted him to be safe somewhere away from me."

She stayed out of sight in case the captain had lied about removing the guards.

A company of troops dressed in light blue coats and white pants with golden brocade accoutrements marched through the corridor near her room. Their shiny black boots hit the ground in unison as they thundered along the path. It was well after midnight now. Maybe this was some ritual new recruits had to endure as part of their training.

"Maybe the captain lied," she whispered. But as she watched the men march through the halls, she realized they were not looking for her.

A tall man stood to the side and gave orders. His dark mustache covered his mouth. "The trooping of the guard is one of the most important parts of the royal wedding. We will be practicing this until it is perfect."

"They're preparing for my wedding?" She shook her head. "This is ridiculous. They'll be too tired to perform perfectly if they stay up late tonight." She couldn't help but whisper the words aloud.

She watched them from the shadows for a few more moments. One soldier stood out among the others. He wasn't meant to. They all should have looked the same. Uniformed. Completely indifferent from each other and to the enemy.

He was a boy from her town. They hadn't known each other well, and he'd be unlikely to recognize her, but she knew him. He had come to the mill with his father to have his grain milled. He was younger than she was. She remembered him as a little boy, barely as tall as his father's hip. Now he could rival any man in the village in height. As the drought set in and crops failed, she had seen less of him.

"Did the king conscript these men or did they volunteer?" She leaned against the cold stone. "Even as volunteers they might not have had a choice," she whispered to herself.

She stayed in the shadows long after they passed. If she escaped, there would be no coming back to the castle. She would be free of this life and all the expectations. There would be no marriage or magic or expectation of the riches she could produce for the kingdom.

Gwen made her way down the winding streets of the kingdom's capital city. It was dark, and the lamps had long dimmed. A north wind chilled the air, and no one walked the roads. In her haste, Gwen had not grabbed her woolen black cloak before she left. Her body was more than a little exposed.

It hadn't been the best idea to leave in the middle of the night, with the chill of winter setting in. But the garden had been pleasant, protected by its magic, no doubt. If she had had more time to plan, she would have prepared for a journey.

She couldn't remember where the stables were and was afraid to visit them. The guard who brought her to the castle might be lurking. So she ventured into the city streets without much of a plan other than to make it home.

They looked familiar. Without realizing it, she wandered onto the first place Prince Ryland brought her to.

She cupped her hands around her eyes and pressed her face to the glass. The store was darker than the street and empty. The beautiful dresses that had been in the storefront were gone. A single headless mannequin stood at the back. Though it was difficult to make out the gray silhouette.

Dissatisfied that she had caused this downfall, she tugged at the door. It easily swung with her slight tug. Surprised it opened at all, Gwen accepted it as a sign that she must investigate the dress shop.

She took tentative steps through the empty room. Dust had already collected on the floor. She rubbed the frigid skin on her arms to warm. Though the place was clearly vacant, it was much warmer than outside. She needed to get out of the city as quickly as possible, but it was too difficult in the dark and the cold with no supplies.

The inset couches and dressing runway were still there. Gwen sighed. At least she could rest until morning. Then she would make an actual plan to run home.

She lowered herself and lay down. Sleep overtook her.

Gwen felt it before she heard it. A gentle shake of her shoulder and then a harder poke in the ribs.

"Gwen darling you can't squat in my store."

She pried her eyes open. They had crusted over in her sleep, but she wiped that away to reveal who spoke to her.

George stood over her. She gasped, suddenly more awake and ready to bolt. She looked around the shop. It was still dark outside.

"George what are you doing here? The king will find you and behead you."

George laughed. "The king is going to do no such thing. I only let him think he has driven me out of town. But you are going to blow my cover."

"What are you talking about?"

"You are sleeping in my vacant store front. I'm the one who gets to ask the questions."

"Yes, I suppose this does look rather suspicious. But I was cold and this was the only place I knew. I took a chance."

George looked at the front glass and back at Gwen. "We can't stay here. Come with me." He grabbed her hands and pulled her up.

He led her through the maze of fitting rooms and through a hidden door, which revealed a set of stairs that led to a well-lit basement. They traveled through another concealed entrance and into a workshop. Hundreds of gadgets with needles poked holes through fabric and pushed thread through. A man or woman sat at the devices to ensure everything worked correctly. They barely looked up as she passed by.

"George. What are these people doing?"

"They are making dresses."

"But you were closed down."

He rolled his eyes. "I was forced underground. Literally."

"But won't the king know?"

"He already knows. He chooses to ignore it. If he wanted to have me killed it would have happened long ago. Though he does have his favorites and he likes to humiliate me from time to time. He feels powerful to put others down. And my staff are loyal to the bone." He gave a hollow laugh. "It helps that I pay them well, of course."

Gwen smiled. "Of course."

He continued to walk and led her through another set of doors. It was much quieter in this room. Gwen realized this was where George brought his creations to life. He had drawings of dresses hung on every available wall space. And some were taking shape on two or three headless mannequins.

"On the other side of this space is another small office where you may sleep, but before you go in there, I must ask why are you not at the palace? I heard of your impending nuptials."

Gwen looked down at her hands and fidgeted, wringing them together. She swallowed once and sighed. "I'm not who he thinks I am. They want a princess who can do magic and turn the tide of the war. That person is not me."

George leaned on his desk. And crossed his arms over his abdomen. The vest of his suit crinkled, but he didn't look a bit rumpled even at such a late hour. He narrowed his eyes.

"And who are you exactly?"

She stood before him. Completely vulnerable. It was time to be honest with someone, at least. In just a few hours, Prince Ryland would hate her, possibly hunt her down and have her and her father murdered. Tears began to form and spill over the rims of her eyes. She hadn't thought of that possibility. George didn't move.

"I don't have magic. I don't know why my father said that. I can't spin straw into gold."

"You have survived this long you must have managed a way somehow."

"It wasn't me."

"Gwen. You don't have to tell me this. I will do my best to hide you."

"I need to tell someone. Someone to share this burden."

"I'm not that person. I like you. But the royal children have unburdened themselves on me too often. And though I have weathered it well, it has cost me dearly."

Gwen wiped her eyes and nodded. "Yes, I see where that would be unfair. I'm so sorry to have bothered you. Truly, I thought your shop was vacant and I…" She lifted her head to the ceiling to keep more tears from falling. "I just needed a place to rest until I can find my father."

George pushed off the desk and approached Gwen with open arms. She stepped into his embrace as he closed them around her. The tears she was trying to hold back broke like a dam and soaked his linen shirt. He rested his chin on the top of her head and let her cry. When the tears finally subsided, he released her.

"There's nothing like a good cry," he said, patting her on the back.

Gwen nodded and wiped her cheeks.

He put his hand on each of her shoulders and met her eyes. "Whether you have magic or not, is not important. I saw how Ryland looked at you. He is smitten and I know personally he has done everything in his power to make this wedding happen. Not because he needs you, but to protect you."

"Protect me? He said my power can help in the war with the white witch. He put me on display for all to see."

George rolled his eyes again and walked back to his desk. "He doesn't need magic to defeat the white witch. He needs a powerful queen who believes in him. Your power is not in your ability to spin gold. It is in your ability to inspire loyalty. And if he did anything it was to protect you."

"I suppose…"

"You don't believe me?"

"No. I'm a nothing miller girl."

George swiped a paper from his desk. "This portrait is hanging in all the local taverns. The town square, anywhere people gather."

She held the edges of the canvas. Her green eyes and golden hair looked back at her. A white glow had been painted behind her, giving her face a look of innocence. Her pouty lips turned upward in a friendly smile. "Why would my portrait be there?"

"The people love that their future queen will be like them. They hope you will represent them."

"But I…"

"Have no power?" he shrugged. "It doesn't matter. They think you do."

"It's a lie."

"These portraits appeared right after you entered the castle. Before I made you a dress, before you spun gold the first time. They don't care if you have magic. They love that you are one of them."

"But how?"

"It doesn't matter. They are singing ballads about you. If you abandon them now, I fear this kingdom will fall further into a darkness that we may never recover from."

Gwen's shoulders drooped.

"The choice is yours." He pointed at the door behind him. "You can rest in there if you want. The exit leads to a tunnel. Left is to the road through the woods, right will take you back to the castle."

"Thank you George. For everything." She lifted herself onto her toes, pecked his cheek, and whisked herself through the back doors.

Regardless of her actions, the soldiers, like the little boy from her village, would continue to die. They would be sent to the front lines of a new battle against the White Witch. Ryland believed Gwen was the key to winning the war.

"I don't have magic." Looking down at her hands, she took a step out of the shadows. "Do I?" Her hand shifted to the braid that hung neatly over her shoulder.

She looked over at the door from George's shop. "But if I leave I will do nothing except whither away in the corner of my father's house. What good will that do anyone?"

She took a step back. "But if I stay. If I marry the prince, and become a princess. Perhaps I would have the power to help in some meaningful way."

* * *

Back in the palace at last, she kept to the shadows. The horizon had lightened with the promise of dawn. Through the doors, a few men from the stables stalked into the hallway. None of them wore smiles, but they stood tall and proud.

"Tomorrow will be different," the leader of the group said.

Another grumbled. "It's never different. Always the same. Day in day out."

The leader flashed a brilliant smile. "But tomorrow the prince marries."

"How will that make anything different?" another younger man said.

"Because he is not marrying a princess. He is marrying the last person in this kingdom with magic."

"We should throw her to the white witch. Let her go be with her kind."

"Besides she doesn't have fighting magic. She can barely even spin gold."

"Well it doesn't matter what she can or can't do. What matters is that the white witch is defeated."

"How is the prince marrying a farm girl with magic powers going to defeat the white witch?"

"They say when the prince marries his curse will be lifted and all magic will be restored to land."

"I don't believe that old tale."

"It's true. I was there when he was cursed."

"What was the curse?"

"The kingdom will wither until the prince finds a bride. He must marry a girl with magic. No one else can break the curse."

The men laughed. "That's a horrible curse. No one even dies."

"Some say a magical bride would be a curse."

"Why doesn't he just go marry the white witch?"

"That old hag. She wouldn't have him."

Gwen held her breath and pressed herself further into the shadows as the group of men passed.

"Harold, shut the door! Were you born in a barn?"

It slammed as they traipsed away from her hiding spot. Their voices faded into the vast hall.

She pressed both hands over her mouth to keep from screaming. Tears built in the corners of her eyes. Prince Ryland? Cursed? And he was relying on her to lift it.

Preparations

Gwen allowed Avonlea to use her as a living doll. She washed, dried and combed her hair. Then stretched it into a tight mass atop her head.

"Did you sleep at all last night?" Avonlea dotted a white powder over her face, then swiped it with a soft brush.

"A little. Why?"

"You have dark circles the size of grapefruits under your eyes and I've used every trick I know to hide them."

"I must look atrocious," Gwen said. She didn't really care how she looked, but didn't want anyone to think she was less than thrilled with the marriage. She cleared her thoughts and lifted her chin, pulling her lips into a radiant smile.

"No. Even now you are a beauty." Avonlea stopped her brushing and leaned against the vanity. "What is it?"

"What do you mean?"

"There is something more than a loss of sleep bothering you."

Gwen slumped against her chair. "I'm doing my best to hide it and forget all about it."

"Would you like to share?"

Gwen shifted her eyes away from the princess and toward the light of the window. Debating for a moment whether anything should be said. Did it matter if the prince loved her? She would have to marry him either way. Finally, she sighed and spilled her worries to Avonlea. "I overheard some men talking last night."

"I won't even ask how you were able to overhear them talking," Avonlea went back to brushing her hair.

"It's a long story. But they mentioned that Ryland is cursed."

The brush in Avonlea's hand clattered against the stone floor.

Gwen noticed the horror in the princess's eyes. "So it's true." There had been a chance to escape, and she ran right back to the chopping block. She wanted to kick herself. Instead, she resigned herself to her fate once again.

Avonlea began pacing in small circles next to the dressing mirror. "Yes. But you will break it today and there is nothing to worry about."

Gwen sighed and pulled her lips into another smile. One that didn't reach her eyes.

"You are still going to marry my brother today?" Avonlea pleaded.

"I don't have a choice. But I'm not the person to break the prince's curse."

"Yes you are. You are the last one in the kingdom with magic."

Gwen remained slumped in her chair. "Of course. How could I have forgotten?"

"Are you ready?" Avonlea asked her for the nine hundredth time.

Gwen plastered on the smile she had practiced in the mirror. "I am ready to be your sister in law. Ready to be the prince's wife and put this terrible business behind me."

"Have you finally been convinced that you are not going to die?"

"Avonlea? If I marry Ryland today and the curse isn't lifted. What do you think will happen?"

"You'll be…"

"Killed. So no I'm not convinced." She stood at her vanity. "I'm not convinced at all."

"I hope that someday we can all feel secure in our positions. Your marriage to my brother is the first step."

Gwen took her hands. "It's not terrible to be prepared for death. It's helped me to live in the moment and enjoy whatever comes."

"That is one good thing I suppose."

Gwen in her night robes moved to sit at the breakfast nook. The women were quiet until Avonlea grabbed her hand and gave it a gentle squeeze.

Leaving the conversation behind, the princess filled her in on all the details of the impending nuptial day.

"The ceremony will take place first. You'll wear that gorgeous gown, but afterwards we'll change you into something more suited for the reception."

She pulled out a new evening gown with lines and cuts similar to the dress she wore to the first banquet. It was bright and beautiful.

Gwen's jaw dropped open. "How will this even work?"

"Don't worry. I'll help you change."

Avonlea's words were cut off when stone scraped against stone. And voices filled a space between her closet and bookshelf. Gwen grabbed a butter knife from the table and leaned toward the noise. As she took a step forward, a door concealed in the framework slid open. Avonlea sat back and crossed her arms.

"I'm telling you she left. She is not in her room," Drake was saying as he and the prince emerged from his adjoining suite.

"What is the meaning of this brother?" Avonlea immediately jumped in front of Gwen. "You are not meant to see the bride until she is beside you at the alter."

"Relax sister." He pointed to the captain. "Drake thought Gwen might be missing. We were merely trying to alleviate his concerns."

Gwen's lips lifted in a wry smile at the sight of Captain Drake's gaping jaw.

He finally found his words again. "Yes. We can see that she is here. So glad she's safe and sound in her rooms." He shifted to go back through the hidden doorway.

"Nuh, uh uh. I think you owe my betrothed an apology."

"Right you are." Drake turned in the direction of Gwen. "My apologies, my lady. You are obviously not missing. I should never have questioned your integrity. I hope it is for the best that you have remained in your chambers and are prepared to take on the responsibilities marrying the prince entails."

Gwen sat back down in her chair. She narrowed her eyes at him. "It is a challenge I gladly face head on."

"Good." Drake turned to Ryland. "Now that we are satisfied, let us return to your chambers and prepare for your wedding."

"Indeed," Ryland said. Though she couldn't see him, she could hear the rustle of the prince's garments as he dipped into a slight bow. "Ladies. Please forgive our intrusion."

"You're forgiven. I'm sure you can make it up to your wife this evening," Avonlea said.

Gwen heard the prince chuckle, a few quick steps, and the door scraped closed.

Avonlea turned to Gwen with a sigh. "Come on. Let's get you in that dress."

* * *

Hours later, Gwen faced the arched wooden doors. They were easily double the size of the tallest man she knew. Beautiful bouquets of silk flowers adorned either side. The smoothed stone floors were polished so she could see her own reflection. Layers and layers of golden fabric draped around her. Avonlea had called in maids to help, and they had pulled it so tight she could barely breathe. Three maids assisted her to the entrance in the dress and then left. There was no turning back now.

She was alone in the hallway. Her father was absent. The circumstances prevented his attendance. A note had arrived at her suite announcing his regrets. A frown pulled at her lips, and the sting in her eyes threatened to ruin Avonlea's hard work. She breathed deeply and cleared the thoughts away. "I will not let it ruin this day," she whispered.

The master of ceremonies had instructed her to knock when ready to open the entrance.

She lifted her hand to do just that and noticed the familiar red lines extending up her arms. It moved faster than it ever had. In seconds, the welts appeared on her upper arm. Instead of knocking on the door, she clutched her throat, gasping for air through her quickly swelling windpipe.

Her eyes rounded in terror and filled with tears. Too late, she realized the couturier had used the spun gold as thread throughout the dress.

She spent the last of her strength to throw herself against the wooden doors. She managed at least one rasp.

Darkness crept into the corners of her eyes, and a figure moved out of the shadows. Dressed in all black, he caught her as she collapsed and the doors swung open.

What Gwen didn't see — the crowd, the prince, and the king most certainly did — was Mr. Woolworth holding her up as she draped backward over his arm. He swirled his hand above her with a sparkle of magic and pulled her into the shadows with him. She didn't see Prince Ryland's face contort into rage or the smile play at the king's lips.

She couldn't have seen because she was half-dead.

Kidnapped

Gwen rubbed her head as she sat up. "Where am I?" she groaned. Her eyes split open slowly. The light from a nearby fire illuminated her surroundings.

She lay on a twin bed pushed into a corner of a small room. Four walls formed from cold mossy stones. Gwen tugged the thin blanket up, thankful for the burning logs.

A workbench stood in the opposite corner, cluttered with tools, vials and… her locket!

She threw the blanket away from her and tumbled out of the bed. Wobbling on shaky knees, the frigid floor scraped against her knees. Her hand slid over the edge of the bed to the foot. Gwen's body and legs strained to follow. The tips of her fingers brushed the bedpost. Clinging to the varnished post, she raised herself to standing. A breath expanded deeply into her lungs. She turned back toward the workbench where her mother's locket hung.

With one hand on the post, she stretched out with the other to stay upright. She released the post, her knees buckled, and she fell forward. The narrow door by the bench opened. A dark figure stepped through in time to catch her. Her arms wrapped around his neck as he held her hips.

Her eyes narrowed, and her lips pinched. Blood and heat rushed to her face. "You!"

He had no right to smile, or to look so handsome doing it. "Me," he replied, his voice silky. She loathed it.

"Let go of me."

He leaned closer. "You first," he whispered.

She peeked behind him at the workbench. She hated to give up on her mother's locket, but she also detested his hands near her. Unfortunately, she would collapse without his support. He glanced over his shoulder, noticing it himself.

"Let's get you to bed," he said, his voice quiet and polite.

"I don't want to go to bed. I want to go home," she whined.

"You definitely can't go to the castle where they just tried to murder you." He tucked his ring finger under a strand of hair and pushed it out of her face.

She leaned aside. Shaking her head to get away from whatever that feeling was that grew in the bottom of her belly. "What have you done to me? Why can't I walk? Am I your captive?"

He carried her to the bed and pulled the blankets back over her.

"You are not a prisoner. I saved your life. Multiple times actually. You kind of owe me. You wouldn't come with me willingly. My warning went unheeded. I had no choice but to extract you."

"I owe you?" She tried to lift herself up again to give him a piece of her mind. Remembering the inability to hold her body upright, she pointed her finger at him and squinted her eyes to show her exasperation instead. "Just what do you think I owe you?"

He stepped away from the bed and sat on a stool near the bench. "Relax princess. I'm not here to collect."

Despite her anger, Gwen breathed a small sigh of relief. "Why did you bring me here?"

"To save you." As if the conversation were over, he turned his back to her and began working. He pulled down glass vials, powders, and liquids. He poured a bit of it into a clean bottle and gave it a little twirl.

"I have lived every day thinking it's the day I die. I made peace with the fact that my life will be very short. Why exactly did you need to rescue me?"

"Because princess…"

"Stop calling me that."

"Despite what you believe, you are worth saving." He held his work in the light of a candle.

Gwen crossed her arms over her chest, realizing she was dressed in a simple shift and nothing else. She pulled the plush blankets up to her neck. "I have nothing and I am nothing."

He shrugged and kept his back toward her. "Just because you don't know who you are doesn't mean you are not valuable."

"My life only has value because of what everybody thinks I can do."

He nodded in agreement. "Not everyone believes that every person should be valued." His head bowed, and he would not meet her eye. His fingers steepled between his knees. "Some will and do see your significance only in your gifts."

He handed her the vial he had just mixed. Absentmindedly, she took it from him.

"The elixir will give you some energy. I can't do much to speed your healing, unfortunately."

She sat it on the small table beside the bed. "I don't have any abilities, as you well know."

He huffed with a smile. "You still have no idea. But you will." He picked up a tool from his bench and twirled it between his fingers absentmindedly.

"What do you want from me?"

He turned his head and met her eyes. "For you to live."

"And what value does my life bring to you?"

He went back to working. "Only the peace that there is someone else like me in the world."

"Ha. I'm hardly similar to you."

"You are."

"I have no magic."

He pumped his jaw in frustration. The war within himself leached onto his face. After a few agonizing minutes, he stood. "It's time to discover who you are."

"That seems difficult when I can't leave the bed."

He nodded as if just remembering and pulled his hand away. "Fine. We'll wait until you are fully healed. No more questions."

"How long will that take?

He growled. "You were in anaphylaxis. You stopped breathing. Your heart almost arrested. Another minute and I couldn't have brought you back." He picked up the liquid she had sat beside the bed and shoved it at her.

Her lips flattened out. Despite being kidnapped, Mr. Woolworth had never tried to harm her and had only ever helped her. She tipped the potion into her mouth. She forced her throat to contract. The thick liquid slid down, leaving a bitter aftertaste. The corners of her mouth turned down. Her tongue slid out. She barely held back a retch.

He lowered himself onto his stool, but didn't turn away from her. "Give yourself time to heal."

"Why couldn't I have healed at my home?" she asked.

His eyes never left hers. "That castle was not your home."

"Not the castle."

"The mill isn't either."

She opened her mouth to say something else, but he popped off the stool and was next to the bed, within a breath. He swept his thumb across her forehead. "Sleep Princess."

Her eyes drooped, her head fell back, but she slurred a few words. "I said.. don't call me Princess."

Ryland

“How could this have happened!” Ryland paced between the door of his father’s study and the window. His dress coat, still rigid over his torso. He pulled at the collar once again. Something inside him wanted out, but he had no way to release it. Long ago, he was told it would take magic to fix the problem. Magic no one had. He learned tricks to deal with it, but when stress mounted against him, it was difficult to remember them.

“Relax, Ryland. It’s all handled.”

He froze mid-step and turned toward his father. “You did this?” His voice was a growl he could barely contain.

The king leaned back in his chair behind a long mahogany desk. “Watch your tone *Son*.” He almost choked on the last word as if it were ash in his mouth. “If I did, it was for *your* benefit. And the benefit of the kingdom.”

“You wouldn’t understand the first thing about what benefits me or the kingdom, *Father*.” Ryland returned the tone the king had used with his name.

“Well, look who’s finally growing a backbone. I’d say you’ve already benefitted from this fiasco. You won’t need to marry that trash commoner, who obviously doesn’t have magic, and the kingdom is ready to rise up in her defense. This is playing out better than I had planned.”

Ryland narrowed his eyes and glared at the king. His eyes flashed with the color of crushed barley oats, but immediately returned to their icy blue. “You planned this,” he growled.

“No. The seamstress planned it, after she discovered your little commoner’s allergy to the very substance she had to create. I had wondered how she was surviving all those nights. Seems we have our answer now."

"You have no right…" Ryland raised his voice. He stepped forward with a lifted fist.

The king stopped him with a single raised eyebrow. Rights didn't matter to the king, and Ryland knew it. "If you lay a hand on me, you will never be king. If I am killed by your hand, your inheritance will go to Avonlea."

Ryland dropped his hand, but he did not unclench his fist.

Satisfied that Ryland had controlled himself, the king sat forward, leaning his elbows against the desk. His fingers steepled, and he narrowed his eyes. "The dark prince has been visiting this castle and saving that girl. Three times. You realize what that means."

Ryland scrubbed his fingers through his hair. They fisted and tugged until he thoroughly ruffled the normally meticulous style. "She's mine, not his," he growled.

The king pulled his lips into a knowing smile. "And what are going to do about it? You don't have magic."

"You know that's not true."

The king pushed his steepled fingers against his lips. "You don't have access to it. And the only way to get access to it, is by destroying the barrier to Mystrim."

"Is that where he's taken her?" Ryland asked.

"Of course, son," the king purred. "Mystrim is the only haven for magic users. The only place the curse, the drought, has not touched."

"Then I will burn it to the ground to get her back."

The king signed a piece of paper in front of him with a flourish. "Approved. Take as many men as you need." He pushed the paper toward Ryland.

"What's this?"

"What you've wanted all along." The king tilted his head. "A declaration of war."

Discovery

Gwen counted the copper tiles lining the ceiling for the fortieth time. She had not seen Aurius for days, but she couldn't take lying in bed anymore. Throwing back the blankets, her skin immediately prickled at the loss of the warmth. But even the comfort of this bed could not draw her back in.

She stretched a leg toward the floor, and her nightgown rode up over her knee. The very tip of her toe met the cold stone floor. While the heat of the fire warmed the room well enough, it did very little for the floor. Still, she pressed on, letting her foot push onto the floor. Her other foot landed moments later. Drawing in a deep breath, she rested against the bed, then lifted her body to standing. She willed her knee to bend, the muscles in her thigh to flex and lift, to pitch her body forward. Everything obeyed. A giggle erupted from her throat.

"I didn't think that would work!" she said to the empty room.

Her legs shook from the exertion of a few steps, and she had to grab the post at the end of the bed. Her victory was short-lived. With the next step, her knee buckled, and she collapsed in a heap on the floor. The cold seeped through her thin fabric of her nightgown and nearly into her bones. She reached to grab the bed, but noticed something shoved underneath. Her hand twitched to reach into the darkness, but paused at the place where light blurred into darkness. Fingers inched past that imaginary barrier, tingling with fear. Her breath caught in her throat. Curiosity lent her courage, and she dared reach for the item under the magician's bed. Dangerous as it might be.

Gwen stretched her hand into the darkness and pulled it back. She could not quite reach. Her shoulders sashayed toward the edge of the bed. Her hand shot back into the darkness. The tips of her fingers brushed something. She was able to press her thumb and finger together over the edge, pulling it closer. Scooted a bit. Pulled it again. She sat up to reveal her treasure. A book so big she could use it as a tray.

Her fingers dug around the edge. The spine cracked as she lifted it, but before she could delve into the words, she heard a noise at the door. She froze.

The doorknob jangled.

She lifted herself onto the bed faster than lightning. With the book, she snuggled in beside her and threw the covers over herself. She leaned back against the pillows and closed her eyes as the door opened.

It shut behind Aurius with a gentle click. His shoes made no noise, but Gwen could feel his presence move closer to the bed. "Hmm. Still asleep?" he whispered. "The potion should be working by now, perhaps I will have to increase the dose to give her a bit more energy."

The stool in front of the workbench creaked as he sat down. Papers shuffled, a tinkling noise, then the dark prince whisked out of the room. The door clicked shut again.

Gwen cracked an eyelid open. "He can use shadows to travel but he insists on using the door?" she said.

"I can use shadows, but I don't like to sneak up on people."

A scream erupted from Gwen, and eyes opened fully in terror.

"I thought you might be awake." Aurius grinned, leaning on the wall near the door, one foot over the other with the tip of his toe resting on the floor. His arms crossed over each other. He was wearing a loose-fitting white shirt that was opened at the top, revealing a decent amount of dark hair, and a brown leather vest. It was the most rugged she had ever seen him.

Gwen threw a pillow at him. He caught it with one hand and threw it onto the end of the bed.

"What are you doing here?"

"Checking on you. I thought I would take you for a walk."

"I'm not going anywhere with you."

"Not even to a magical garden?"

Gwen narrowed her eyes at him. "How magical?"

"More magical than the garden at Aurum."

She sighed. "I could be persuaded."

His lips pulled into a knowing smile. He threw her a thick robe. "No need to dress. It's just outside on the other side of the corridor, and we'll make it a brief visit."

Gwen pulled her legs out of the blankets, making sure the book stayed hidden beneath. She clutched the robe to her, quickly threw it over her shoulders and threaded her arms through it. She tied it in the front and pulled her braided hair over one shoulder. The effort took a toll on her arms and legs. Aurius stepped forward and held out an elbow. And though it felt as if she was giving up something, she took it without complaint. Her legs felt as though she were trudging through molasses. She spent too much energy flying back into bed like she did.

She leaned on him more than intended.

"It didn't take much persuasion at all."

Gwen offered a small smile. "Turns out, your room is tedious."

"Not when you're sleeping."

"I can't sleep all the time."

After escaping his suite and a few steps more, Aurius twisted the handle of an ordinary door. He pushed it back to reveal the most beautiful garden she had ever seen. Soft rays of light danced along the tops of weeping willows. Little yellow and pink butterflies flitted this way and that. Songbirds echoed their chirping lilts to each other. Water from a brook trickled along the pathway, adding to the cadence.

She leaned on Aurius, stopping to close her eyes. The warmth of the sun's rays warred with the damp shade, creating the perfect temperature. A soft breeze lifted the ends of a strand of her golden hair. Gwen expanded her chest, letting the fresh fragrances of the garden fill her completely.

"How long have I been asleep? It was winter and already it's spring?"

Delight twinkled in his eye. "Magic garden. Still winter everywhere else."

Aurius tugged her arm, pulling her out of her moment of bliss. They took a few more steps down the path to an arranged seating area. The gardener had positioned the bench off the path and nestled it into the landscape, while the pathway led deeper into the garden. Gwen longed to explore, but her legs shook with exertion already. The stone bench was cool against the back of her legs, but Aurius radiated warmth as he lowered himself beside her. She found she didn't mind so much.

"Did you make this garden?"

Aurius huffed and smiled. "No, but the creator hasn't been around in a while."

Gwen's face fell. "Oh. I was hoping I could meet her."

"Him. It was the former king."

"Oh?" Her eyebrows lifted. "I shouldn't have assumed something so beautiful would have been created by a woman."

"King Nolan was very powerful and very creative. He created this garden as a gift for his wife."

"That's sweet."

"It's self sustaining. It doesn't need magic to continue."

"No just water," Gwen sighed.

"And sunlight," Aurius added.

"At least you allow people to visit. Are there any former queens buried that keep the magic going?"

He shook his head. "Not needed here."

Gwen smiled at him. "There are people in my village who have never seen a garden. The flowing brook alone would be a dream come true."

Aurius let his chin fall to his chest. "I know," he sighed. Gwen waited for him to find the words. "Saving your village. It might be impossible," he finally finished.

"Do you know what needs to be done?"

He nodded. "I have an idea, but I don't know if it will work."

"Is there something I can do to help?" she asked.

His pinky brushed against hers as he leaned forward, sending a little tingle racing up her arm. Her breath hitched at the unexpected contact. "You're the catalyst. I think your role in this will become clear to you in time."

"But you won't tell me what it is?"

"I think it's best if you discover it for yourself."

"Aurius. My village is dying. If there is something I can do to help I want to do it now."

He had the audacity to smirk at her. "Spoken like a true princess."

Gwen narrowed her eyes at him and pursed her lips. "We both know I'm not a princess."

Aurius slapped his hands on his knees. "Well, I have work to be getting on with. Shall we return you to your rooms?" He stood and lifted an elbow out to her.

She looked up through her lashes. "After you tell me what a catalyst is."

He dropped the elbow and pressed and hand to his chest. "Did I say catalyst? I meant miller's daughter. No one of importance at all," he said, smiling like a kitten who'd just caught his first mouse.

"Fine. Keep your secrets." Gwen huffed and stood on her own, ignoring his crooked elbow. She lifted her chin and took two steps. Her knees buckled. Aurius's arms wound around her, saving her face from smacking a rock. He lifted her into his arms as if she were a bushel of wheat.

"We need to work on strength and stamina," he said. She nodded against his chest. "Two walks per day. Each time I want you to go ten steps further than the last."

"What if I fall?"

"Get up and try again," he said.

He lowered her legs when they reached the door to his suite so he could use one hand to open it. But he left one arm wrapped around her back. Her legs trembled, and her eyes wanted to slip closed. She was determined to walk to the bed, hoping to keep her discovery a secret. The door swung smoothly. Gwen took a step before Aurius could crouch to lift her again. He didn't stop her, but kept a firm hand between her shoulder blades.

By the time her toes sunk into the blankets, her legs were a wobbly mess. She breathed a sigh of relief.

Aurius smiled down at her. "Before long you'll be running through the garden. Don't worry."

Gwen's eyes drifted closed in response. She could hear the tap of his shoes as he retreated away from the bed. "Don't get too comfy, princess. I'll be back for round two after lunch."

She groaned, but the argument she might have mounted died as she drifted off.

* * *

Gwen shifted on the bed. Her hand running along the book tucked into the blankets with her. Her eyes popped open and shifted around the room. The light had shifted, filling the rooms with long shadows.

She sat up. Clearly, Aurius had not returned to pull her into another walk. But as she rotated in the bed, she noticed a tray of food beside the bed. Steam rose from the bowl. She lifted the note from beside it.

Eat Princess. We'll start your recovery tomorrow.

Gwen growled at the nickname Aurius refused to stop using. The smell of beef stew found its way to her. She ignored her annoyance, pulling the warm bowl to her chin, glad to be alone as she ate so she could slurp to her heart's content. She scraped the bowl with a spoon and noticed a slice of bread waiting on the edge of the plate.

A giggle escaped as she swiped the bread around the bowl to absorb the last of the broth. It melted on her tongue, and she sank into the bed a little more, closing her eyes to savor the taste of warm bread.

With her belly full, she placed the bowl back onto the tray and pulled the book from under the blankets.

She ran her hands over the decorative gold foil inlay once again. The spine creaked as she pulled it back. Thick yellow pages felt stiff against her fingers. The first page was blank, but the second held a dark script scrawled through the center.

The Chronicles of the Goblin Kings

Gwen tilted her head. "Hm? Why would Aurius have a chronicle of goblin kings under his bed?" she asked the silent room. She shrugged. The pages rustled as she slid them against each other. "Maybe he borrowed it and forgot to return it." Which was reasonable. He seemed to be a busy prince.

She flipped through illustrated pages that read like children's tales. Goblins performing unbelievable feats with unbelievable magic, always the hero of the story. The next-to-last story, titled *The Last Goblin King,* featured a baby born with raven hair. His mother struck a deal with a neighboring kingdom so that he could learn to use his magic. He longed to return home, but his mother died before he could.

Gwen found herself wiping a tear from the corner of her eye. She wanted to curl into a ball and weep for the boy, but her fingers turned the page.

The Goblin and the Queen. Her eye snagged on the first line. *Rumpelstiltskin was a clever goblin king.*

The story detailed how he saved the queen three times. And because it was three times, she owed him anything he asked. Of course, what he asked for was her firstborn daughter. The queen had little choice, so she reluctantly agreed, thinking she might never have a child at all. She signed a blood oath with a goblin. An unbreakable blood oath.

Gwen couldn't pull herself away from the story. She had to keep reading to see what happened to the queen.

The queen realized she was pregnant soon after and grew worried about her agreement with the goblin. The Goblin King, Rumpelstiltskin, being ever the hero, offered to allow the queen to keep her daughter if she could solve the riddle of his true name. Of course, she solved the riddle. The Earth gobbled him up, leaving a rift through the land and the goblin prince behind. The story didn't say what happened to the queen, but hinted that even though Rumpelstiltskin was gone for good, the contract was still binding as long as his descendants and those of the queen lived. So he still won in the end, even though he made some questionable choices regarding the queen.

The book ended even though there were still blank pages waiting to be filled.

Gwen tapped her lips. "Are these stories true? I wonder who the goblin prince is then? Is he handsome?" The goblins in the pictures didn't look grotesque at all, other than their green-tinted skin and protruding teeth.

Gwen shook her head. "That doesn't matter," she decided.

She set the book aside. It was interesting, but it had revealed nothing of use. She pulled the blankets away from her legs. "Time to get moving." Her breath rushed out of her as she built up the desire to do the work.

Her toes touched the floor, and she straightened her body. The tray needed to be placed in the hall for the staff to pick up. The silverware tinkled together as she lifted it. She released the bed and held the tray with both hands. A small step forward and then another. A few more got her to the door. She pulled it free easily, surprised to find it unlocked.

She sat the empty tray in the hall, closed the door and returned to the bed. The chronicles of goblin kings had vanished. "I know I laid it here."

She crouched below the bed, but it wasn't lying there in the dark. Gwen stood and looked around the room. "Am I losing my mind," she whispered, shaking her head. Exhaustion tugged at her again. She gave up the search and crawled into bed with a shrug of her shoulders.

Recovery

The next few days went much the same way. A tray would appear with delicious food and a promise or excuse from Aurius. Almost as often, a book would appear on his workbench or on the mantle, enticing her out of bed. She took to sitting by the fire, which reminded her of home, but she tried not to think of it. It seemed many years ago, though it had only been a few weeks.

The food and light exercise built her stamina. Her steps became surer with each passing day. She hadn't seen Aurius since their walk in the garden, but she was sure it was him caring for her.

The latest book was heavy on her lap. A fire blazed in the hearth. The radiant heat nearly burned her legs. She didn't want to move them away, feeling comforted by the warmth. She wondered about the garden. It was winter, but that little garden seemed stuck in perpetual spring. Perhaps the right magic could defy the cycle of death winter brought. She shrugged as she pushed open the book in front of her.

This one wasn't a history or a storybook. It was a dictionary of magic. Her face pulled into a bright smile, and she wiggled in the chair. She wasn't the type of girl to clap her hands together with excitement, but she barely controlled the urge. Little butterflies fluttered around in her belly at the anticipation of finally learning more about magic.

She flipped straight to the section on catalyst magic.

CATALYST MAGIC:

Speeds up a magical process or makes the magic stronger. Very rare. No known catalyst has had other abilities. If one were ever found, they would be too powerful to allow to live. The catalyst usually bonds with a powerful magician for protection. Even a mediocre magician could become most powerful with a catalyst bonded mate. Catalysts cannot be forced or coerced into using their magic.

The entry ended. That was it. Nothing to explain how it worked. No magic words.

She slammed the book closed and threw it toward the fire. Just as the book was about to hit the golden flames, she thrust her hand towards it with a word of regret. The book froze in midair. Gwen's eyes rounded as her outstretched hand shook. Flames licked the pages, ready to consume them forever, but Gwen willed the book back into her hands. A squeak escaped from her lips as she wrapped her thin fingers around the edges of the book.

"How?" she whispered.

The tears that had built burst over the edges of her eyes. Her grip tightened on the book as if that were the only stable thing in the room. If Aurius was right about her catalyst magic and she could levitate items. She shuddered to think what might happen if anyone found out. If she really was more powerful than any catalyst that had ever lived.

Gwen set the book aside.

"It's ok. That didn't really happen. I couldn't have levitated a book. It must have had a spell on it." She paced back to her bed. "A spell that kept it from being destroyed." She ran her fingers up the side of face and into her silken hair. "I'll ask Aurius when I see him again."

She looked through the papers on the workbench and found a blank piece. Scribbling out the note, she left it where he could find it if he returned.

As she turned to go back to the place by the fire and contemplate her life, she noticed another book. She didn't mean to snoop through Aurius's belongings again, but she couldn't help but notice the title.

"How to break curses and contracts," she said. Her eyebrows pushed into her forehead. A squeal escaped unbidden, and she covered a giggle. Perhaps there is something here that can break Ryland's curse. She pulled the book from its place, careful not to disturb anything else on the table. As she flipped it open, a slip of paper floated to the floor. It was creased where it had been folded and unfolded many times. The paper was thick in her hands. She meant to set aside without reading it. It wasn't her business, after all, but curiosity was a powerful motivator.

She tugged the paper back and down. As her eyes scanned the contents, her mouth dropped open. This had to be a replica. Why would anyone keep this in a book on a worktable? But as she finished, the words at the bottom said *Original*.

Above those words was a signature in deep red, Queen Liora Macaluso. The same queen in the *Chronicles of the Goblin Kings*.

The lock on the door twisted, and she heard Aurius say the magic words to enter the room.

She quickly folded the contract, placed it back in the book, and put the book back where she had found it.

Gwen had no time to return to her bed before Aurius stepped into the room. He had returned to his rogue prince outfit; black on black. He pulled his lips into a half-smile. "I'm glad to see you doing as I asked. Are you feeling well?"

Gwen smiled and almost squeaked. "Yes," she looked down at the note she had left. "I was just leaving you a note. I've seen so little of you."

"My apologies. I didn't realize you were missing me."

Gwen's smile faltered. "I'm missing... everyone."

Aurius pressed his lips together. If Gwen wasn't mistaken, he looked... concerned.

"I've come to see if you would like to join me for a meal."

Gwen looked around the room. The magic dictionary taunted her from where she'd left it by the fire. Her hair was a mess, and she had dressed in a simple gown from the choices she had.

"I'm not dressed for a meal."

"Nonsense. You look beautiful."

The words slipped from Aurius's mouth as though he meant them. But surely he did not, because he had only kidnapped her for her power, whatever it was. Gwen tilted her head and narrowed her eyes, replaying her interactions with the dark prince from a new perspective. Perhaps there was more to it than that.

"Well, if my attire is acceptable then I should like to join you," she said.

Aurius held out an elbow, and Gwen gladly took it. She looked once again over her shoulder.

"You can bring the book if you like."

She shook her head. "It's not that. I just," her eyebrows scrunched together, "does the book have a spell on it to protect it from destruction?"

He shrugged. "Any magic user can see a spell."

Gwen tilted her head.

"Watch." He waved his hand over the door, and the familiar shimmer sparkled over the opening. "If you had no magic, you wouldn't have been able to see that."

"So it only happens when the magic is active."

"Precisely." He tugged her through the door.

"Then if I had tried to destroy the book and it didn't shimmer? There was no spell."

"Why on Earth would you try to destroy a book?" Aurius asked, as if that was the most concerning part of what she said. She waved away his concern with pursed lips.

Gwen's steps were slow as she allowed Aurius to lead her, though she paid no attention to where he was leading. Her thoughts were consumed by the implication that the book didn't shimmer when it stopped over the fire.

"You seemed worried about something. Do you want to talk about it?"

His question pulled her from the storm building in her mind. "Oh? No. It's just something I was thinking of."

"Well if you go around throwing books in the fire you'll be banned from the library and you haven't even seen it yet."

"How can I see it, when you bring me all the books I need?"

Aurius gasped in faux outrage. "I have merely aided you in your time of need."

She shrugged a shoulder. "You've fed me and brought me books. I can't really ask for more than that."

"You needn't ask for anything. But would you like to see the library?"

"Is it more magical than the garden?"

He shrugged, and the corners of his mouth turned down. "It has books."

"Then it must be more magical."

Aurius's smile, accompanied by a deep laugh, stole Gwen's breath. She forgot her afternoon troubles as they stepped into the magical garden, lit with lightning flies. A table for two spread with at least three courses had replaced the stone bench.

The dark prince led her to the table and pulled her seat for her, then took his place across from her. There were no others in the garden. The chirping of garden creatures created a natural symphony. The cool night air reminded her of a summer as a child at the mill. She put that thought aside, wanting to enjoy the world as it was here.

"Are you impressed?"

"Impressed? No. Astonished? Absolutely."

Aurius grinned and began scooping food onto her plate.

"Where are the servants?" she asked.

"I gave them the night off."

"We're here alone?"

"You have been in my room for many days. But there is no impropriety. Anyone in the castle can look out on us at any time."

Gwen's shoulders slipped a fraction. She scooped some of the creamy salad onto a roll and popped it in her mouth. She barely kept herself from groaning as the flavors popped over her tongue. Even as the bite slid down her throat, the mixture of tastes and textures combined to bring a new note to the concoction.

"Gwen. There's something I need to discuss with you."

She did groan at his tone. "I knew it was too good to be true."

"It's about your heritage. And the reason the miller said you had magic."

Her hand paused halfway from the plate to her mouth.

"I guess we couldn't avoid the subject forever."

Aurius smiled again, but it didn't reach his eyes. "No. I guess we couldn't."

"So lay it on me. Why did my father sell me to the king?"

"Gwen. The miller is not your father."

Her hand dropped to her lap, and she leaned away from him. The cold metal of the chair bit into her back. Her eyes narrowed as she tried to find meaning in what he said. She motioned her finger in a circle, indicating he should continue.

"He was just somebody your mother found to hide you, and take care of you until you came of age."

"What proof do you have of this?"

"The book you found under my bed." He raised his eyebrows at her. "Yes, I knew about that," he said, answering a question that she hadn't spoken. "It has the story of a goblin who tricked a queen in to giving up her first born."

"A children's story."

"A true children's story."

Gwen's teeth ached from crushing them together.

"The Queen was your mother," he said, as if it were as normal as the sun rising in the east.

She squeezed her fingers into a fist to keep her hand from shaking and lowered her voice. "Again. I'm asking for proof."

He seemed unaffected by her behavior and kept buttering the roll in his hand. "You have catalyst magic."

"So?"

He lowered his chin and looked directly into her eyes, finally expressing the importance of this conversation. "It has only ever been found in one family line." Aurius held up a finger to prove the point.

Gwen lowered her head and unclenched her fist to sip her tea. "Maybe your information is mistaken."

"I'm not wrong."

"Do you feel strong enough to visit the library?"

Gwen nodded and sat her tea beside her plate. "I have gained strength in the last few days. Thank you for your attention to the matter."

Aurius ignored the comment, but his lips twitched at the corner. "We'll go as soon as you are finished with the meal."

"This late? Won't the library be closed."

"The benefit of having a library in a castle is that it is available whenever the need arises." He popped the bread he had buttered into his mouth.

Gwen nodded her agreement. "Alright," she said and found the will to eat every morsel on her plate.

Tales

Aurius reveled in the look on Gwen's face as he pushed open the oak doors. They were as tall as an ogre. The race of ogres had died out many years before, but they could have enjoyed this library, too. As remarkable as the doors were, the library was more so. A plaque on the door read, "knowledge is power". Unlike King Aric of Aurum, Queen Helen had upheld the belief in empowering her people. The library remained open to all citizens of Mystrim.

Tomes lined the walls from floor to impressive ceiling, the likes of which would impress the Alexandrians. Gwen's eyes rounded. She searched the room, trying to find a place to look. Aurius had to admit it was likely overwhelming. "We will be in this alcove over here." He tugged her along as she stumbled in awe.

The library's design featured circles and tiers. On the bottom tier were twelve booths equally spaced around the circle. Six on the left in a semicircle and six on the right. Between the two half circles was the entrance door. A much smaller door to the librarian's office and living quarters was opposite the entrance.

The librarian did not allow patrons beyond the office door and hardly left the sanctuary. Many considered being in her presence a true honor. Her magical gifts meant she usually knew exactly what a patron needed before their arrival.

The booths were identical and afforded some privacy, separated by tall cases behind the bench seats. A passerby would still see and hear them, but they would be alone. Behind the blue velvet seats, ledges held more books.

It was as if they had sat in a carriage with bookshelves for walls.

As they lowered themselves onto the seats across from each other, a lamp descended from the curved ceiling.

"I'm surprised the library allows candles," Gwen commented.

"The light is provided by glow worms."

Gwen's eyebrows pressed together in concern.

"There's no need for concern. The worms are quite satiated. They wouldn't glow at all if they were not well fed and cared for."

She released a small breath. The wrinkles on her forehead softened.

"So we're here. What is it you wanted to tell me?"

"This is not a place for telling. It's a place for showing." Aurius pulled a book from the pile behind him.

The cover was dark brown but embossed with ornate, gilded swirls. The spine cracked as he flipped it open. His thumb ran along the edge of the pages, the paper fluttering against his skin. He pulled back the page he was looking for. The smell of dust and old paper floated over them.

The paper was thick and yellowed, but the ink was a dark black as if it had just been written.

Gwen leaned in. "But before I read this, I have a question."

Aurius raised an eyebrow.

"Before my kidnapping, you visited me three times. Prince Ryland seemed to think that was significant. What does it mean?"

Aurius looked down at the book. "Traditionally, it means I can claim you. I can make a demand you must obey."

Gwen's eyes rounded in horror.

"If you passed the test you would get a magical benefit or remedy, if you failed a curse."

"And are you a traditionalist?"

"It doesn't apply in this case."

He passed the book to her. Waiting for her to absorb the story.

Her eyes shifted from left to right across the pages. She turned three pages and leaned back. "This is a children's fairy tale."

Aurius pursed his lips.

"My father told me this story countless times as a child. And I read it… recently," she said. Even though he already knew she had found his book, it seemed like losing something if she admitted it. "The story of Rumpels…"

Aurius pressed a finger to her lips. "Don't. Speak his name. Why do you think he told you this story so often?"

Her eyes clouded with the familiar sting of tears, remembering easier times with her father. There wasn't enough oxygen in the room. Her lungs seemed to collapse. She shook her head, trying to clear away her confusion. She leaned away from him and pushed his hand away.

"I know you say story is real, but why would my father care to tell me about a queen and a goblin king?" she asked between gasping breaths.

"Better question. Do you want to know the answer?" Aurius asked, never taking his eyes off her.

She looked over the book again, slowing her breath. "Say I believe this story is real. After the past few weeks its not hard to see where one might conclude that it is. Obviously you are…" she gestured up and down. "him."

He shook his head.

She tilted her head. "So you can't spin straw into gold?"

He rolled his eyes and tapped the book. His arms crossed over his chest as leaned back with a deep sigh. "Keep reading."

She turned her attention back to the story.

After a few minutes, she leaned away from the book again. Her jaw was slack.

"I know this is shocking," he said.

"Let me out." She scooted to the edge of the bench seat.

He beat her to the edge and blocked her path. "We need to talk about this."

She stepped around him. "I'm not talking about it. I want to go home."

"You can't go home," he said, grabbing her wrist lightly, not hurting her, but keeping her in place.

She yanked it away. "So I am a prisoner."

He stepped within inches of her face. He barely hid the anger warring within him. His voice lowered. "If you go back to that castle, you will be imprisoned and used for your power. Isn't that exactly what you were trying to save me from."

"And what exactly is that power? I can't spin straw to gold. "

"No."

"Then what? What is it you are trying to protect?"

Aurius didn't pull away. His fierce eyes burned into hers. "The reason my father wanted you. Bargained for you…"

Gwen yanked her wrist away from his and crossed her arms over her chest, waiting for his explanation. She was done with the riddles and innuendos.

He pointed to the ancient book on the table. "The reason he bargained with the queen. Your mother."

Gwen rolled her eyes. "I'm listening," she prompted.

Aurius lowered his voice to just above a whisper. "Is because you are the catalyst."

"The catalyst? You keep calling me that, but you won't tell me about it." The book she left behind, the levitation, the power she felt swirled through her thoughts. Her eyes darted away from his as she sorted through it all.

"A catalyst is rare. You are unique. In all instances a catalyst speeds up a reaction."

She nodded. "Or makes a reaction stronger."

Gwen sat back in the booth with hunched shoulders. She was quiet for a long while. "Is that why you took me?"

He scoffed. "I don't need your power."

"But it makes your magic stronger," she argued.

"Yes. But I don't need it."

"But you want it."

"It's difficult not to want you… your power."

Gwen stared at the table, oblivious to his stumble. "How does it work?"

"Your power?"

She nodded. "Can someone just take it? Does it give someone more power by being near me?"

"No." He studied her hair and took a strand between his fingers.

She slapped his hand away again. "It's my hair?"

He looked into her eyes. "Yes."

"So is that how you turned the straw to gold?"

He pulled away. He flipped the book closed and wouldn't meet her eye, stacking the books. "This is a lot and you're still recovering. We should get back to my chambers."

"Answer my question."

The oak doors swung open.

He lowered his voice to a whisper. "I promise to answer any question you have. But not here."

"We just got here. Why didn't you just bring the book to me, if you didn't want to have a public conversation?"

Aurius looked over the selection of books he had gathered. "You needed to get out of the room. Now that you know where the library is you can come any time. But this particular book can't leave the library."

"I supposed it's spelled."

"No. Its just in the reference section. I do follow rules."

Gwen rolled her eyes. "Fine. If I'm not a prisoner, when can I have my own room?"

"When I've made it safe enough here for you." He stepped away from the booth.

"Another riddle."

"I'll tell you more in my quarters."

He held out his hand.

She stood on her own and ignored his hand. Her anger and curiosity seemed to strengthen her legs and help restore her balance.

Agreement

The trip back to the room was much faster now that Gwen knew the way. She needed more answers before she bought into Aurius's story.

"So Rumpel…"

His glare cut her off.

She narrowed her eyes. "Will saying his name summon him? I thought he was dead."

He carefully pushed his door closed with a click and twisted the brass lock to ensure it set. He whispered a few words and waved his hand over it. "You never know and we can't be too careful."

"He was your father."

Aurius nodded.

They took a few steps into the room. He escorted her to the bed. She didn't need as much help as he was insisting upon, but it seemed to satisfy his need for recompense. The heat from his hand on her waist brought immediate tingles in her belly and a crimson blush to her face. She sat and allowed him to move away before taking a deep breath. The smoky smell of the fireplace wrapped around her like a warm blanket. The knot in her stomach unwound, and she leaned back against the feather pillows. They conformed around her as she sank into them. She almost groaned, but as the sound started its escape from her lips, she remembered she had company.

She cleared her throat. "And he created a deal with my mother. Was she like me?"

"She had a weak catalyst magic. From what I can tell in my father's writings, it was not as potent as yours." He fiddled with a tool from his workbench.

"And the king took her and forced her to spin straw to gold. Just as he did with me."

"Different king. I'm only a few years older than you, but that's the tale I've read."

"Except she married him and became pregnant with me."

"That's where the story gets…" He cocked his head to the side and shrugged a shoulder. He squinted one eye and rocked his flattened palm back and forth. "Of course, the tale is that she became queen. The truth is, she was already married to the king. Your mother was the sister-in-law to our current queen."

Gwen's eyes rounded. "The white witch is my aunt?"

Aurius pressed his lips together. "Propaganda from the king of Aurum. It's an effective technique and has worked well on the prince and his people."

Gwen pulled herself onto the bed as Aurius continued his story. "Your mother was married to the king, your father. He locked her away when he found that she had catalyst magic."

"Why would he do that?"

Aurius shrugged. "Maybe to protect her. Maybe for the same reason the king of Aurum does what he does. Magic scares those who don't possess it, in more ways than one."

"Not everyone is afraid of magic."

"Ha. They are either afraid of magic or they want to use whomever holds it."

"That is a very cynical view."

"A view forged in experience."

Gwen tapped her cheek. "Ah. And the reason you didn't want to talk in the library."

His lips turned down as he nodded in agreement.

"What happened to my father?"

"Maybe that's a question better asked of Queen Helen."

"So I am not related to Prince Ryland?"

Aurius took a deep breath. "This is your kingdom. Not Aurum. I know very little about Ryland's parentage, but you can rest assured you aren't relatives."

"What a relief! At least I didn't almost marry my brother." She laughed. Aurius didn't, so Gwen changed the subject.

"Is it possible for catalysts to do other magic? If my mother had been trained to work spells and use her magic, could she have done something to save herself?"

The dark prince smiled. "What you are really asking is do you have the ability to perform magic."

Gwen tucked her chin, a little embarrassed he had read her so easily. That wasn't all she wanted to ask. The book she almost threw in the fire was still troubling her. But she nodded her head. The movement was so small Aurius barely perceived it.

"It usually looks for balance. It is unusual for catalysts to be able to cast or use spells because they would be too powerful. Their catalyst magic is not very useful to themselves. But when they team up with a magic user, even a mediocre one, it becomes more potent."

"If the story is correct, your father was already so powerful. He didn't need my mother's catalyst magic. But he helped her anyway. Why?"

"He didn't need the power, but he wanted it."

"Power?"

"I'm assuming. But that was his M.O. Everything he did was for power. He did a favor for a queen. He expected it would be a great return on investment. And it would have been if he had gotten his hands on you."

"But she outsmarted him." Gwen smiled at the thought, but her reverie was immediately popped.

Aurius held up a finger in protest. "Her captain outsmarted him."

Gwen lifted a shoulder. "It was a team effort."

He nodded. "And the Earth swallowed my father. Leaving me an orphan. And most of the world without magic."

"So the death of magic happened with your father's disappearance?"

"Yes."

"Not with a curse on Prince Ryland?"

A suppressed growl came from his chest. "The prince is not cursed."

"I heard he was."

"He's not."

"The curse is the death of magic. And he has to marry the last person in the realm with magic and it will be restored."

"Gwen, the prince is not cursed. That is a terrible curse anyway. It doesn't even hurt the prince in any way and no one dies."

"Yes, I heard that as well." Gwen changed the subject again. She didn't want to think of Ryland. "Sorry to bring up a sore topic, but did you lose your mom as well?"

He shrugged a shoulder. "Not really."

"I have a feeling there is something you aren't telling me."

"There is."

"I want to hear all of it."

"You may think less of me."

"I already think less of you. You kidnapped me on my wedding day."

He rolled his eyes. "Yes. Yes."

Gwen lifted her eyebrows.

"Fine. There is only one creature that can spin straw to gold."

Gwen leaned forward. "Go on. What type of creature is that?"

"They are extinct and their kingdom no longer exists. Likely because of their ability."

"That can't be true. You can spin straw to gold. I'm assuming you are one of these creatures."

He nodded. "Something like that."

"Well, what kind of creature are you?"

"A goblin."

She laughed. So much so that she grabbed her stomach. "You thought I hadn't worked that out already. I literally thought you were Rump…"

He didn't smile. "He's my father, remember." Aurius stooped into a low, sweeping bow. "The goblin prince, at your service."

Gwen composed herself. "But what I can't figure out is why you are handsome, not knobby and green or short."

"Handsome?"

Gwen felt her cheeks grow warm. "Forget I said that."

"Impossible."

"I'll never admit it," she said.

Aurius pulled his full lips into an alluring smile. "No need. Your secret is safe with me."

"What happened to you when your father died?" she asked, to pull his attention away and save her dignity.

Aurius's smile faded. He tinkered with a tool on his workbench. "I was already living here in the palace as the queen's ward."

"Who is your mother?

"Unknown."

"Not a goblin then?"

"There are no female goblins. My father was the last full-blood goblin. As far as I know, I am the last creature with any goblin blood at all."

"You are half goblin then?"

He shrugged.

"So that's it. That's the big secret?"

"Despite the effort of the chronicles to turn all goblins into heroes, goblins were hunted out of existence for their ability and their malfeasances."

Gwen leaned back. "Well, if your father is the example I can see why."

"Really?"

"He tricked my mother into giving up her first born."

He nodded. "I agree he wasn't the best. Given the prejudice I try to keep my heritage on the down low. However, the queen is aware and has permitted me to retain the prince title which affords me a room at the palace and more resources than I would otherwise have."

"That's not so bad."

The conversation paused as Aurius wrestled with himself. His hand trembled over his coat pocket. "There is one more thing." He turned to his workbench. He tilted his head to the right, pausing a moment before pulling the book Gwen had put back just hours ago. The folded paper fell from the cover, and he handed it to Gwen.

"What's this?" She unfolded it and skimmed over again, finding a new meaning considering all she had learned that evening.

Aurius leaned against the wall with his arms folded over his chest. He watched her eyes roam over the words and the full weight of their meaning take hold.

He knew the moment she reached the end. Her jaw dropped open. Gwen let the paper fall to the bed where she was sitting and looked up at him.

"This is a contract?"

He nodded. "Signed by your mother."

"So when you said earlier that the three rescues didn't apply it was because of this?"

"Yes."

"Tear it up." She shoved it back toward him. He let her hand hang in the air, not moving to take the wrinkled paper.

"Tried. I can't. It's magically binding."

"This can't be happening." She dropped the contract, letting it float back and forth. It crinkled as it hit the post of the bed and rested on the floor. "I'm betrothed to Prince Ryland. I can't be betrothed to *you*."

Aurius ignored the paper on the floor. "You are."

"I wasn't even born yet."

"The magic doesn't care about that."

"So you are going to force me to marry you?"

He shook his head. "I don't force people to do things. As you well know. I absolutely could have made you come with me in the garden. But you will find me much different than your Prince Ryland."

"Ryland didn't force me to do anything."

Aurius held her eyes.

"He didn't. I could have said no."

"If you had, you would have been locked in the dungeon until you died of something horrible. Let me guess. Ryland claimed you and begrudged any other who put a hand on you." He swooped down and picked up the ragged paper, rolling it and tying it back with a bit of leather. He shoved it into a metal tube, and it disappeared from sight.

"It was romantic."

"Mmm-hmmm. In any case, the contract is binding, princess. I can't get out of it any more than you can."

"Why didn't the contract break when my mother figured out your father's name?"

"My father was tricky. He only promised he wouldn't take you if she guessed. Not that I would not. Plus he never imagined she would discern his name. He would have taken greater precautions if he had. He certainly wouldn't have been gobbled up by the chasm."

Gwen pressed her head between her hands. "This is.."

"Unfair?" Aurius finished.

Gwen dropped her hands and nodded.

The bed dipped with his weight. "If you truly wish to be released from the agreement there are a few things we can try."

To his surprise, she placed her hand on his forearm. "You have been so kind to me. Most of the time. But this was not my agreement. It was made before I was born, by a desperate woman and a tricky goblin. I would never choose to marry someone under those conditions."

He pulled his lips back into a kind smile. "I understand completely. Although I wonder how these conditions are worse than your previous betrothal."

"I'm beginning to see that as well. Has Ryland even attempted to find me?"

He patted her hand. "The Prince has been spotted on the front lines, leading attacks against the magical barrier." He took a few steps and stood by the fire. "I can only guess it is to retrieve you. It seems the people of Aurum have a renewed purpose in the war. An effort to save their future queen."

Gwen rose from the bed. And slipped on her shoes. She didn't remember taking them off. "I have to go to him. Tell him I'm ok."

"He is aware of the fact that you are recovering from an assassination attempt."

"Assassination?"

"What else could it have been? The fabric of the dress you wore was woven with the threads of spun gold."

"Which is straw that only looks like gold."

Aurius nodded.

Gwen wanted to ignore that complication. "Only a few people knew the gold affected me." She narrowed her eyes at him, clutching the blanket tighter to her body.

"Then you should think twice about trusting them. Do you have an idea of who it could be?"

"The seamstress would be the top of the list. She hated me. I'm not sure how she knew the gold would trigger the reaction."

"Who else knew?"

A lump formed in her throat. She tried to swallow it, but tears formed unbidden.

Aurius grabbed her shoulders. "Who else?" he growled.

The words came out strangled by a sob. "Ryland, Avonlea and possibly Drake." She shook her head as her shoulders collapsed together. The room was suddenly stifling. "But I can't believe they would want me murdered." She threw the blankets away and jumped from the bed, racing toward the door.

Aurius blocked her from the door.

"Are you holding me prisoner?"

"No."

"There was one other person who knew."

Aurius narrowed his eyes. "Who?"

"Don't you think its a little too convenient to need to rescue me one last time?"

She reached around him for the door again. The walls closed around her, and her clothes felt too tight. The crackle of the fire was too loud. Everything was too much.

"You can't go to the barrier," Aurius whispered.

"Yes. I need to get out of here."

"It wasn't me. I've only ever helped you."

He held her at the waist with one hand and placed a gentle hand behind her neck. His fingers dug into her hair. He searched her eyes, and a little voice deep in the recesses of her mind said it wasn't him.

But she needed to see Ryland. Her hand barely touched the knob.

"If you do, the barrier may react to your magic. It will be strengthened, sending out magic to push back the army that attacks it."

Gwen's mouth dropped open. "I wouldn't be saving him. I might even kill him."

"On second thought maybe we should go to the barrier." Aurius pulled his lips back in a wicked smile.

She turned back to him. "You can't want Ryland to die?"

He shrugged a shoulder. "It would save us a lot of trouble. But no that isn't something I wish to happen."

Gwen pulled her hand away. Her slow and heavy footsteps pounded against the floor. The bed creaked with her weight as she sat, her shoulders slumped forward, her eyes on the floor.

"I have researched for years how to break the contract, but perhaps with your help we can find something. Maybe a drop of your blood or signing a new contract. When the contract is broken I will take you back to Aurum myself if that's what you wish. Even against my better judgment. You will never see or hear from me again, unless you call upon me."

"Can we transfer the contract to someone else?"

He shook his head. "Nontransferable, except on death and it transfers to your child."

Gwen's shoulders slumped further. "Your father certainly closed those loop holes."

"Yes."

"We'll think of something. You can't really want to marry me either." She tapped her full pink lips. "Perhaps a…"

He turned to face her. "What princess?"

She glared, which only earned her a devilish smile.

"A kiss? Perhaps a kiss would fulfill the contract or break it?" Gwen asked.

He pushed his eyebrows together. "How so?"

"Well it didn't go into much detail, so perhaps we could fool it with a kiss."

Aurius shook his head. "It would have to be a genuine kiss."

Gwen shrugged. "I'm willing to try."

The bed dipped as Aurius leaned himself toward her. He took her hand in his. This time, she didn't pull away. She could smell his deep musk, which made her head spin. His loose-fitting black shirt was open slightly at the top, giving her a view of a portion of his muscular chest. Her breath hitched as he leaned closer. She waited for his lips to touch hers. He lifted his hand and caressed her jawline with his thumb, ending just under her chin and lifting her face towards his. Her eyes met his, daring him to close the space between them.

Aurius smiled, and she could feel his breath mingle with hers. He patted her hand and swiftly stalked to the door. "Get some rest. You will meet the queen tomorrow. You can ask to send a message to your prince."

Gwen fell backward at the loss of his weight on the bed. "The queen?"

"Yes." He tapped his temple. "You'll need your wits about you."

"What should I wear?"

"The peridot dress. It matches your eyes," he said without hesitation.

He left the room, discussion over. He let the door shut behind him before he fell back against it.

She hadn't read the fine print either. No one ever did. "Time is running out," he whispered.

Falling

The door burst open and startled Gwen awake.

"It's time to get up princess!" Aurius announced.

"What? It can't possibly be time to meet the queen."

"No. The queen has been called away to the front lines. Don't worry I've sent a message to the prince that you are alive. But I have you to myself today and I intend to make the most of it."

Gwen fell into the pillows and groaned. "There is nowhere I would rather be than lying in this bed."

"You mean my bed? Perhaps I shall join you then."

Gwen sat straight up. "No. No. I'm up. Give me a few moments to dress." She pulled the blankets tighter to her chest. "Is everything ok at the barrier?"

"Hmm? Oh yes. The Queen is just reinforcing it with her magic. Nothing to worry about."

Prince Aurius pulled his lips into a satisfied smile. "You have ten minutes. I'll be waiting in the corridor. The maid has already laid the clothes for you in the washroom."

"Goodness. I must be a heavy sleeper."

"You are. Now get moving."

"Fine." Gwen grumbled as Aurius drew the door closed behind him.

She stumbled to the washroom. There was a large metal tub full of steaming water. "If Aurius wanted me to hurry, he shouldn't have ordered me a bath," she mumbled. After undressing, she slipped into the water, letting the liquid slide over her skin. It drew the last of the ailment from her body and seemed to renew her energy. The bright scent of gardenia awoke her senses and got her moving. She quickly rubbed the nearby bar of soap over a cloth and cleaned herself. To her surprise, she was out of the bath and dressed within the ten-minute time frame Aurius had given her.

The maid had left her a set of brown stretchy pants, a long-sleeved oversized shirt and a pair of brown knee high riding boots. "These might have been Aurius's clothes when he was younger. But it looks like we're going on an adventure today." The idea lit up her face with a smile.

Gwen yanked the door open to an awaiting Aurius. She had left her golden hair unbraided and flowing over her shoulders in soft waves created by the humidity of the bath. Aurius tucked a bit over her shoulder.

He parted his lips, quickly closed them again, and lifted them back into a shallow smile. His eyes narrowed, and he offered her his arm. "Shall we be off?"

She hesitated for a moment, debating at what it might mean to link her arm around his when she didn't need the assistance. She didn't want to give him the wrong idea. Her need to get out of his room won out, and she placed her arm in his, choosing to see it as a purely gentlemanly gesture.

"Where are we going?" she asked.

"You'll see." He tugged her faster down the corridor to an exterior door.

He pushed it open for her and she stepped into the most beautiful and serene forest she had ever seen. He followed her through with a broad smile at her expression.

"Is this a portal?"

"Of a sort."

"What sort?"

His face became somber. "It's a secret. You can tell no one you've traveled here."

"Who would believe me?"

"There are a great many who would kill to find this place."

Gwen put a palm over her chest. "Your secret is safe with me, besides I have no one to tell."

"What about your betrothed?"

"My betrothal is on rather shaky ground at the moment."

Aurius accepted her promise and grabbed her hand. "Alright, let's explore."

A gasp escaped Gwen's lips. "Aurius. Have you been here before?"

"Yes, many times. As a boy I used to disappear here for days. I would plan grand adventures. And play with my forest friends."

"Your forest friends?"

He took a shaky step around a moss-covered boulder and winked. "You'll see."

The trees were lush green, towering massively over the land. They blocked out the light from above, and yet the forest didn't seem to dim at all. Lights twinkled above them as they picked their way along a winding stream. She couldn't discern where the light emitted as she had to watch her steps. The clear water of the stream flowed over rounded gray stones with lush mossy tops.

They had already walked for several minutes when it dawned on Gwen to ask, "Is it dangerous?"

"All the best places are." Mischief danced in the goblin prince's eyes.

"I've never been anywhere dangerous," Gwen said as she stepped over a decaying tree.

That stopped Aurius in his tracks. "When I found you, you fed me watery broth with a few vegetables floating on top. Before I could return, the king kidnapped you and threw you in the dungeon, where I discovered you almost dying."

"You were the old man that visited the mill?"

He paused before answering. "It's my disguise. I do some clandestine work for the queen. But when I heard someone in Aurum had magic I had to check."

Gwen stopped. "Would you have taken me if you had gotten there first?"

"I did get there first. I was speaking with your father in tavern about you, until Prince Ryland and his crew came in. When they heard him mention you had magic and he made his offer I had to check on you. I needed to make sure it was true. I might have convinced the miller to allow your return here, but the prince moved quicker than I anticipated. And I told you before I don't make people do things."

Gwen smacked her head. "That's where I had seen the prince before. I went to the tavern when Papa returned to settle his tab if I could. The prince rescued me from some Rowdies." She started walking again. "Maybe that's why he moved quicker. He was afraid someone else would snatch me up before he could."

He took her hand and helped her over a wider part of the stream. She met his eyes as he pulled her over. "You look a little like him you know."

"Prince Ryland?"

"Yes."

He offered her a weak smile. "I've never heard that before."

"It's the eyes," she said.

Their conversation faded as the trees opened onto a meadow. The sun beamed down on thousands of tiny purple flowers arranged in a semicircle. In the center of the semicircle was a magnificent horse. Her white coat sparkled in the sunlight. Her mane draped over her neck in platinum waves. Protruding from her forehead was a small iridescent horn.

Gwen's hands flew to her mouth. "Is that a..." she lowered her voice to whisper, unable to believe what she was about to say.

"Unicorn?" Aurius finished for her.

Gwen nodded with wide eyes, still not moving her hands from her face.

"She is THE unicorn."

"The only one?" she whispered.

"There can only ever be one."

"How lonely."

"Hmm. Would you like to meet her?"

"Of course. Will she let us approach?"

"She's asked to meet you."

"She. Asked? To meet me?"

He nodded and took a step forward. "Follow my footsteps, exactly. The meadow is beautiful but also treacherous."

She nodded and stepped in his footsteps until they reached the unicorn.

Aurius took a knee in front of her and bowed his head. "Madam Prisma."

"Prince Aurius. You have returned almost grown."

Behind him, Gwen whimpered with barely contained excitement at the sound of the unicorn speaking out loud.

The prince lifted his head and smiled. "It's been a while."

"Is this her?"

Aurius nodded.

Prisma shook her head and snorted as horses do. "Please child, come forward."

As she stepped around Aurius, still on bended knee, he mouthed to curtsy. She complied.

"Princess, it's my greatest pleasure to meet you."

"And mine as well."

"Please sit with me children."

Though Gwen and Aurius were not children, they sat before the unicorn.

"Aurius, why have you come?"

"The princess and I have a contract. And we would like for it to be broken."

Gwen's jaw dropped open. He had been true to his word in looking for a way to break the contract. It was utterly shocking, given his lineage.

"A magical contract I assume, since you seek my assistance," Madam Prisma said.

"Yes. A blood contract written by my father and signed by her mother."

Aurius presented it to Prisma.

"I can try to break the contract but as you know magic everywhere is weakening and I've never been a match for a goblin king."

"Please. I'm to marry another and this contract isn't what we wished it to be," Gwen said.

The unicorn turned her attention back to Prince Aurius. "After all these years searching, boy, you found her betrothed to another?"

Gwen tilted her head, examining Aurius with wide eyes.

Aurius cleared his throat. "The contract please."

If it were possible, it appeared the unicorn rolled her eyes. "Very well, place it before me."

Aurius placed the contract at her feet. Prisma rose as the prince and princess scampered out of the way of becoming trampled. The sunlight hit the unicorn's horn and broke into a million light beams of different colors. Prisma reared onto her hind legs and pedaled her front hooves in the air above their heads. Aurius pulled Gwen back further and wrapped his arms around her as the unicorn slammed her hooves to the ground on top of the contract. Gwen was surprised to find that she enjoyed the contact and felt safer than she had anywhere with anyone, even her father.

There was a burst of magic that spread through the meadow in a circle around the unicorn. Gwen and Aurius were blown back a step by the force. Trees shook, and the tiny purple flowers lay over in the onslaught.

Gwen thought for sure Prisma's magic would overcome the magic of the contract, but it remained intact.

"I'm sorry Gwen. This agreement cannot be broken by my power."

Gwen's shoulders slumped forward. She had been so hopeful. "I appreciate the effort." She pulled a single strand of hair from her head. "Let me do something for you in return." The princess held her hand up to the unicorn. The hair floated in the breeze. Prisma bowed and allowed Gwen to approach. She took a small piece of Prisma's mane, lined up her hair and twisted the strands over each other into a small, imperceptible braid. When it was complete, a golden glow slid over the unicorn and then faded.

"Thank you for this gift child. I feel better than I have in ages. If you ever have need of me again please visit the meadow and find me."

"Thank you," Gwen said and bowed to the unicorn.

Prisma swung her head toward the prince. "Aurius. Make your way to the fair folk."

"The fairies do not want to hear from me."

"They may have a way to break the contract."

"Thank you for the advice but we will be avoiding that bit of the forest."

"Very well. Suit yourself."

The unicorn's dark eyes shifted to Gwen. "Gwen even though you don't believe it, you have great power."

"Thank you Prisma, but even Aurius has told me I can't perform any magic."

"Power doesn't come from magic. Magic comes from power and when all the worlds are losing magic, it's interesting that you have the most powerful catalyst magic I've ever felt."

"I'm not sure what that means."

"You'll figure it out some day. It is my hope that you do so before it's too late for the rest of us."

Gwen looked up at Aurius, whose expression matched her confusion. "We'll be off on our journey then, Madam Prisma."

Aurius bowed and placed a hand on the small of Gwen's back as he guided her out of the meadow.

Grinhelda

As they stepped back into the forest, Gwen took his hand. "Thank you for trying. I appreciate the effort. What happens if we don't break the contract and we don't fulfill the terms?"

"My life is forfeit."

"What do you mean?"

"I mean, dear Gwen, that I will die."

Gwen stopped walking. "What? Why didn't you tell me?"

He placed his hands on her upper arms. The warmth seeped through her loose shirt. "It's in the fine print, and I was hoping that when I found you, you would want to fulfill the contract making it a moot point." He raised his thumb to her cheek. "And I've seen your kindness and how you sacrifice yourself. I didn't want to influence your choice with my plight."

He turned toward the stream and began the journey anew. Gwen could do nothing but follow him. "Since you don't want to, we must find another way."

"You're not giving up?" she asked.

"Gwen. Our options are to fulfill the contract, break it, or die."

"Why not force me to fulfill the contract?"

He took a big step over onto a boulder and reached a hand back to help her onto it. "I think I've answered that enough times."

Gwen opened her mouth to respond, but Aurius held up a finger to silence her. He tilted his head, listening to the forest sounds. His eyes roamed the canopy, searching for the disturbance he felt. Finding nothing amiss, he whispered. "Did you hear that?"

She froze and listened. In the distance she heard a cry of an animal in distress. "A creature. I think that way." She pointed across the stream and deeper into the forest. "It's hurt I think."

Aurius looked in the direction she was pointing and took a step in the opposite direction.

"Shouldn't we investigate and see if we can help?"

He squinted his eyes at her. "Nothing good will come of it."

"How can you say that?"

"Because I've learned my lesson in this forest, but if you need one, by all means be my guest." He swooped his arm in the direction she pointed.

She jumped off the boulder toward the sound. "I won't turn my back on a creature in need if I can help."

Aurius smiled. "Lead the way, princess."

She took a breath and a moment to evaluate her options. As Aurius was just about to turn once again, taking a step in the cry's direction. It seemed closer, or perhaps louder. But unmistakably, a creature needed help.

"This way," she whispered. She knew better than to take off running toward the danger. The knife in her boot felt weighty for the first time since she had slipped it there. She assumed Prince Aurius would trust in his magic to defend him, but what magic could she use? She silently cursed her useless catalyst magic. They maneuvered past trees until they came upon the creature that made the noise.

A small fawn was trapped in a net against the ground. It struggled to rise against the fine wires of the snare.

Gwen took a step toward it to untangle it from the net. But Aurius grabbed her forearm.

"You can't rush in there to save it."

"It's just a net. We pull it off and the baby runs away."

Aurius pursed his lips and exhaled with a growl but backed up to allow Gwen to follow through with her rescue. She pulled a small knife from her boot and knelt beside the net. She did her best not to step on it, in case Aurius was right and this was a trap for them.

"Where did you get the knife?" Aurius stood behind her, looking about the forest to ensure nothing attacked them.

"I have learned some lessons recently myself. One of those is that even innocent maidens can be kidnapped from their homes and I thought that perhaps it was time to start arming myself with more than magic." Her words held a hint of sarcasm.

"That is a good plan princess. Especially since I won't always be here to protect you or save you."

That comment earned him a glare, but she couldn't spend too much energy on it, as she had work to do. "I've been kidnapped twice, actually."

"That knife will do nothing against this net. It's magical and can't be cut with a blade."

Gwen looked over her shoulder from her crouched position. "Then how do we take it off?"

"Only the witch who wove it can remove it." An unfamiliar voice joined the conversation.

Gwen twirled to get her back toward the tree, which was a feat from her original position. The voice hadn't come from behind them. Aurius didn't look the least bit surprised that the distressed fawn had turned into a beautiful woman. She was out of place in the forest, wearing a red sequined evening gown. Her ice-blond hair was neatly styled without a hair out of place. Bright red lips matched her gown. The net disappeared with a wave of her hand.

"Grinhelda," Aurius grumbled. "I should have known."

"You did know. It was this kind heart that should have heeded your warnings."

He stepped toward Gwen. "She does have a kind heart and you will not lay a hand on her."

Grinhelda stood. Every movement was fluid and elegant. "Relax. I'm not here to hurt her."

"Me then?"

"Not to curse you. I heard you were working to break the contract."

Aurius's look of alarm was all Gwen needed to know they were on dangerous ground. Grinhelda must have been very powerful to have frightened Aurius.

"News travels fast, but Grin, you know there is nothing between us," he said. Caution laced his voice.

A moment of silence drug on for eternity. Grinhelda threw her head back and grabbed her stomach. Her laugh would curdle blood.

Aurius moved one foot back and readied his hands to fight. Gwen hated that Grinhelda was between them. But if it came to it, perhaps she could grab the woman and keep her from attacking Aurius.

The sound stopped abruptly. Grinhelda stepped toward Aurius, completely unfazed by his stance. She cupped his cheeks between her thumb and fingers, puckering his lips. "Oh Aurius. You were always so cute."

He pulled his face from her hand.

"Didn't you hear. I am betrothed myself to someone much more powerful than you."

"Congratulations on your betrothal. And since there is no one to rescue we will be off."

"There was a point to this little... test, Aurius."

Aurius shifted his eyes to Grin. A fire lit behind them. He pumped his jaw, but waited for her to explain.

"Don't worry. She passed and she shall receive a blessing."

"We do not need your blessing." The way he turned the last word into a sneer had Gwen thinking that perhaps a blessing from Grinhelda would not feel as though it were.

"But you'll get it all the same. I have a favor to grant and this will fulfill it. You know how your father's deals are. Binding and perpetual even in death." Her voice was becoming angrier. Gwen stepped up to distract Grinhelda from Aurius for a moment.

"Then we definitely do not want your blessing." The words spilled from Aurius as Gwen said, "I will gladly accept whatever your blessing is."

Grin whirled around to face her. "Oh. You're still here. Yes. of course. Everyone wants a blessing from me." She winked at Aurius, who never took his eyes off of her.

Grin lifted her arm and unfolded her hand in a graceful twirl. A puff of smoke appeared and disappeared, leaving behind an envelope.

Gwen lifted the stationery from her outstretched hand.

"Goodbye Gwen, until we meet again."

Grinhelda faded from sight, but her horrible laughter remained until it was carried away on a breeze.

"That wasn't ominous at all." Sarcasm dripped from Gwen's words. Something that had been happening more often since leaving the Kingdom of Aurum.

She looked at the envelope in front of her.

"A gift from Grinhelda could also be a curse. Be careful when you open it." Aurius's light warning did not match the serious tone of his voice.

"You assume I am opening it."

His voice softened. "It is natural to be curious. That's the point of the packaging."

"What are our other options?"

"Leave it behind, but Grinhelda will definitely see that as a slight and it would cause problems later in life when you are least expecting it."

"Nix that option."

"Or open it later.

Gwen shifted her eyes to him when he stopped talking. "And?" she said, urging him to continue.

"We don't have much time and if you wait to open it I might not be around to help you deal with the consequences."

"What if I just never open it?"

"Grin will know and also take that as a slight."

"Who is she?"

"A powerful witch, you don't want to offend."

"So the only real option is opening now."

His dark eyes met hers. He reassured her with a smile, stepping closer, and put his hand over hers. "Don't worry," he said. His breath tickled her ear. "I'm here with you to face whatever it is."

Gwen swallowed hard and nodded. Aurius moved his arm over Gwen's shoulder as she broke the seal of the envelope. She leaned away from the incursion of golden light. When her vision cleared, the pair were no longer surrounded by natural forest, but were instead in front of an abandoned cottage.

She shrugged, wondering if they had moved or if the cottage had appeared from nothing. "Abandoned cottage. A little cliche' but not as bad as I was expecting."

"Don't move princess,"Aurius whispered into her hair. Somehow, while magic poured from Grinhelda's envelope, he had shifted himself behind her, wrapping her in his protective arms.

She tried to turn toward him, but he held her tight. "Don't. Move." His voice was firm. His arms covered hers and kept her in place.

Gwen froze and waited.

She felt the wind of the arrow more than she saw it coming toward her. It stopped within a breath of Aurius' neck. When Gwen opened her eyes, it dropped to the ground.

Aurius didn't look at the arrow that almost took his life; he looked at her. "What was that?"

"What?"

"You stopped the arrow?"

"I..I.." Her lips opened and closed like a fish, but she couldn't deny it. "I didn't do it on purpose, I just I felt the arrow and… and I didn't want you to die so I took control of it with my mind." The words spilled from her mouth to explain.

He pulled her into his chest and stroked the back of her head. "Shh, shh." He pushed her away and grabbed her shoulders to look into her eyes. "You will never use this magic in front of anyone ever again. Not even to save my life. Not even to save your life." He shook her shoulders when she didn't agree right away. "Do you understand me?"

She nodded.

"It is better to die quickly than have someone discover you have dual magic."

"But you have dual magic? More than dual."

"I'm a goblin. We're supposed to be the most powerful magic users. But even so I'm no match for a magician with a catalyst as powerful as you. No one will allow you live with dual powers. And you will die in the worst way imaginable."

"No one? Not even you?"

"I am bound to you. I can't harm you."

"But if we break the contract?'

"I don't think breaking the contract is going to change that," Aurius said and stepped away. He searched the ground for the arrow that had nearly ended his life.

It shimmered in what little light that was left in front of the cottage. He bent and retrieved it from the grass mound it had fallen into. With the arrow in one hand, the prince released her and stepped toward the cottage.

"We can move now?" she whispered.

He reached back, grabbing the tips of her fingers. "Stay close."

She followed him cautiously. Aurius approached the door. It hung on one hinge, and all the windows were boarded over. Moss grew up the outer walls. The air smelled earthy and wild.

Even though the door was barely hanging and more leaning against the wall, there was a notch in the wood in the arrow's shape. He snapped it into the groove and rotated it.

The cottage twisted and turned. Walls shifted and grew taller. The moss receded, replaced by polished boughs and branches. Sweet scents of blooming wisteria replaced the smell of death and decay. The old cottage transformed into a royal palace.

The door remained open. Gwen followed Aurius's tentative steps into the estate.

"Aurius! You've returned just in time for the ball."

Elves

A lithe woman with pointed ears leaned against a roaring fireplace. The room was bright and warm. There wasn't much in the way of furniture. Tree branches and roots bent together to form places to sit around the fire. Polished stone served as the floor. Gwen couldn't comprehend whether this room or the abandoned cottage was real.

"Grinhelda must have given you our invitation," she said. Her voice was light and airy. It tickled Gwen's ears when she spoke. It wasn't unpleasant, but not something she would want to listen to for a long time.

"She didn't mention who it was from but yes, we received it." Aurius spoke for them.

"We?" The woman looked around Aurius. "I was under the impression you were alone."

Aurius took Gwen's hand and pulled her from behind him. "No. Elanil. This is Princess Gwen," he turned toward Gwen. "Gwen this Elanil, Princess of the Four Realms of the Enchanted Forest."

The elf princess bowed her head slightly. "Well met Princess Gwen," she said.

"A pleasure to meet you also Princess Elanil," Gwen replied, following the protocol Avonlea taught her. With that thought, Gwen's lips turned down at the corners, but not long enough for anyone to notice.

"What land do you rule?" Elanil asked.

Gwen took a deep breath to clear the memories of the royal siblings from her mind. There was no time to dwell now.

"Uh, Princess Gwen is between lands at the moment," Aurius answered for Gwen before she realized a question had been asked.

The elf princess switched her gaze from Aurius to Gwen. She narrowed her eyes. Her lips parted as if she had a question, but she closed them before she asked. A look of confusion passed over her face, and then she shook her head as if deciding not to try to understand how a princess could not have a land. She turned and motioned for them to follow her.

"Come. We have prepared a room for you, Aurius. We'll find a place for Gwen as well."

"We are not lodging in the four realms," Aurius said.

Elanil waved her hands and tsked. "Don't be silly. There is a ball. Everyone lodges here for the ball."

Aurius grumbled and had some choice words for Grinhelda. To Elanil, he said. "Then Gwen will be staying with me."

"Are you married?" she asked.

"No. Gwen is under my protection and she will not leave my side."

"You know that will not be possible and she is in no danger here."

"Then I want an adjoining room."

"Gwen is in no danger here," she repeated.

"These are my terms or we're going home."

"You would refuse an invitation from my brother for this human woman?"

Gwen stepped forward and placed a gentle hand on Aurius's forearm. "Maybe, it's…"

Aurius ignored Gwen. He kept eye contact with Elanil. "Yes."

Gwen tucked her chin and pulled her hand away. Elanil pursed her lips. Her eyes shifted to Gwen, then back to Aurius. She sighed in the elegant way of elves. "Very well, we can prepare adjoining rooms. This way." She turned from her previous course to the left instead of the right.

Elanil guided them through the tree house of twisted branches and paths so narrow they could only pass in single file.

"Are they fairies or elves?" Gwen asked when she thought she was no longer within earshot of the princess.

"We are elves, though the fairies are under our jurisdiction," Elanil answered.

Aurius pressed a finger to his lips and motioned for her to wait to ask her questions until they reached their rooms.

The elf princess stopped abruptly in front of doors that were intricately carved with images of more trees and branches. "Here we are. Adjoining rooms. Gwen, you will find a wardrobe appropriate for the ball which will begin within the hour. Aurius, your wardrobe has been moved to this room. This room will be reserved for you alone for the remainder of our friendship." Elanil clasped her hands in front of her. "I don't mean any rudeness, but I must leave to inform my brother of your arrival, prepare for the ball, and soothe Elora. She will be devastated with your news."

"We take no offense. Thank you for accommodating our needs and providing us food, shelter, and clothing," Aurius said.

"As you say."

Elanil nodded her head once and walked back the way she came.

Aurius held up a hand as Gwen opened her mouth. "I know you have questions, but this is not the time or place. I will do my best to explain everything when we are away from here."

"Are we in danger?"

Aurius shook his head with a sigh. "Just dress for the ball and don't drink the wine." A little growl tainted the end of his sentence.

Aurius entered her room and locked the door after her. He checked all the usual hiding places for anyone who might be ready to ambush them. Behind the bed built from woven tree branches. (The cushion on top of those boughs looked comfortable enough.) Inside the wardrobe, filled with dresses ornate with their simplicity. If there had been corners of the room, she was sure he would have stabbed them all. But the area was oval.

Gwen was unsure what he was searching for. She could breathe easily for the first time since her father had come home from the tavern. She felt it the moment her foot crossed the threshold into the forest. The weight of her looming death lifted. Aurius opened the adjoining door to his room and performed the same routine.

He poked his head back through when he finished his examination of the rooms. He ran a hand through his dark hair with an exasperated sigh. "You can lock this door if you like. If something does happen I will be able to access your room through shadows."

"Why did you make a big deal about adjoining rooms then?"

"To send a message."

"What message?"

"That you are important to me. You are under my protection and you are not on the market."

"Oh."

"I'm sorry Gwen. But you do not want to get caught up in Elf politics and as a princess any noble here would have a right to your hand in marriage. And since your father is not here, I am your protector."

She sat on the bed. It was even more comfortable than she had imagined moments before. "Wouldn't that be easier if you just announced we are betrothed?"

Aurius raised an eyebrow. "Are you ready to fulfill the contract and make that announcement?"

Gwen remained silent, pressing her lips into a thin line.

"I didn't think so. The Elf King may be able to break it. But I have to convince him to do so."

"How do you do that?"

"Making it clear that I will not marry his sister while the contract is still in place."

"Oh? You are engaged to his sister?" Gwen's throat felt tight. She swallowed the jealousy choking her. She had no right to it.

"Elora and I were friends a very long time ago. She decided we were to be married. I had nothing really to do with it."

"If there is no contract, will you marry Elora?"

Aurius's lips formed a tired smile. "I don't know."

"You have every powerful woman in the enchanted forest falling all over themselves to marry to you and yet you are stuck with me. I'm so sorry."

"Gwen." For a few long minutes, nothing followed, as if he were trying to find words to explain all this and came up very short. "None of this is your fault," were the words he chose instead. He took her hand and squeezed it between both of his. "I have hated my father for a long time for his manipulation of everyone in his life including me. But I could never be angry with you. And," he pushed a wayward strand of hair from her face and tucked it behind her ear. "I'm thankful this contract has given me the few moments I've had with you."

She didn't move away from the touch. Her eyebrows pressed together. "But even now you are willing to find a way to break it?" she asked.

He smiled and lifted her chin. His eyes held hers for the longest moment. "For you, I will."

She waited for his lips to touch hers, but he stepped back instead.

"Get ready for the ball. I'll meet you there." He disappeared into the shadows of the wardrobe.

Ball

The dresses in the wardrobe were elegant in their simplicity. They were all the same cut and style. The stitches were even and perfect. The only differences were the color and fabric. There were silk, velvet, and linen. The colors were all shades found in nature. Foam left behind by the sea after the tide had turned. Grapes pressed into flowing liquid. The bright feathers of a male peacock.

She picked the silk sea-foam dress and slipped it over her head. It immediately adjusted itself to her body for a perfect fit. The cut in the front dipped below her collarbone and rested just off her shoulders, forming two points. The sleeves extended down her arms, ending in sharp angles over the back of her hands. Fabric flowed over her thighs, over her knees, to the tips of her toes. Soft and silky, as if the elves had wrapped her in a cloud.

She wiggled her feet into the pointed flat shoes that matched the dress. Music began floating through the room.

It was quiet, but it called to her. The waves of sound laced themselves around her heart and pulled her to the ballroom floor. Her feet took her, though she didn't know the way. She was helpless to resist the call to dance. Many others were as well.

As her slipper touched the polished oak floor, the soft, lulling music turned more dramatic and desperate. The beat of her heart was now driving the rhythm. Or was it the other way around? She couldn't tell.

She was breathless. The tension built in her chest and spread to her arms and legs. But the dance demanded she wait for a partner. She knew in that moment that the partner she wanted was in this very room. His dark eyes hadn't left her from the second she entered.

He hopped off the table he had seated himself on and placed a mug aside. His black leather brocade jacket bulged in the arms and hung behind him to the back of his knees. He let the white shirt underneath hang loose at the top. But the dark belted pants hugged the muscular curves of his legs. He didn't look a bit out of place in this rugged forest Elven ballroom.

He stepped to her side and placed a gentle hand on her opposite hip as the dance called for. All the attention of her nerves went to that spot on her body. As the beats grew louder and wilder, he twirled and spun her around the room. The members of the Elven community faded away, and it was just Gwen and Aurius on the dance floor. They spun around each other. He lifted her hand, encouraging the final spin of the dance. But instead of ending with a bow, she stepped into his embrace. Their breaths intermingled, and she found herself looking into his eyes and hoping again he would close the inches between them.

Their chests rose and fell together. Aurius moved a fraction toward Gwen. Her lips tingled in anticipation.

The Elf King clapped his hand loudly on Aurius's back. He jerked away from Gwen and spun to stand beside her. Gwen almost fell forward in his absence. "Why does this keep happening?" Gwen whispered, wondering if her lips would ever touch another's. There had been many close calls over the past few days.

"Aurius. I'm so glad to see you again."

The king was everything Gwen expected elf royalty to be. The top of his head towered over everyone else in the room. White hair hung in straight, pointed strands over his shoulders. He wore a crown that looked as if its creators had woven twigs and dipped it in gold. The crown itself was beautiful, but on top of the head of the Elf King, no one would even appreciate it.

His face was chiseled out of marble and brought to life by magic. Dark eyes sat under furrowed brows. Between them, a sharp and straight nose. His lips were full and rounded into the perfect bow. Not to mention his strong jaw and the deep timbre of his voice. A linen doublet covered his broad shoulders in a color similar to Gwen's dress.

Aurius crooked a finger under her chin and clicked her mouth shut. Had she been drooling? Her dress also changed from sea foam to a charcoal grey, which startled her back into reality. She had matched the elf king, and now she was his opposite. She tilted her head and looked at Aurius with a raised eyebrow. He ignored her unasked question, choosing instead to keep his eyes on the elf king. Had he changed the color of her dress?

The king lifted the corner of his perfect lips into a knowing smile. "Will you join me in my study, Aurius? I would like to talk about your request."

Aurius looked down at where the elf king gripped his shoulder. The king lifted his other hand to take a strand of Gwen's hair between his finger and thumb. "And perhaps later Gwen and I could come to an agreement about her power as well."

Aurius turned his body, shielding Gwen from the king's attention. "If it comes to that, it will be a mutual agreement. No one forces her to share or use her magic."

The joy left the king's face, and he dropped his hands to his side. "My study, Aurius."

Aurius stepped in front of Gwen, took her hand in his and brought the tips of her fingers to his lips. "I'll find you when we're done. Stay here and have fun, but remember what I told you about the wine."

Gwen plastered a smile on her face as she watched him walk through the crowd. The balconies twisted around the dance floor as if they were a crown. The shadows it created made the setting more intimate. While focused light from above the bough filtered to the center floor with bright intensity, sconces dotted the walls under the balcony. Cozy was the only word Gwen could find to describe it. Cozy yet elegant.

Aurius and the king ducked under a balcony and disappeared through an ornate door toward the back.

The music began again, but with her partner gone, Gwen visited a banquet table on the opposite side. Someone handed her a goblet filled with a fizzing pink liquid. As she lifted the silver cup to her lips, her disappointment at the near kiss turned to determination that it would not happen again.

* * *

Aurius stepped into the king's study and closed the embellished wooden door behind him. He didn't bother with a spell to silence the room to intruders. The Elf king already had one in place. It would be rude not to trust it.

Aurius barely had it closed before the king was speaking.

"You would allow her to share her power with me?"

"It is hers to do with what she pleases, Erym."

"But you would allow this?" he asked again.

Aurius pursed his lips and looked at the ceiling. "My father was the one who manipulated and forced people into contracts they did not want. I'm striving to be better than that."

The elf king pulled a decanter from a shelf behind his desk. Pulling the stopper from the top, poured the brown liquid into two crystal glasses and replaced the decanter on its shelf.

He handed one of the glasses to Aurius, who graciously accepted, but did not sip. Elf drink was more potent than fairy wine. Being of goblin descent, it wouldn't affect him as much as a human, but he needed his wits about him for this conversation.

The elf king lowered himself to the edge of his large desk. "You possess the catalyst. You can be more powerful than any goblin, even your father. And yet you refuse to enforce the contract and save yourself."

"I possess nothing. Gwen is not an object. She is a person. I will not take her freedom to save mine."

Erym leaned back at his words. His eyes widened, and he grinned. "You fell in love with her."

"I do not love the princess," Aurius said. His voice was flat with denial.

The king laughed. "You love her and you are willing to give up your life for her."

Aurius remained silent for a few moments, tinkering with bobbles on the table. "If you break the contract, I won't have to give up anything."

"Except true love."

Aurius scoffed. "True love doesn't exist."

"It exists and it is more powerful than any magic."

"You've let the fairies tell too many tales."

The king laughed again and drained his glass. "It just so happens the tales are true."

"Gwen doesn't love me. She loves Prince Ryland. I want to give her her hearts desire."

"Stop denying you love her."

Aurius's fingers tightened on the glass. He considered breaking it, but just as he felt the glass shift under his fingers, he relaxed his hand. What was the point of fighting it any longer? "Fine. I love her. Will you break the contract?"

"No."

Aurius stood. "Why ever not?"

"Because she loves you too."

"She has made it very clear she does not." Aurius sat the glass down before he did something he'd regret.

"How long have you been in this forest?" the king asked.

"A few hours."

"Only moments in your realm."

"Yes."

"And has she mentioned this other inferior prince in those few hours?"

Aurius crossed his arms over his chest. "We've been busy trying to break the contract so that she can return to him."

"But has she spoken of him?"

"No."

"There's your answer. If she truly loved him she wouldn't shut up about him, trust me. I have three sisters. I know."

Aurius remained unconvinced Erym knew anything about love. The elf king leaned in. "I saw the way she looks at you. She is as in love with you as you are with her."

"Did you see how she looked at you?"

The king scoffed. "Everyone looks at me like that."

Aurius didn't dare to hope. "Will you break the contract or not?"

The king stepped away and lifted his chin. "No."

"Because you believe us to be in love?"

King Erym poured himself another drink. "No, because I haven't the power to do so."

"You are the most powerful being in the forest."

"And yet I am no match for a blood contract created by your father. Besides magic is dying everywhere as you know. I can't expend energy on a fruitless endeavor."

Aurius sat in a nearby chair. "You have condemned me to my fate."

The king shrugged and turned his lips down in thought. "Fulfill the requirements of the contract and you will avoid it. Otherwise it might not be so bad being the goblin king."

"You know how bad it will be. I'm more powerful than my father. I'll be worse than he ever was."

"Perhaps you will not give yourself wholly to the goblin."

"I'll have no choice. I won't be able to control anything once the Goblin takes over."

"Your only hope is Gwen."

"But she will never agree in time."

"Not if you are in here belly aching to me. Now go and dance until your feet fall off."

Aurius groaned. "Please tell me you don't mean that literally."

"No, of course not. Enjoy the party. You have little time left."

The prince drained the brown liquid from the glass and sat it back on the table. "Goodbye, Emyr."

The king tilted his head in a slight bow. "Until we meet again."

Aurius rose to leave. "Emyr… about Elora."

The king waved his hand. "Let me worry about her. You have enough problems. But please don't allow her obsession to keep you away so long next time."

Aurius bowed. Pulling the door shut behind him, he whispered, "If there is a next time."

Prince Aurius returned to the ballroom floor to find Gwen twirling with other girls her age. At least, they looked her age. They were probably hundreds of years older than her. Still, her smile was intoxicating, and her laugh was the best thing he had heard in months. And then he felt the thing he had been dreading. His acceptance of the Elf King's observation must have been a new type of catalyst. The cage slammed shut around his heart. Admitting that he loved Gwen was the final lock, setting in motion the countdown, in addition to his approaching birthday. He had mere days to convince her to return his love or he would lose himself to his goblin blood forever.

He stepped onto the ballroom floor, hoping Erym was right. Could Gwen love him as he loved her?

* * *

He found Gwen speaking and laughing with a group of young elves. The musicians had taken a break, and everyone ate, drank and laughed while the magic of music waned.

He took the cup out of her hand. "What did I tell you about drinking the wine." His voice was low.

Gwen looked up at him and frowned. "I was only holding it so as not to be rude."

As he set the cup aside and pulled her away from the crowd, the music began again. Gwen's body swayed in response.

"Gwen. We must go."

Gwen's eyes refocused as she turned back toward Aurius. "Everyone stays until morning. Dance with me. Once more."

"We cannot stay." He tried to tug her away.

Gwen frowned. "I suppose the king couldn't break the contract."

"No."

She wrapped a daring arm around his waist and looked up through her lashes. "A dance and then we shall go."

"I thought you said you were only holding the cup."

"I might have taken a sip. I don't see what's so dangerous about it." She

208

giggled.

Aurius sighed and shook his head. "It only removes your inhibitions and reveals your deepest secrets."

"I have no secrets. Except that I want to dance with you."

The dark prince, despite his better judgment, relented and let Gwen pull him to the center of the room. She wrapped her arms around his waist. He placed his hands on either side of her beautiful face. His head bent over hers as she looked up at him. The music thrummed around them, and while others moved around the circle; they stood immovable.

"This isn't dancing princess."

Gwen responded with only a slight movement of her lips into a small smile.

"No. I suppose it is not. But I've never been a very good dancer."

He slid a hand down her arm and took her hand in his. Lifting it to his chest. He placed her other hand on his shoulder, and his went to her waist. The elves danced in their own revelry and paid the couple no attention. He swayed with Gwen in his arms to a rhythm much different from the enchanted musicians played.

"And what about you?" Gwen whispered.

"Me?"

"Have you drank any fairy wine?"

"No wine for me tonight. But it doesn't effect goblins the same as humans."

"Half-goblin."

"Mhm."

He continued to sway. With her in his arms, he could almost pretend this was his court, his ball, his... wife.

Gwen looked up at him, and the cage around his heart tightened another degree. If this continued, he would be a goblin by morning.

She smiled at him, lifted onto the tips of her toes, and pressed her lips to his. The movement was sudden. Her lips were as soft as he had imagined they would be. It awakened a need deep within him. It was his undoing. And he knew if he stayed with her any longer, he would force her hand in marriage. He wouldn't be able to control the greedy goblin growing within him.

When she pulled away, he searched her eyes for regret. Finding none, his fingers dug into the hair at the back of her head, pulling her face to his as he crushed his lips to hers. While the first kiss was sweet and testing, this was all-consuming. A kiss. There was no escaping, no coming back. It felt like a fleeting moment and an eternity all at once.

The ground shook beneath their feet. A few couples screamed and scurried from the dance floor. Aurius immediately pulled Gwen into his body and wrapped protective arms around her.

Dust poured from various places, and the leaves of the branches twirled to the ground.

"What was that?" Gwen asked, pushing her hair away from her face as Aurius released her. He couldn't answer her because he wasn't sure. His eyes searched for the Elf King and found him in the balcony's shadow near where his study met the ballroom. Emyr looked as if nothing had happened at all. He met Aurius's gaze and lifted his glass toward him and then to his lips.

Aurius pursed his lips. His nostrils flared. "I think the curse has reached the Elven woods," Aurius whispered. "And the king is trying to force me into action."

"What's to be done about it?"

"Nothing tonight. It's time to go."

Gwen looked around at all those leaving the ballroom and heading away down corridors. "I suppose the party is over now."

She followed Aurius toward their rooms. He paused before he opened the door and turned toward her. The glazed look in her eyes had cleared slightly. "We need to talk about the…" He couldn't bring himself to say the word.

"I didn't mean to make it awkward," she said with a little giggle at the end.

His eyes narrowed. "How much fairy wine did you drink?"

She held up her pointer finger and thumb to her eye to indicate a small amount. Aurius sighed.

He placed his hands on her arms. "I am so sorry Gwen. I had hoped I would never have to do this."

Gwen's eyebrows pressed together in confusion. A polished crystal sphere appeared in his hands. The gem was cool in his palm, but pressed against Gwen's temple it warmed. He pressed his lips to her forehead. "Thank you for showing me what it is like to love."

Gwen smiled at him.

He couldn't bring himself to take the adventure from her, but he wanted her to choose him. The fairy wine wasn't fair to her. It tainted her choice. He wanted her to have the full function of her mind when she chose him.

"Gwen Miller you will not remember anything after your first taste of fairy wine tonight," he said. The air shimmered around him. A glow emanated from the gem, lighting the space in front of their adjoining rooms. Gwen's eyes drooped and her knees buckled. He caught her while carefully putting the gem in his treasury and carried her through their adjourning rooms. He placed her on the bed of boughs.

He set a hand on her forehead and eased his thumb over it. "Sleep well, Gwen. Until we meet again."

Safety

It had been two days since she had seen Prince Aurius after their return from the enchanted forest. He had been right about breaking the contract. It wasn't possible. After the Elven ball, he had barely spoken to her. And she didn't have the nerve to bring it up. The elves allowed them to return through a portal door. Exhausted from their adventure, Gwen slept soundly in Aurius's room.

The following morning, he left a note for her with her locket, explaining that he wanted to check on one more avenue for breaking the contract. She had lost hope that he would be successful and sighed at the thought. "At least he was true to his word and tried for my sake."

Approximately three weeks had passed since she had seen Prince Ryland or Princess Avonlea. There was no way to tell after her trip to the forest. "Are they still looking for me?" she wondered at her lonely breakfast nook.

The meeting with the queen? Never rescheduled. Gwen guessed there was not much time to meet with lost girls with no parents. Even lost nieces with rare magic that everyone supposedly wanted.

Moments after she found Aurius's note, they whisked her away to another suite. Gwen couldn't tell if it was an enchanted note to notify the staff she was awake.

Now she had more space than she had ever had in her life, although it could hardly compare to the rooms at Castille de Alfur with the elves. Still, she wished they had allowed her to stay in Aurius's room. At least there, she might have caught a scent of him.

She rolled her eyes at the thought.

"I don't care for him. Why would I want to remember how he smells?" she told herself.

She tried to remember what had happened after her first sip of wine. It was an absentminded, foolish thing to do. "I guess the wine took my memories as well."

After a quick tour around the suite, she opened the large French doors to a small balcony. There was barely space to step outside, but the view was unlike anything she had ever seen. Large trees shaded the cropping. Even though she was on the second floor, a large hill rose and brought the trees with it, which blocked any view beyond. A cool dampness enveloped the ledge, and disappointment wrapped itself around Gwen's heart. The quiet hope that had bloomed, that she might see her homeland, died.

"I suppose I would like this view better than that of the courtyard, though it is likely strategic to place me where no one can see me and I can see no one," she said to the paned glass.

Her meals appeared outside her door each day like clockwork, but she never saw another soul.

"You are not a prisoner, but for your safety you are not to leave this room."

She replayed the gruff words of the guard over in her head countless times. To her surprise, the doorknob turned when she tried it moments after they left. It swung open onto an empty hallway. She shut it immediately after, not wanting to be caught trying to leave the room, certain a summons would arrive for the meeting with the queen the next day.

But no one arrived. No maids to help her dress. No person appeared at all. She fell asleep at night and woke the next morning to a spotless room. Either the maids were mice or the room was enchanted to clean itself. Those were the only acceptable explanations. She didn't want to think someone had come into her room while she slept.

Several nights had come and gone, and the routine was the same each morning.

Another ripe grape slipped over her lips into her mouth. The crunch was more than she could bear. The sweet juice wet her tongue, but she had the hardest time swallowing. "How can I sit here and enjoy this amazing fruit when my friends, my father, could be searching for meals?"

She spat out the grape.

"No. I will not eat another thing until I speak with the queen." She swiped the tray from the table and overturned the food onto the rug. It was unlike her to do such a thing. She didn't know who she was anymore. She had expected to die when she ran out of food and every night since. Nothing had seemed right from that moment until this.

It was difficult to get into the peridot dress. The one that did indeed match her eyes. Without a maid, she had to get creative in tying laces and latching hooks, but managed the complete ensemble of lace and silk.

Standing in front of the door to the suite, she took a deep breath. Her slender fingers graced the brass knob and stopped. Her hand pulled back to her lips. "What will happen to me if I leave the room? They said it wasn't safe." She paced to the middle of the suite, thinking of what to do.

The image of her father lying dead in the dirt flashed into her mind.

She lifted her chin and reached for the knob again. It didn't matter what happened to her. She had to make sure her family was at least fed.

It turned easily, and the door opened. There were no guards stationed outside, and nothing stopped her from leaving.

Her slippers dipped into the plush navy blue carpet. The ceilings of the hall were at least four stories. Directly across from her room was a set of carpeted stairs. There wasn't much else in this part of the castle. No wonder no one had bothered her.

She descended the stairs to another corridor. The guards stationed at the bottom of the steps did not stop her from passing. They were so still, Gwen wondered if they were statues at first.

She followed the voices heard from an open room. It was not yet midday, so perhaps this was a breakfast party.

Gwen entered without being announced. Several modestly dressed men and women sat around a long table. A vast spread covered the middle.

The woman at the end of the table appeared bored until everyone noticed Gwen. Slowly and then, all at once, they stopped eating and conversing. Every eye shifted to her and back to the woman.

Gwen's mouth dropped open. It was as if she were looking in an enchanted mirror that showed her slightly older self.

She could only assume this was the queen, the so-called White Witch. Her father's sister. She hadn't imagined they would look so alike. Her father had always said she looked like her mother.

Gwen lowered herself into the shallow curtsy Avonlea had taught her.

"Gwen!" The queen clapped her hands together. "It's so nice of you to finally join us."

She looked around the vast dining room. This single space was bigger than her entire house at the mill. "I was told it would be dangerous to leave my quarters."

The queen laughed, and her guests followed suit.

"And what made you finally leave the safety of your suite?" Gwen watched the queen's thin red lips form the words and her penciled eyebrows lift.

Gwen almost begged right then and there, but she took a beat to think before she answered. "Loneliness."

The Queen's lips turned down in sadness. "I suppose safety can be rather lonely. Would you like to join us for breakfast? It was just served and is still warm." She motioned for a seat to be brought to the table and another setting.

"Actually." Gwen took a step forward. She wrung her hands together. "I was hoping to speak with you about the food."

The queen's eyebrows raised again. "Is it not to your liking?"

"No, the food is very tasty. It's that…"

"Spit it out child I'm sure my guests would like to finish their meal."

"There's so much of it. And my father, my town is starving."

The queen's features softened. She motioned to the seat beside her. "Come sit. We'll discuss. Everyone please continue your breakfast."

A man dressed in a white coat with long tails and navy blue patent blue shoes ushered her to a seat beside the queen.

Gwen lowered herself into her seat, hesitant to relax.

"That is a lovely dress dear. How ever you did you get into it?"

"Carefully."

The queen's laugh was pleasant and not at all shrill, as Gwen had expected. "I'm glad you've finally decided to leave your room."

"As I said I thought my life was in danger. Aurius said…"

"Aurius? You've spoken to him?"

"Your majesty? Were you not aware that he brought me here?"

"I am aware of the manner of your arrival. I just hadn't known you spoke with the prince."

Gwen chose her words carefully. If Aurius hadn't mentioned her presence for three weeks, perhaps it was better that she didn't either. "We had a very enlightening conversation."

"I'm sure that it was. Will you have tea with me later today?" The queen winked an eye as if she was letting Gwen in on some secret knowledge.

"I can accept your invitation as I have very little on my itinerary."

The queen leaned away with a knowing smile. "Excellent."

"Your highness…"

"Please. There's no need for titles here. You are amongst friends and I dare say family."

Gwen ignored the mention of family.

"Please call me Helen."

"Helen?"

"Yes. That is my name. Queen Helen of Mystrim."

"Forgive me… Helen," A name without a title felt disrespectful. "I would just like to request that food be sent to my father if it can be spared."

"Does your kingdom not receive the rations we send?"

"My town has never received rations."

The queen's frown returned. "We've heard of the drought that plagued your land. We have given monthly rations of food for years. It is up to the King to distribute it to the people."

"Unfortunately, I think it is just enriching the king all the more."

"It sounds as if the rations may need to be revoked."

Gwen reached out to the queen. She remembered herself and let her hand fall to the rail of the chair rather than clutching the queen's hand. "Please is there something that can be done to make sure the people are getting the food rather than the king?"

Helen lifted her chin and narrowed her eyes.

"My people need it. If there is a way to ensure it reaches the people, it would be beneficial and endure you to them. The king is known for his harsh laws. He has very few friends in the villages," Gwen said.

The queen pursed her lips in thought.

"It is very difficult to bring oneself to fight against the one that feeds you," Gwen added.

"So you know about the war?"

"War?" Gwen pinched her eyebrows together.

"The one started against us, in your name."

Gwen's eyes widened. She searched her memory for any mention of it.

The queen pursed her lips. "You don't. I wonder how long you've resided in my home?"

Gwen let the question hang in the air. Her eyes met the queen's, and an understanding passed between them. Aurius hadn't informed the queen he had been hiding her. The silent moment passed in a heartbeat.

"Does the king not spread lies about how dangerous magic users are?"

"He does. Full bellies may yet convince them that magic isn't all that bad."

"Until their bellies are empty again."

"Perhaps I could go as an ambassador?"

"No."

"But you said I wasn't a prisoner."

"You, my dear, are not a prisoner, but you are also not going back to the king who kidnapped you to use you to fill his coffers and fund a war against this kingdom."

Gwen dropped her eyes. "I understand. I appreciate your generosity." She pushed her seat away from the queen and stood. Her curtsy was not as low as it had been when she arrived. "I'll look forward to our tea later today," she said without meeting the queen's eyes.

"I'll send for you. Will you be in your rooms?"

"Yes, Your Highness." She turned to leave before the tears could spill over the edge of her lashes. Her behavior was uncouth for a royal breakfast chamber. Entirely disrespectful, especially to the one who held her life. But there were no audible gasps, no cries of "Off with her head." The conversation simply carried on without her, as if her presence were of no consequence.

Choices

Gwen paced her room, wondering if the Queen's tea would happen as planned. She longed for Avonlea to walk through the door and tell her what to wear. She had learned during her stay in Aurum that clothes were weapons or armor. A weapon that had almost killed her. If it hadn't been for Aurius, she would have been dead by now.

A knock startled her from the memories of that day. She turned toward the sound and held her breath. Who stood on the other side? Could it be an assassin, or had Aurius returned? She didn't know which she feared more.

"Miss. May I come in?" The voice at the door was soft, but abrasive.

"Who are you?"

"I've come to help you dress for the Queen's tea."

Gwen crossed the room and opened the door.

A young woman stood in the hall in front of her door. Fancier clothes than Gwen expected adorned the young woman. The maids in her previous palace experience had dressed in black shifts and blended into the background. This girl would fit in at any royal affair.

"Are you going to let me in or what?"

Gwen startled and stepped out of the way. "Of course please come in."

She sauntered in with all the grace of a petulant child and stopped in the middle of the room. "So where's the dress?"

Gwen shut the door and followed her. "I haven't decided yet."

The maid rolled her eyes. "So not only do I have to help you get dressed, I have to choose a dress as well?"

Gwen tilted her head to the right a bit. "Isn't that your job?"

The girl laughed. "Of course not. I'm not a maid."

"Ah. That would explain…" Gwen motioned to her dress.

"My mother is the Queen's secretary. I was voluntold to help you. Now let's get on with it. You don't have much time."

"What's your name?"

"What difference does it make?"

"I would like to know."

"Fine my name is… None of your business."

"Oh? That is a long name. Would you mind if I called you Nun for short?"

"Lady, you can call me whatever you want as long as we get this dress on you and you are not late for your tea."

"Do you have another appointment?"

"What I have is…"

Gwen raised a finger. "I know. None of my business." She waved to the closet. "Well, let's get on with it then Nun. What do you suggest I wear?"

Nun crossed her arms over her chest and shifted her head. Her body language telling her that in no way, shape, or form was she going to help her choose a dress.

Gwen ignored her and crossed to the closet. There were too many options. "Where did all the dresses come from?" she had wondered more than once. And no one could blame her for wondering if she could trust the maker. But she had to decide on something.

Her hand hovered over a black dress with sheer sleeves. Nun grunted. Gwen had her back turned to the girl, and a smile played at her lips. She clutched the dress and drug it out of the closet. The billowing skirts swung around her legs.

"Seriously?"

"What? This is pretty enough."

"Oh it is beautiful, but you can't wear that to tea."

"Why not?"

"Because black is the color of love."

"Love?"

"Romantic love."

"Why would I even have a black dress in my closet?"

Nun shrugged her shoulders. "I would say its because someone loves you. Romantically."

Gwen pushed it away, horrified. The only person here that could have provided a black dress was Aurius.

"This would be a sweet wedding dress. But if you like it I could probably change the color for you."

"You have magic?"

The look on Nun's face said Gwen was stupid. "Lady. I think you'll find everyone here has some kind of magic."

"Ok. Let's see yours," Gwen said with a twinge of giddiness. She hadn't seen magic outside of Aurius using her hair to turn straw into gold and the enchanted forest. She didn't dare say that. The warning not to tell others of her ability or Aurius's was at the top of her mind.

Nun held up a hand. "Ok. First. You can't just go around demanding to see people's magic. It's rude."

Gwen's eyes rounded. "Oh? I apologize. I've never seen magic before," she admitted.

Nun squinted her eyes. "I heard you came from the other kingdom, but I can't believe you would be here if you have never seen magic."

Gwen was silent for a few seconds but decided Nun deserved some kind of trust if she was going to show her what she could do. "Aurius saved my life with a potion. I wouldn't be anywhere, least of all here, if he hadn't performed this magic. I owe him my life in more ways than one. But I didn't get to see his magic on the account of being unconscious."

At her admission, Nun stomped over and touched the dress. It burst into a bright pink. Gwen swallowed loudly. Nun grabbed it out of her hands and untied the bodice.

As she held the dress for Gwen to step in to, she spoke softly. "It's Prince."

"Prince?"

"Prince Aurius."

"Oh. Yes. I heard that he is a prince."

"Yes. And you should use his title since you are beneath it."

"I...I apologize again. I have been told titles aren't important here. But also..."

"Who told you that?" Nun insisted.

"The queen."

Nun pulled the laces so tight Gwen could barely breathe. "Who are you?"

"My name is Gwen. I'm a miller's daughter from the kingdom of Aurum."

"Gwen Miller. The queen may be willing to let her title go. But I am not willing to allow you to disrespect the Prince. So his name is Prince Aurius."

Gwen waited silently for her to finish with the dress.

"You are ready for your tea with the queen." Nun left without another word, although the door slammed into place.

"Ok. That was interesting. I guess I'll find my own way to the Queen's suite."

As she proceeded to the bottom of the stairs, she asked the guards where she could find the queen. Neither of them answered and only stared straight ahead.

"Could you least point me in the correct direction?"

One guard looked as if he was doing everything in his power not to snicker.

Gwen squinted. "Why do I feel as though I'm the butt of a joke?"

The other guard cleared his throat and shifted his eyes to the right. Gwen took it as a direction and thanked the guard.

She passed only a few people in the halls of the castle, but those few did a double take and hid a snicker behind their hands.

Gwen finally arrived at an elaborate door.

She raised her hand to knock, and it opened without a sound.

"Please come in, Gwen."

Gwen entered and walked into the most ornate room she had ever seen. The queen sat on a sofa near the end of the second chamber.

"Oh dear," the queen said.

"Did I do something wrong?" Gwen asked.

"Did you choose this color?"

"Well..."

"Did Josie do this?"

"I don't know who Josie is?"

"The lady's maid I sent to help you dress."

"Oh, Nun?"

"Nun?"

"Well she said her name was none of my business. I asked to call her Nun. She didn't object."

"I see."

"Did I misstep?"

"I don't think the color of the dress was a result of your nickname."

"Is it a problem?"

"Well. It is the color of jealousy and usually worn by courtesans. Though we don't typically have many in this kingdom at all."

"Oh." She looked down. "Now I get the reason for the snickers. Well, the last time I wore a wedding dress I nearly died, I guess this is the least of my concerns."

"The dress was originally black?"

"Yes. It was in my closet and Nu.. Josie offered to change the color for me since I liked the design. But then she got offended by my using Aurius's name without his title and... "

"I see. You've had more than just a conversation with him." The queen folded her hands in her lap and then offered a gentle wave. A faint breeze floated over Gwen and the dress changed to a dull grey.

Gwen ignored the statement. "And what does this color mean?" she asked.

"Unrequited love. Fitting don't you think."

Gwen looked up with a soft growl. "Ugh. How did my life become so complicated?"

"It was always complicated my dear. You are just now discovering it." She motioned to an armchair near her. "Please sit. Let's discuss those complications."

Gwen sat in a cushioned white chair across from Helen.

"Why would Nun... I mean Josie turn my dress pink?"

"I imagine she is jealous that Aurius gave you black wedding dress."

"It's not as though I asked him to do such a thing. I hardly know him."

"But he knows you, my dear, quite well. And I suppose we never ask for the most important gifts. Josie should never have done such a thing. I will have her reprimanded."

"Oh no. Please don't. I wouldn't wish her punished for my ignorance, nor would I want to give her reason to hate me even more."

"I see. I'll give it some thought. But that is not why I asked you to tea."

The queen dismissed her staff, closed her eyes, and lifted her hands in front of her face. She crossed them and then waved them in a wide arc above her head. The air sparkled in the arc as if a protective bubble formed around them. The pops of glitter were the only sign the queen had used magic.

"We won't be heard or disturbed."

Gwen nodded, waiting for the queen to explain.

"Where do I begin?" Helen asked.

"I suppose the best place is at the beginning."

"Yes. This is not your first visit to this castle. In fact, you were born here."

"Aurius explained some of it. But I still find it outrageous. I am the daughter of a miller, born in Aurum."

"That was the story your mother made up and how she hid you all those years ago. But she was not a miller's wife. She was the Queen. The man you know as your father, is not," said, as if the act of saying it made it fact.

"Though I read Aurius's book, I believe that to be impossible."

"Gwen. I need you to let me get through this. It will be shocking and even a little scary for you. But it is time you know the truth. You have some tough decisions to make."

Gwen closed her mouth and swallowed the questions she had. She would give the queen a chance to explain.

"When you were just a few months old. Rumpelstiltskin came to collect you."

"Aurius's father?" Gwen asked. Her mouth clicked shut with a withering look from the queen.

"Aurius was only a handful of years old. The Queen, my sister in law, had signed a contract with him. Something you should never do with a goblin. Especially a goblin king and one as crafty as Rumpel. His contracts were ironclad.

"But for some reason, he had a soft spot for your mother. He allowed her leniencies where he had never allowed them before. You've heard the story. She had three days to guess his name, to keep you from being taken. And well, she cheated, of course. When she guessed his name, the earth opened up and swallowed him whole and that's how she got out of giving you up. But the contract didn't end. And Aurius is bound by it, just as you are."

"I still think it is unfair that we're bound by a contract that we didn't agree to."

"Yes. It was a blood contract and it continues perpetually until it is satisfied. When your mother died the contract was transferred to you. And had you had a child it would have transferred to her upon your death. It is outdated and barbaric and why they are rarely used. But your mother was desperate at the time and so was the goblin king."

"I can relate."

"History does tend to repeat itself."

Gwen grabbed her forehead between her thumb and forefinger. "No. No. There is no way that I am actually a princess."

"Unfortunately, no. My brother, your father, died only a few weeks before you were born. When Rumpel disappeared your mother became paranoid. We had no proof that he was dead. So she decided to go into hiding. She abdicated the throne to me and took you out of Mystrim. I had no idea where she took you at the time and I've spent many years looking for you."

"Except Aurum doesn't have magic."

"Though that would make it the perfect place to hide you, it wasn't always so. When the Earth swallowed Rumpel, magic changed. As if he was the source of magic and his death caused a vacuum. We have managed to stave off the blight and form a barrier. But every day it gets harder and requires more energy. I'm getting weaker. Soon someone else will have to take my place."

"You are dying?"

The queen nodded.

"How long do you have?"

"A few months at most."

"I don't know what you expect from me."

"The abdication contract required you become my heir."

"You want me to be queen?" Gwen placed her arm over her stomach. "But I'm a miller's daughter, if not by birth then by practice. I have no skills or training for this."

"I want you to marry Aurius and complete the contract. It may not break the curse but it might give us more time."

Gwen's mouth dropped open. Not for the first time. "The contract my mother tried to break."

"Yes."

"A marriage contract for an infant?"

"You weren't even a thought when she signed it. She was just trying to survive."

Gwen closed her eyes and took a deep breath. "Trying to survive because your brother put her in the dungeon and asked her to perform impossible magic." Gwen realized she had raised her voice.

"My brother was trying to protect her. Coralynn summoned the goblin thinking she could persuade my brother with gold to release her. All she did was bring about the thing he was trying to avoid."

Gwen pursed her lips, not sure whether she believed it. "Putting that aside. How is me completing the contract going to help?"

"I believe the curse is related to Rumpelstiltskin, and therefore Aurius. If you marry Aurius it might be broken. I will be able to live much longer. My magic will not constantly be drained. I'll have time to train you to become queen. And it will save Aurius. He is one of life's greatest surprises and I would like to see him live."

"He mentioned his life would be forfeit?"

"If a Goblin is not married by their twenty fourth birthday they cease. And since he is in love with you already, it may speed up the process. The contract is meant to guarantee a compliant human girl."

Gwen's attention snagged on one word. "Cease?"

"Are you dense child? His human side will die."

Gwen stood and paced behind her chair. It was poor manners, but she couldn't help it. "That's what he meant? That he will become a goblin and lose himself. What about me? Is my life tied to the contract?"

"You will not die, but you will still be blood bound to the contract."

"Meaning I can't marry anyone else. The contract will pass to my first born. Or I'll have to marry Goblin Aurius."

"I've only just learned its full extent, and I've done my best to find a loop hole in the contract. My only suggestion is that whatever you think of marriage to Aurius, not marrying him will be much worse."

"And when does Aurius turn twenty four?"

"In seven days."

Gwen almost swallowed her tongue. "A week?! Why am I just now learning of this? Why didn't he tell me? I only have a week to determine if I want to marry him."

"No. You have a few minutes to decide whether you want to save your lives, save magic, and save this kingdom."

"A few minutes."

The Queen nodded. "I negotiated a deal with Prince Ryland. He's declared war on Mystrim. The only way to end it is for you to return to him. It's fortunate we got him instead of the king. I negotiated a temporary peace to allow you the choice. In a few minutes this protective silence will disintegrate. You'll go down the front steps and enter a carriage. The driver will take you anywhere you want to go. You can go back to Prince Ryland and prevent a war, but magic will die along with Aurius. Or you can go to Prince Aurius and save us all."

"But if I marry Ryland, our child would still be bound by the contract. How can I make an impossible choice?"

The queen smiled, but it didn't reach her eyes. "I've said all I can say. I've been bound from saying more." She bent her head, and a tear slid down her cheek. After a few moments, the queen lifted her chin again and straightened her back. "Your stay here has ended. The choice is yours. But you must make a choice indeed."

"And how would I even find Aurius? He left without saying goodbye and…"

The queen extended her arm and opened her palm. In the center lay her mother's signet ring.

"My mother's ring?"

She pushed her hand toward Gwen. "Take it. It is spelled to find what most you seek. It will guide you."

"I didn't know you could do such a thing."

"It's a family heirloom. Aurius brought it to me when you gave it to him. It is how he proved who you were."

The bubble burst, and the sound rushed around her again.

"It is time to go. I'm looking forward to your decision." The Queen clapped her hands. Two tall guards charged in and grabbed Gwen by the arms.

"Lady Gwen has decided to leave the castle. Please escort her to the royal carriage. It is prepared and waiting."

The guards lifted her and turned her toward the door. Gwen struggled in their arms. "NO! No." But her screams did nothing for her. She looked over her shoulder at the queen, who sagged against the sofa.

"But why would you do this to family?"

The queen didn't respond. Her face was unreadable, but she refused to wipe away the tears that moistened her cheeks. It was the last glimpse Gwen saw of her aunt before the guards pulled her through the door. The walk to the carriage was short between their lengthy strides.

They unceremoniously shoved her toward the carriage and shut the castle doors behind her. The loud bang of the door finalized her fate. The choice was now.

"Tell the horses your destination. They will take you where to instruct them to go." The groom on top of the carriage called down to her. She turned at the sound of his voice, willing the tears away with a deep breath. She lifted her chin and pulled her shoulders back. The queen had given her a gift. She wasn't being kidnapped or whisked away at dawn. It was her decision and though the options were few, she had them. Aurius, Ryland, her father, or somewhere new.

She gently approached the horses. Stroking the nearest's neck and scratching behind her ears, she whispered. "Where should I go?"

The horse nickered.

"No, I don't supposed you would be able to tell me."

As she ran her hand against the dark mane, a thought occurred to her. If a magical horse could understand her, maybe it could decide for her. With renewed hope, she whispered to the horse. "Take me home."

The horse tapped a hoof on the ground. "That means she understands," the groom yelled.

Gwen left the mare and entered the carriage with the help of the second groomsman.

As soon as she settled in, they lurched forward. Her shoulders slumped in disappointment and her belly filled with acidic dread. Was this the right decision? A part of her had hoped it wouldn't move at all. But deep down, she knew better. This castle wasn't her home.

She leaned back and crossed her arms, resolved to allow her fate to play out.

* * *

The queen watched Gwen at the window. The tall presence warmed her as he put his arms around her waist and kissed her neck. "Did she believe your story?"

"I think so. It was close enough to the truth."

He nodded. "I guess now we wait and see. Where do you think she will go?"

The queen faced him but ignored his question. "Remember our wager?"

King Aric raised an eyebrow. "The wager you tricked me into? I remember. If she marries Aurius and saves magic, you send me all the gold they make every month and I stop the attack on our shared border. The Changling you traded marries Avonlea and we have an alliance. If Gwen shows back up at my doorstep I imprison her and trap the goblin when he comes to claim her. Your son will be sent home in exchange for the plans and ability to ensnare the goblin king."

The queen sighed. "It is no small thing to sacrifice a beloved child. Even if it is for the good of everyone. Your need for gold will be satiated and the war will be over."

He wrapped his forearm around her waist and pulled her to him, pressing a kiss to her painted lips. "What if I want more than gold?" he asked when he pulled away.

The queen's lips pulled into a knowing smile. "What did you have in mind?"

* * *

Want to join the conversation? Subscribe to my free newsletter on Substack or follow me on Facebook @EvangalinePierce

Acknowledgments

As always, I must thank you readers. Without you, I would just be satisfying my need to quiet the voice in my head. You are the ones that make these stories special.

Thanks also goes to my family, who support my efforts to make this hobby into a career. My daughter for inspiration and market research and especially my husband, who lets me have conversations with handsome men in my head and then share it with you. He also supports every crazy idea I get, like driving fourteen hours to Tennessee in the winter to meet new readers.

My beta readers Jocelyn Beck, who reads all the things, and Friar Jak. This book wouldn't be where it is without you.

And above all, I thank Jesus for his grace and blessing.

Also by Evangaline Pierce

A Sword of Plated Gold

So many curses so little time.

After being faced with a terrible choice, Gwen must mount a daring rescue. She learns of a magic sword that will solve everything. Just one problem: it is in the King's treasury. Can she retrieve it in time to save everything she loves.

Don't miss this dramatic conclusion to the Magic and Gold Series.

Sacred Series
A secretive guardian angel. An obsessed demon. Where do her loyalties lie?

After a series of tragic losses, Alle teams up with her too-gorgeous, totally off-limits guardian angel to travel through the veil. Although Gabriel seems to have her best interest at heart, but he has secrets. Secrets that could shatter the idyllic life she had built.

When she catches the attention of the demon realm, the prince becomes obsessed with her. With his offers to help she has a choice to make. Trust Gabriel or her new frenemy?

With danger lurking around every corner, Alle must risk everything to save her daughter and discover the truth of her past. Will her faith lead to victory or cost her everything she holds dear?

Winner of the 2023 Firebird Book Award in Christian Fantasy, Outstanding Creator Award in Christian Fiction, and finalist in the Reader's Favorite Awards for Christian Fantasy. Indie BRAG Medallion Honoree.